**Prai**

# "Miss?"

**Third Edition**

Laurel McHargue

ALPHA PEAK LLC    Leadville, CO

### "Miss?"

THIRD EDITION 2016

Published by Alpha Peak LLC
Leadville, CO

Library of Congress Control Number: 2016906983
McHargue, Laurel, Author
"Miss?"
Laurel McHargue

ISBN: 978-0-9969711-4-0

Cover Design by Alex Tibio
Back Cover Photo by *Tonya's Captured Inspirations LLC*

PRINTED IN THE UNITED STATES OF AMERICA

## Dedication

To students everywhere struggling to learn
and to your teachers who are struggling
to help you.

There once was a teacher named "Miss?"
When she talked to her students they'd hiss;
But she *would* keep on trying
And hide all her crying,
She'd save her kids from the abyss!

~ Laurel McHargue (a.k.a. "Miss?")

# "Miss?"

♡
Laurel

## ~ 1 ~

MAGGIE MCCAULEY HIT THE SACK knowing that when she awoke the next morning, her new life would be a breeze. Having spent the past two years never knowing if she would see the light of the next day, her only struggle now would be adjusting to the mundane 8-5 requirements of her new job as a 7$^{th}$ grade English teacher.

Well, she also had to earn a teaching certificate, and that meant taking classes nights and weekends, but those requirements paled in comparison to the ones Maggie experienced during her recent tour of duty in the Middle East as a Signal Officer in the Army. Yup. Civilian life would be a piece of cake.

"Bones, no!"

Despite her confidence that she could teach a bunch of 13-year-olds blindfolded with her hands tied behind her back, Maggie was restless, and her 60-pound floppy-eared rescue mutt translated her uncharacteristic nocturnal fidgeting as an invitation to play. Confused by the unexpected censure, Bones cocked his head slightly, then resumed pouncing on different body parts moving beneath the covers.

"Oh, all right," Maggie gave in, realizing that since she probably wouldn't fall asleep for the next hour anyway, she might as well take her frisky pup for an evening stroll. Sliding her feet into the battered running shoes by the door, she didn't even consider putting on real clothes. No one would notice her Wonder Woman pajamas and overall disheveled appearance this time of night, and even if they did, she didn't care.

"Bones, come!"

These distinct commands, which her slobbery side-kick of only two months had quickly learned, never failed to make Maggie smile. She attached the leash to the camouflaged collar and opened the front door of her small end-unit apartment. The unusual heat of the Denver summer night transported her for a moment to a time when a strong, handsome two-legged side-kick kept her company during evening walks. Sam had been the one to make her laugh when all seemed lost, when she longed to be safely home with indoor utilities and a comfortable bed, when she felt that what she was doing in that godforsaken part of the world was meaningless.

After spending two years stationed together in a war zone, she and Sam talked about where they'd live when they returned to the States and had already named their future dog. Sam had always wanted to name a dog "Boner," not only because it was inappropriate—and he was as much a rebel as Maggie was—but because they'd share endless laughter at any training command that would start with the dog's name. Sam was funny and smart and strong, and Maggie couldn't imagine her life without him.

But Sam didn't return with her, and would never be there to help train the pup. She'd have to endure the horrible reality surrounding his death for the rest of her life. Maggie hoped that by adopting her dog, she would—in a tiny way—keep Sam's memory alive, and more often than not, Bones was able to make Maggie laugh. For the sake of propriety and because she was alone, she modified her dog's name, but always enjoyed the secret joke.

By the time she and Bones returned from their fast-paced tour of the surrounding homes and apartment complexes—Maggie never did anything slowly—Bones was ready to lap up the contents of his water bowl and plop down, gracelessly, at the foot of the bed. Maggie finally felt ready to give in to her fatigue. Fortunately, she had two days to set up her classroom and get to know her new civilian peers before her "troops" would arrive for the first day of school on Wednesday.

~~~~~

The 6 a.m. alarm startled her awake, freeing her from a recurrent panic-filled dream. While childhood friends laughed at their clichéd showing-up-naked dreams, Maggie often woke in a cold sweat from smoky visions of chaos and blood. Lots of blood. And screaming. Her military unit was supposed to be in a safe zone, but everyone knew that there were new rules for this war. No one was ever safe.

Maggie walked out to the tiny patch of grass behind her new home sipping her mug of black coffee while Bones completed his business. The morning was warm and overcast, and although Maggie was excited about her plans to make her classroom special, the atmosphere did nothing to break her nightmare mood.

"Who's a good boy?" Maggie praised her little buddy, who came wagging back to her ready, once more, to play. She deposited her mug, threw on her shoes, grabbed the leash and took Bones for a fast run before prepping for her first full day in her new work space. The school was a 15-minute drive, and Maggie felt fortunate to have found this little treasure of an apartment. She'd be able to bop home to let her puppy out at midday, and he'd already demonstrated that he could be left alone for several hours without becoming too mischievous.

At 7 a.m. she was out the door, her conservatively cropped hair looking wild from her towel-dried styling and her brightly-patterned Capri pants topped with a blouse over which she threw an unnecessary—but funky—belt. Years of wearing the same uniform 24/7 had left Maggie with a desire to express her inner artist through her outer-wear. She could use teaching kids as an excuse to be as flamboyant as she wanted.

She opened the passenger door to her Jeep and tossed in her backpack, then turned back to grab what she had purchased from Target to eliminate the clinical feel of her classroom.

"Oh! Good morning, Harry! I didn't think you'd be out so early today!"

"Well, I couldn't very well let you start your new assignment without giving you a good luck hug, now, could I?"

Harry Wilson stood just outside his door, holding open the screen and appraising Maggie with a smile of approval. An 83-year-old WWII veteran, Harry had taken an immediate liking to his new neighbor when she had moved in with her dog at the beginning of the summer. They had some past experiences in common. Harry had lost his wife of 60 years over a year ago and now passed his days watching the comings and goings of his neighbors, completing the crossword puzzle in every newspaper, and occasionally waiting until 5 p.m. to savor his first scotch.

Maggie approached her neighbor with arms open and was surprised by the little knot that rose in her throat. Although she had purposely chosen to teach in Denver because she and Sam had talked about settling there, a place neither had lived before, she missed her parents in New England. Harry reminded her of her father. Equally surprising was the strength of the old Colonel's hug.

"Now go get 'em, Captain!" Harry emphasized the "Captain" as he held her at arm's length and then chuckled. "You sure do know how to make an entrance, don't you?"

"Yeah, well, I figured if I wear some crazy clothes I may be able to keep their attention. I've heard these kids have the attention span of a gnat." Students had two more days of vacation, but many were showing up to complete registration requirements. She anticipated that more than a few would end up at her end of the hallway to check out the new teacher.

"I'll be coming home to let Bones out at lunch, but if I don't see you then, I'll come by this evening to give you my report." Maggie turned and headed down the sidewalk.

"Well, I don't want to keep you, but you know I wouldn't mind letting the little guy out while you're gone if you can't make it home. Just thought I'd offer."

"Thanks, Harry!" Maggie stopped briefly before hopping into the Jeep. "Let's see how he does today and we'll talk tonight. And thanks for the hug," she called out the open passenger window before driving off.

~~~~~

North Middle School was in full bustle. Teachers lugged items from cars to classrooms, administration manned the entries and directed new students and parents to late registration tables, custodial staff buffed floors and completed final touches for opening day and small groups of students darted around finding and testing new lockers and peeking into classrooms. This was exactly what Maggie had expected to see Monday morning. What she didn't expect to see, however, was the scary-looking security guard standing in the background down the hall.

Having just met her teacher peer group briefly the previous week and not knowing any of them well enough to feel comfortable chatting,

Maggie focused on her own mission: to create a positive environment in which her students would be happy to learn. It took several trips to empty the contents of her Jeep, and it was time to decorate.

She moved the teacher's desk, a metal monstrosity, to a less conspicuous location at the back of the sterile room. She wanted the entire area in front of the chalk board clear and didn't *ever* plan to sit while her students were working. Nevertheless, she taped a huge yellow smiley-face to the front of the desk for the infrequent times she might engage a student there. One of her education instructors was focusing the following week's assignment on how the arrangement of desks in a classroom can influence participation, and Maggie had already decided the days of uniform rows were over.

Pushing the old student desks and chairs to the edges of the classroom, Maggie spread out a multi-colored 5'x7' carpet in front of the chalk board. This would be the focal point upon which she intended to deliver her vast knowledge to eager ears. She arranged the student desks in staggered semi-circles around the carpet. After drawing a sketch of the arrangement, she assigned names to seats, decisions she realized might need to be tweaked once she got to know her kids and how they interacted with one another.

Her students would soon figure out she wasn't like their other teachers, many whom Maggie suspected might be jaded from year after year of the same routine. Maggie—all 5'4" inches of her—was young and resilient and tough. Her funky hair and wide eyes belied her inner strength. She had combat experience. She had jumped out of airplanes, trudged countless miles in full military gear, and knew how to defend both herself and the soldiers in her charge. Her students would respect her and would tell others how lucky they were to have the cool new English teacher.

Maggie couldn't believe her eyes when she finally looked up at the clock and realized she'd worked through lunch; it was one o'clock. Bones had been home alone for six hours, longer than she'd ever left him before. She locked her classroom and ran out of the building, nearly slamming into Roger Jones, the full-time security guard assigned to walk the halls of North Middle School, home of the Eagles. At 6'2" he was built like a brick wall.

"Whoa there, little lady, there's no runnin' in these here halls," he said with a twinkle in his eyes, "unless there be a fire, and I don't see no fire."

"Sorry! Sorry! I've got to go! I'll be back soon!" Maggie apologized to the amused man, and out she ran.

~~~~~

As soon as she opened the door to her home, Maggie realized six hours was about two hours too long to expect a year-old dog to entertain himself appropriately.

"Awww, Bones, what have you done?" She laughed at the mottled fur bag who looked up at her through half-averted puppy eyes, tail wagging guiltily between shaky back legs, an unknown papery white substance hanging from his whiskers. It was her fault.

After stepping over what could have been a much larger pile by the front door, Maggie walked through the small apartment. The contents of what had been a few small pillows on her hide-a-bed couch decorated the living room. The lamp on the foot-locker by the window—Maggie's reading area—lay smashed on the floor. Following a narrow white paper trail from the living room to the bathroom, Maggie gasped at the condition of the bathroom. There was surprisingly little damage in the kitchen, but the upturned water bowl made for slippery footing.

"Come 'ere, Bones, it's okay," she called to her pup, who appeared to sense he'd done something wrong but didn't understand what. Bones shuffled over to Maggie, tail still wagging low between his legs, and sat by her feet.

"Looks like we've got some work to do when I come back tonight, huh boy?" When her tone convinced him everything was going to be all right, he took a quick dash around the apartment, losing it on the slippery kitchen floor and slamming into the cabinets.

Maggie opened the back door to the tiny yard and let Bones romp outside while she threw a couple of towels on the kitchen floor, made a mental note to find tip-proof feeding bowls, cleaned up the mess by the front door, and did what she could to remove any potential dangers for the next few hours. She thought Harry might pop his head out for a quick hello, but he didn't. She made another note to swing by the hardware store for an extra key to her place that afternoon.

"Okay, Bones, be back soon! You're a good boy!" She ruffled his head and drove back to add the finishing touches to her classroom. In one more day, every seat would be filled with fresh young minds to influence. Maggie knew how important first impressions were and wanted to ensure her new troops left her classroom feeling excited about what they'd learn this year.

~~~~~

The atmosphere in the main entrance was the same as when she had left the school, but walking down the hall to her classroom, she saw two boys standing against the wall with Roger towering over them and addressing them sternly. She walked past the situation quickly, not wanting to interfere, but was surprised that although the boys were standing there quietly, their faces expressed disinterest. Maybe even cynicism.

Noted.

She felt better stepping into her classroom. The bright carpet, the half-moon desk arrangement, the smiley face and the two beanbag chairs already presented an uplifting change. Maggie decided to leave the beanbag chairs behind her desk; she'd come up with a plan for who could use them and when. She liked the idea of having a special reading corner, and students would have to earn the privilege of using it. *Yes, this will work*, she thought.

She arranged six bright plastic baskets—her "in" boxes—on the counter against the windows on the far side of the room, then sat down to arrange the contents of her desk before finishing her seating charts. The swivel office chair—probably as old as she was—creaked and nearly tossed her over when she leaned back. No, she wouldn't be sitting much this year.

Not knowing any of the students, Maggie decided on a boy/girl/boy/girl arrangement for each of her classes and quickly filled in her charts. Each chart went into a clear plastic sleeve on which she could take attendance with a dry erase marker. On a butcher paper tablet she replicated the arrangement for each class and taped them to the front board.

She would direct students to the charts to find their seats upon entering the classroom.

She covered the large cork board by the door with bright yellow paper and stapled a sparkly star border around the edges. This is where she would post student "exemplars." Those who did outstanding work would have their efforts rewarded for all to see. Stepping back to take in the whole scene, Maggie was pleased with what she saw. A perfectionist by nature, she'd apply everything she was learning in her licensure program to her job and then go one step further by adding her own unique flair. She was about to close up and head to the hardware store when Kirby Cohen, the science teacher on her team, entered the room.

"Wow, nice rug." There was no enthusiasm in her voice. Kirby was slightly older than Maggie and was a commanding presence in the room. Physically, she was the antithesis of Maggie and bore a striking resemblance to the poster of Einstein Maggie had taped to the back wall. She had a mad professor look about her, kinky wild hair and all. Meeting her for the first time during in-processing the previous week, Maggie sensed her new peer—who didn't attempt to hide her sarcastic wit—could become a friend. This was her ninth year teaching middle school science at North and Maggie could tell there was wisdom behind the wisecracks.

"What? You don't like it? These rooms are so ugly! I thought it might make the kids smile when they walk in." Maggie was surprised by the defensiveness of her response; after spending five successful years in military leadership positions, the latest being in high-risk environments, she wasn't used to having her decisions questioned. She was the low-man-on-the-totem-pole at school, and this was unknown turf.

"It'll make 'em smile all right," Kirby shot back, this time with a smirk. "I see you've already made your seating charts—can I see them?"

Maggie handed her the spiral notebook with each chart in the proper order.

"You'll want to move Kevin away from Brad, and Mateo away from, well, everyone. I wouldn't put Trevor next to any of these girls. Bernicia is pretty smart, but she'd rather be a pain in your ass, so don't expect much from her. She and Shareena are trouble together, so watch out for that." Kirby looked up and saw the distress on Maggie's face. "Hey, listen, don't worry about this. You'll figure it out pretty fast, and maybe they'll be better for you than they are for me. I probably shouldn't be saying anything before you meet them."

"No, that's okay, I probably should've talked with you before making my charts." Maggie realized she knew almost nothing about pre-teen dynamics in this inner-city school.

"Just remember—you're in charge and you can make changes whenever you want. Let's eat lunch together tomorrow and I'll fill you in on a few more things before Wednesday," Kirby offered as she left the room.

"Thanks, okay." Maggie hoped Harry's offer to let Bones out at mid-day was still on the table once he learned of the pooch's earlier shenanigans. On her way out of the building, she approached Roger, who maintained his cross-armed brick wall composure until she was within greeting range.

"Sorry about earlier. I'm Maggie McCauley, the new English teacher." She extended her hand and he took it, cocking an eyebrow as she matched his grip. He held on for too long. "Ah, I had a dog crisis," Maggie stammered, anxious to retrieve her hand.

"Ain't nothin' but a thang," he replied in a smooth, deep voice, finally releasing her hand. "Roger Jones, security, but everybody call me Razz. You'll be seein' a lot of me this year."

Maggie could tell he was checking her out and wasn't sure how she felt about it. As a single woman in the Army, she always had to arm herself with a tough-girl façade, something Sam was able to break through within weeks of meeting her. It was hard for her to believe she'd been single for over a year since Sam's death. Now that she was a civilian, she wasn't sure how to act. Still, she sensed a distinctive need to protect herself from this swarthy security guard. The irony wasn't lost on her.

"Why would that be?" she asked, taking a step back and re-arming herself.

"You'll see . . ."

"Ms. McCauley!" The school's principal broke in, approaching the two. "I was hoping to see you before you left. I see you've met Razz. He'll take good care of you."

David Martin was cool and professional, mid-30s, slightly balding and in great shape. Maggie had liked him from the minute she met him during the interview process. He was engaged to be married—not that she'd ever consider a relationship with her boss—but she allowed herself to admire his great command presence. She trusted him.

"Yes, sir," she answered, not knowing how else to address him. "He was just telling me I'd be seeing him a lot."

Her boss didn't correct the "sir" and she took it as a good sign. She was comfortable with having a clear chain of command and he conveyed an air of authority she expected from the leader of a school with security guards.

"We'll be having a staff and faculty lunch tomorrow to kick off the new school year, and I'm hoping you'll spend a little time getting to know the other people on your 7$^{th}$ grade team. I know you've got a lot to prep for Wednesday, but remember: your peers are here to help you and so am I."

"Thank you, sir. I'm really excited about meeting all my students and Kirby has already visited."

"She'll be one of your greatest assets. Don't let her scare you."

Maggie suppressed her desire to say there wasn't much that scared her anymore, except, perhaps, the large man whom she'd soon be "seein' a lot of." She smiled and said goodbye to the two men, left the building and drove to the nearest hardware store.

~~~~~

The old Colonel was sitting outside his front door when Maggie pulled up to the curb. Raising himself gingerly from his folding chair, he awaited her report. Maggie hurried up the sidewalk, gave him a quick "Hello" hug, then encouraged him to sit back down.

"Let me grab Bones and we'll be right back," she said over her shoulder as she trotted to her own front door.

Bones was happy to see her, and a quick look around told Maggie the place was no worse off than when she last left it. The dog followed her out to the Jeep, curious to see what was in the packages, and then noticing Harry, romped over to the seated man and threw his front legs onto his lap. Harry laughed, engaging the dog in a playful manner, and was rewarded with a wet tongue under his chin.

*"Miss?"*

"Oh! Sorry, Harry!" Maggie shouted from the walkway, taking in the scene and not sure of her neighbor's comfort level with dogs. "Bones, come!"

"It's okay," he replied as the dog obeyed and ran back to her.

"Be right back!" she called to Harry.

Maggie and Bones disappeared into the apartment and returned ten minutes later with an extra folding chair and a clean, bright tennis ball. She set up her chair, joined her neighbor and tossed the ball over to her front yard. The dog amused himself with the new toy, occasionally bringing it back to Maggie or Harry for another launch while they visited.

"Join me for a scotch?" Harry offered.

"Sure! Why not?" Maggie wasn't much of a drinker and had never had scotch before, but everything about her new life was different and she loved the excitement of anything that removed her from what she considered to be her comfort zone. She embraced change, knowing she'd always learn something new from it; it was one of the reasons she had joined the Army. "Do you need any help?"

"No, you stay there. You can get the door for me in a moment." He returned with two icy tumblers and when they were seated again, he proposed a toast. "To your new life! May those kids at your school appreciate what you have to offer!"

They clinked glasses and Maggie held the first sip in her mouth before swallowing the smooth beverage. Scotch was nothing like beer. She needed to make this one glass last.

"Thanks, Harry. I got a little indication today that middle school kids here might not be like the ones I went to school with 15 years ago back home. Did you know they have a security guard?"

"Well, I don't want to diminish your enthusiasm, young lady, but I've lived here for almost 20 years and I've heard rumors. Some people are saying North Middle might close. Bad test scores, lots of fights, can't keep good teachers, things like that. Doesn't surprise me. This area has been struggling for a long time and with things as they are, it doesn't look like much is going to improve."

"I was wondering why there seemed to be more tension than excitement in the building last week while I was in-processing. Oh well. I'll do the best I can and that's about all I can do, right?" With her glass half empty, Maggie relaxed. They laughed watching Bones charge around the front of the building as if he were on a racetrack.

Which reminded her . . .

"So, your offer to let out my little rascal at lunchtime—is it still a possibility? Because I have a feeling I might not be able to come home too often, and I know I can't tomorrow. When I came home today—obviously too late—I felt terrible because he had an accident." She left out the complete details.

"I wouldn't have offered if I didn't mean it, now, would I?"

"I just don't want you to feel obligated or tied down, and there's always the doggy-day-care center. This would be such a relief to me, and I'll be happy to pay you."

"You'll do no such thing, dear. This'll give me a reason to get out of the house more. Is he leash trained? I could take him for a walk."

"He's great on a leash. I have no idea how he ended up at the shelter, but someone obviously trained him. I think he's only about a year old, but he's a smart boy. I keep the leash on a hook by the front door. Just call his name and give him simple orders like 'Bones, come,' and then make him sit while you attach his leash. He's used to the routine. Oh, and I made you a key." Maggie stood, dug the key from her pocket and handed it to Harry. "Want to call now to make sure he behaves for you?"

"Here boy!" Harry commanded in a firm, but pleasant voice. Bones stopped in his tracks, ball in mouth, and trotted over to Harry. "Sit!" Same tone. Bones sat. "Good little fella," Harry praised the dog, patting him on the head. "I think we'll be just fine," Harry said to Maggie, whose mouth was slightly agape. "I used to have a mutt years ago. He was a good dog. Here, let me take your glass. I know you've got lots to do tonight. If I can't let him out, I'll let you know in advance, deal?"

"Deal!" Maggie answered, handing him her glass and starting to pick up her chair.

"Unless you need that in your apartment, you're welcome to leave it here. I occasionally get a visitor and it's nice to have an extra seat to offer."

"Of course! Thanks, Harry, I really do appreciate this. See you tomorrow." She gave him a quick hug and returned to her apartment with Bones on her heels.

## *"Miss?"*

Lightheaded when she entered her messy home, she realized she hadn't eaten since breakfast and tossed a frozen dinner into the microwave. She set up and filled Bones's sturdy new food station and finished cleaning up the disaster. She ate the bland meal while catching up on the news, then prepared for the next day, setting out the peanut butter to remind herself to make a sandwich in the morning. Maggie fell asleep on the couch halfway through an episode of *Fringe* and woke to the wet kisses of a dog ready for his evening walk.

Dragging herself to her feet, she went through the motions of prepping for what would normally be a fast-paced couple of miles in the cooler night-time air, but found the excitement and stress of the day—topped with the intoxicating new beverage—had sapped her of her usual energy. Fortunately, Bones was just as happy with the slower-paced stroll and the two were in bed and asleep by ten.

For the first time in years, Maggie enjoyed a dreamless, fidgetless sleep and woke to the new day without an alarm.

# ~ 2 ~

MAGGIE'S MORNING RUN with Bones, something she planned to make her habit, was exhilarating. She was eager to spend time with her new teammates and to finish prepping for her students.

Before leaving the apartment she closed off the bedroom and bathroom doors and looked around to ensure the pup wouldn't be able to do much damage. She deposited several types of play toys on the living room and kitchen floors and as was her custom, left quickly with a cheerful, "Later!"

She had read in one of her dog training books that if you don't make a big deal about leaving, the dog won't develop anxiety over the ensuing separation. She'd heard horror stories about clingy parents making a huge fuss over leaving their kids at school the first day and decided there were probably many parallels with pets. Still, she was happy to know Bones would have a capable visitor in a few hours.

~~~~~

The school seemed more upbeat too. She sensed a nervous, excited energy in the air and all but skipped down the long hall to her classroom at the end. Several teachers shouted, "Morning!" as she passed their rooms and although she didn't stop, she returned their greeting.

She loved the feel of her cheery classroom. After filling up the candy bowl by the door with Jolly Ranchers, she set up her front board for the first lesson of her teaching career.

## *"Miss?"*

Along the top of the board Maggie used bright chalk to spell out "Magnificent Monday, Terrific Tuesday, Wonderful Wednesday, Thoughtful Thursday, Frazzled Friday," with corresponding dates over each day. She was hopeful someone in each class would pick up on the alliteration and planned to use this technique each day to help build her students' vocabulary. New words each week would be added to her Word Wall, another gimmick espoused by her instructional teachers.

Day One would be all about introductions and expectations. Maggie sat down to write a parent letter about who she was and how she'd give "more than 100%" to their children throughout the year. She planned to do everything in her power to ensure each child would get the enthusiastic instruction, the materials and the help he or she needed to be successful in class. She signed the letter and rushed to the office to make copies.

"One more day!" she said to Razz, passing him quickly in the hall, not wanting to engage in another awkward moment.

"Mmmm! You look like a ray o' sunshine today," he called as she disappeared around the corner.

And she did. Maggie had spent $150 at the local Goodwill and took home three full bags of the craziest, most colorful outfits she could find. She figured anything she could do to attract and keep the attention of her new troops would be a good thing.

She had to wait in line at the copy machine behind Matthew Green, the 7th grade social studies teacher. Matthew bore a striking resemblance to her favorite middle school social studies teacher, in looks and in temperament. He was slender and tall, soft-spoken and pleasant, and had kind brown eyes. She liked him immediately.

"Ready for tomorrow?" he asked. "I've just got a few more pages to copy."

"Almost. I just finished my parent letter and then I need to make my expectations chart. No hurry."

"And . . . done. Did Kirby tell you we'll sit together at lunch today?"

"Yes, thanks! I'll see you then," she said, turning back to her task and noticing an older woman who had just entered with a stack of papers to copy. The woman appeared miffed at having to wait. Maggie had seen her during in-processing and had overheard a comment she'd made to another teacher which had instantly raised her alert level.

"How much longer will you be?" the woman asked, unsuccessfully masking her irritation with a forced smile.

Not, "Hi, welcome to our school."

Not, "Hello, I'm the cantankerous computer teacher."

Not, "I hear you're our new English teacher."

No. This woman had a serious attitude and she hadn't yet even introduced herself.

"About three more minutes?" Maggie guessed, never having operated the machine before. "I'm Maggie McCauley, the new 7th grade English teacher." Maggie offered her hand, which was grudgingly accepted by the woman who grasped only her fingers, and weakly. Maggie repressed a shudder.

"Elizabeth Cole. Computer Science. Been here 15 years."

Maggie was relieved when her last letter exited the copier.

"I look forward to learning from you this year!" she told the woman, indicating the copier was all hers. She forced a smile and left the office.

On the way back to her classroom, Maggie had to remember to stop referring to her future students as her new troops. The snarky comment she'd heard the previous week was about the "rude awakening the perfect little Army girl" was about to get. This was Maggie's first experience with what she considered to be a personal attack from someone who was supposed to be an ally. She wasn't meant to have heard it, but it still astonished and stung her. It also warned her that not everyone at the school was happy with the selection of a newbie who was fresh out of the military.

Ever the optimist—despite past adversities—Maggie decided to do her best to avoid future interactions with Elizabeth, an obviously unhappy individual.

Opening her classroom door, Maggie was startled to see Razz standing on her carpet and assessing the room.

"Real nice," he nodded, and Maggie wasn't sure if he was talking about the room or her. She propped the door open with a wedge. "Now don't you worry 'bout a thang tomorra'. I'll be by, an' if I hear trouble, I'll be right in."

Maggie chastised herself for secretly judging him on his lazy diction. She was also getting nervous about the strengthening undercurrent of negativity surrounding discussions about the students.

"Good to know, Razz. I don't think I'll have any trouble, though. So you like the classroom?" She attempted to divert his unflappable gaze.

"Yes ma'am. Sure look nice. Kids be lucky to have you teach 'em. Get some sleep tonight. You'll need it."

Maggie thanked him and as he passed, he offered his hand. Unable to avoid it, she did her best to demonstrate she was all business. This time, he didn't linger.

"Yep! A ray o' sunshine," he said over his shoulder as he left the room.

Back at her desk, Maggie wondered if she would, indeed, be prepared for the next day. She finished her "Policies and Expectations" chart focusing on participation, respect, and the expectation her students would make the mature decision to do well when given the opportunity to do so. The last bullet on her chart was, "Be happy you're not a 6th grader anymore!" She was certain her students would smile at that one and would start acting like young adults, if they hadn't already.

Maggie finished her chart just as Kirby stuck her head in the door.

"Let's go! Lunch party!"

Maggie dug the brown bag from her backpack and knew her PB&J would be smashed beyond recognition.

"Unless you really want that," Kirby continued, "the kitchen has a great spread for us, and today's free."

Maggie ditched the bag and joined Kirby in the hall, doubting the middle school cafeteria could provide anything palatable but not wanting to insult anyone unnecessarily. She wondered if this would be a good time to bring up some concerns and decided to go for it.

"Could I ask your opinion about some staff members?"

"Sure. What's up?"

"So what's the deal with Elizabeth? I think if she could've vaporized me this morning, she would've, and she also made a really unprofessional comment about me last week."

"Seriously? That is uncool," Kirby said. "What did she say?"

"Just some snarky comment about my military background and getting a rude awakening. She sounded vindictive and she doesn't even know me."

"Yeah, she's not the most cheerful person on the planet and I think she's been here too long. I actually think *I've* been here too long, but I try not to take it out on anyone."

Entering the cafeteria, they agreed to continue their discussion later. Maggie was pleasantly surprised to see a beautifully stocked salad and sandwich bar awaiting them. Living alone for the past several months had made her lazy when it came to eating well and she craved a huge salad.

They loaded up their plates and joined several members of the 7th grade team at one of the long tables. Kirby introduced Maggie to the group and she shook hands with those she hadn't yet met.

Amber Thompson, the math teacher, gave Maggie the once-over. Maggie could tell she was being judged. Maggie withheld her own judgment on the petite, bordering on anorexic blonde. She sensed a nervous energy in her impeccable comportment and was unsure if it was a good thing or a bad thing.

"Welcome to the best team at North," Amber offered in a heavy southern accent. She had moved to Denver five years earlier to escape the oppressive heat of Georgia, but hadn't lost her distinctive drawl.

"It's only the best because *I'm* on it!" Grant Powell, the school's physical education teacher, tipped back in his chair, raising his arms over his head as he delivered his cocksure greeting to the new girl on the team.

Maggie appreciated the physical specimen stretched out before her and was startled by the tingling rush she felt throughout her body. Flustered, she sat quickly and dove into her salad, hoping her face wouldn't betray her. She suppressed an instant feeling of guilt when thoughts of Sam crept in, but she couldn't deny her sudden primal attraction.

"Yeah, we kinda felt sorry for him since he wasn't really part of any team. He's our mascot," joked Kirby, who enjoyed a more familial relationship with the auburn-haired hunk. Everyone laughed and then turned as the principal stood to address the group.

"I'd like you to join me in thanking our cook staff for this fabulous meal!" David acknowledged the three workers who graciously accepted the applause. "I'd also like to thank you all today for coming back to what will be a very challenging year for our school. I know you've been hearing rumors about the state closing North. The truth is, it's up to us this year to ensure that doesn't happen. We're on our last year of academic watch with the state Department of Education which means any number of things can happen. If we meet AYP this year—that's Adequate Yearly Progress for you knuckle-draggers," he made a point of gesturing toward Grant, which started the whole room laughing good-heartedly, "I mean *when* we make AYP this year, we may be extended on watch. I don't want to talk about what might happen if we don't, so let's not let this news get around the school. Do the jobs I hired you for and we'll all be fine."

"That said," he continued in a more upbeat tone, "I'd like you all to welcome our new 7$^{th}$ grade English teacher. We're lucky to have Maggie McCauley with us this year and I'm sure she'll have a thing or two to share with us about her past life as an Army officer."

A murmur swept through the crowd, mixed with applause, and Maggie realized not everyone knew about her past. A quick scan of the room indicated nods of approval interspersed with looks of skepticism. Elizabeth all but sneered. Maggie caught Grant's eye and was pleased to see a look of surprised amusement in his expression. She felt her face heat up and was grateful when her boss continued.

"Now let's enjoy the last peaceful meal we'll share this year and then get back to work, Eagles!" More polite applause followed and then the team's attention was back on Maggie.

"Does that mean we have to call you *ma'am?*" Grant was the first to speak.

"Only if you want to," Maggie shot back. "You might get my attention faster if you do!"

"Oh, boy, this is going to be a *long* year," Kirby said in her typical deadpan manner, shaking her head at the exchange and already sensing Grant was on the prowl. "So, as leader of the 7$^{th}$ grade team, I need you all to keep your planning hour free every Wednesday for team meetings. Maggie, I've been assigned as your mentor so we'll be meeting more often. I'd encourage everyone to try to visit other classes during your planning period like we started last year. You know the deal. We're all supposed to learn from each other."

"Catch y'all later!" Amber was the first to leave, having barely picked at her sparse salad while the rest loaded up on the free meal. "Feel free to stop on by anytime, Maggie."

Maggie thanked her, suppressing a chuckle at what she considered to be the stereotypical southern belle accent.

"Feel free to stop on by the gym anytime too," Grant offered, playfully punching her arm as he passed. "Just don't kick my ass in front of the class, okay?" Maggie enjoyed watching him swagger out the door and let her mind drift momentarily to what he might look like in gym shorts—or out of them.

"I think he liiiikes you," Kirby teased in a sing-song voice. "Just be careful, though. He's a bit of a playah, if you know what I mean."

Maggie knew what she meant.

"He's not bad," Matthew added, "he just hasn't found the right girl yet." Matthew told Maggie about how he and his own girlfriend had met at a professional development seminar and how great it was to be living together. Matthew's girlfriend taught at the nearby high school, so they had lots to share at the end of each day.

"So, do you need any help this afternoon before the big day tomorrow?" Kirby asked.

"Thanks, Kirby, but I think I've got everything almost ready."

The two said goodbye to Matthew and walked back down the hall.

"So, I've got one more question to ask. Should I be worried about Razz?"

"What do you mean, 'worried'?"

"Well, he's been really attentive when he sees me. I mean, *really*."

Kirby laughed.

"Razz has been our security guard since I started—you don't need to worry about him. I know he can be a little intimidating, but I think that's why he's still here. The kids are afraid of him but I don't think you, of all people, should be!"

"Okay, thanks. That makes me feel a little better," Maggie lied, wondering if the burly intimidator paid as much attention to the married females in the building. Her instinct told her to keep up her guard around him and she always trusted her initial judgment. "I guess I'll see you tomorrow," she said.

The two returned to their rooms and Maggie made quick work of finishing her prep. She was anxious to get home and play with her pup and hoped Harry hadn't had any trouble with him.

## *"Miss?"*

At 4:30 Maggie took one last look around the room, closed the door and left. She was happy not to run into Razz on her way out.

~~~~~

Maggie pulled into her parking spot and smiled. Bones had just returned his ball to Harry, who threw it into the adjoining yard. When the dog saw Maggie, he stopped in his tracks and then charged toward her, his tail wagging his whole rear end. Maggie ruffled the dog's fur, then walked straight to Harry, exchanging what she hoped would be a routine hug, and plopped into the guest seat.

"You first," she said, "and please be honest. Did he give you any trouble?" Bones was back to gnawing on his ball, satisfied that all was right in his world.

"Trouble? Remember who you're talking to, young lady. No, he's been a good boy today. Took a little walk around the apartment at lunch and he was very well behaved. One thing, though," he continued, and Maggie braced herself for what might come next. "Would you happen to have any of those special plastic bags? I don't want the neighbors getting in a huff about 'gifts' they might find in their yard!"

The two laughed and Maggie promised to leave a roll of special bags by the leash the next morning.

"Scotch?" he asked, starting to the door.

As much as Maggie wanted to join him, she declined.

"I don't suppose you're a tea drinker?" she inquired. Maggie could drink hot tea any day of the year.

"Well, not so much, but I might have a box of Lipton in the cupboard. Come on in."

Maggie followed the Colonel to his kitchen, taking in the immaculate condition of the little apartment. He had *real* furniture and several shelves of books all "dress right, dress" along the back wall. She felt a slight twinge of embarrassment when she imagined what Harry must have thought going into her apartment that afternoon, but decided he'd probably seen worse in his day. Feeling instantly at home, she helped herself to the tea and the two returned to their seats outside.

"I have a pretty good feeling about my new team, but I'm not sure about the math teacher. She seems a little uptight. I also had kind of a run-in with the computer teacher. I think she has some kind of grudge against me, or maybe against the Army."

"Some people will never be happy. Have you heard the story about the two little boys who had to spend the day in a room full of shit?" Harry asked, startling Maggie by his choice of words. She decided right then she had discovered her true mentor.

"No, I can't say that I have!"

"Well, at the end of the day their mother asked them how their day was. One boy sat down with his lower lip protruding and told her it was the worst day of his life. But the other one jumped up and down and said he couldn't wait to go back tomorrow, because with all that horse poop in the room, he knew there just had to be a pony in there somewhere!"

"Ha! That's excellent! I've already identified some of my petulant peers. I'll need to find ways of staying away from those grumps!"

They shared local gossip before Maggie returned to her apartment to watch some mindless television before turning in for the night. Eating a bowl of cereal for supper, she decided to shop in the produce aisle of the store the next day.

Bones was ready for his bedtime routine at nine and kept up with Maggie's fast pace as she let her mind drift to the following morning. She was excited, but self-doubt crept in. She quickened her pace and convinced herself there was nothing a bunch of 13-year-olds could do to ruffle her feathers.

That night she dreamt she had shown up for the first day of class . . . naked.

~ 3 ~

WEDNESDAY MORNING Maggie woke with a full-blown case of the jitters.

"Damn it, Maggie! Get a grip!" she scolded herself while running with her carefree pup, who looked at her quizzically. Deciding to forego her second cup of coffee back at the apartment and not having the stomach for breakfast, she dressed in one of her colorful new outfits and left her apartment.

Backing out of her parking spot, she noticed Harry had just opened his front door. He delivered a crisp salute her way which she returned, smiling. It should have been the other way around, she being the junior of the two, but they were beyond formalities.

Maggie arrived at school with a knot in her stomach and was surprised to see groups of students already milling around outside. There were some tough-looking kids in this group, some who looked like they belonged in high school already, and she tried to hide her astonishment at many of the outfits the girls were poured into. There was a dress code, but she wondered who did the enforcing. Students weren't allowed in the school until the bell rang and for that, she was grateful.

Picking up bits and pieces of "new teacher" comments as she strode through the boisterous gaggle, she did her best to look composed and professional. Maggie chastised herself for allowing thoughts of defeat to slip into her psyche. *What if they don't listen to me?* she wondered.

David Martin was there to greet his teachers as they entered the building and Razz stood in the background, unsmiling, arms folded. Today was all about setting the proper tone for the new school year and Maggie had already underestimated her new charges. These weren't the pubescent classmates she remembered from her own middle school days in New England.

"Good morning, Ms. McCauley. Have a great day," David said, shaking her hand at the door. Despite his cheerful tone, Maggie could sense he was on edge.

"Thank you, sir, I plan to!" she returned his firm handshake, nodded to Razz, then made it to her classroom as quickly as she could. Everything was as she had left it. In ten minutes the bell would ring and her first class of 7th graders—still on their summer vacation high—would converge in room 224. Fortunately, there was a bathroom directly across from her classroom. Seven more minutes. She looked at the bathroom mirror and forced herself to smile. It was a trick she had learned years ago and it generally worked to improve her mood. It almost worked.

Three more minutes. She grabbed her candy bowl, positioned herself in the classroom door and jumped when the harsh bell rang. The halls were instantly flooded with chaos, laughter and shoving, and moments later the swarm hit her end of the hall.

"Aw, sweet! Don't mind if I do!" The first boy to arrive dug his hand deep into the bowl and removing it with a fistful of candy. Maggie was shocked, but pulled herself together before the boy entered the classroom.

"I don't think so, young man, these are for everyone." She addressed him sternly, holding the bowl back out to him, and he grudgingly returned several pieces.

"Thanks, Miss," the next girl said timidly, which is what Maggie had erroneously expected from all the students. When the passing bell rang, 27 students were sprawled across desks and chairs continuing their hallway conversations.

Maggie followed the last student into the classroom, closed the door and moved to the front of the classroom, fully expecting her class would quiet down and look to her for instructions. They did not.

# "Miss?"

"Good morning! I'm Miss McCauley," Maggie announced, still anticipating the hush that should have fallen and hearing several loud "Shhhhhhhh" noises from random parts of the room. "This is your seating chart," she indicated the diagram on the front board. "Please find your assigned seat."

More chaos ensued as students stormed the board en masse, unable to find their names, and when they did, unable to make the connection between the pictorial image on the chart and the physical location in the classroom. Maggie accepted her idea was a bust and changed course immediately.

"Okay, now, Juan, raise your hand." When she located the student, she directed him to the assigned seat.

"Linda!" She called each student individually, directing them one by one to the appropriate place, attempting to enforce order on chaos. She would know better for her remaining classes. When everyone was seated, she resumed her position at the front of the class and asked everyone to take out a notebook. After some snickering in the crowd, someone shouted out, "We ain't got our notebooks yet."

"Okay, then," Maggie continued, "if you *do not have* your notebooks yet, please bring one tomorrow, and every day, because this is your English class. You must have something to write with and something to write on when you come to my class. I'm sending home a letter to your parents introducing myself along with my policies and expectations. Please give these to your parents, have them sign acknowledging they've gone over these with you and return them by Friday." Maggie passed out the letters, most of which were shoved carelessly into backpacks while students continued to talk to one another.

"I think we should go over my classroom policies and expectations now," Maggie spoke louder, indicating to the talkers it was time to focus up front, but with no effect. She looked at her seating chart.

"Bernicia, would you please read the first bullet on the chart." It was a directive, not a question. Bernicia turned from her conversation, looking confused.

"What?" she snapped, irritated at having her chat session interrupted. Everyone laughed.

"Please read the first bullet on the chart so everyone can hear."

Bernicia looked disgusted but began, "Cell phones, pagers, and electronic games will remain off and out of site. WHAT? No way, what if there's an emergency and my dad needs to call me?" Others joined in the outrage over this policy and the noise level escalated again.

"Believe me," Maggie jumped in, "if there's an emergency at home, the good people in our main office will come to get you immediately." She cut off further protest by letting them know that although she would confiscate their devices if she saw them being used, she knew they would do the right thing. "Rico, the next bullet, please."

"Aw, Miss, I can't read," the young man said. He looked embarrassed.

Unsure if he was being honest and not wanting to humiliate a student on the first day of class, Maggie said in a playful voice, "Okay, then, who can help out Rico with the second bullet?" Rico looked down at his hands and Maggie felt horrible.

Several students joined in with, "Participate, participate, participate."

"Thank you for your participation!" Maggie offered, attempting to win them over with her sense of humor. They remained unimpressed.

She continued to call names randomly for each bullet on her chart and was surprised at the number of students requiring help sounding out some of the words she felt were basic, certainly for students in the 7th grade.

Maggie read the last one to the group, "We will not make excuses or blame others for our own malfunctions. What's a malfunction, Annie?"

"I dunno," the young girl shrugged.

"OH! That reminds me," Maggie jumped in, "There will be no 'I dunno' responses in my class. Ever. When I ask you a question, even if you honestly don't know the answer, I expect you will at least throw out a guess. I'll work with any answer you give me, except 'I dunno,' and help you figure out a better answer." Maggie was on a roll and excited about being able to teach her first impromptu lesson. "If something is functioning, or functional, Annie, what does that mean?"

"That is works?" Annie shrugged again.

"Right! And do any of you know what happens when you add the prefix 'mal' to a word?" She lost them. They stared at her as if she had three heads, but she didn't want to lose the momentum. "A prefix is something that comes before something else, like a *pre*-game show comes before a football game, or a *pre*vious episode is one that happened before the one you're watching on T.V. now. So in 'malfunction,' we affix the 'mal' to the front of the word and it changes its meaning. Can anyone think of other words starting with 'mal'?"

Maggie had chalk in hand and was ready at the board to write down all the answers.

"This is boring," was the first response.

Ignoring the comment, she asked, "Has anyone heard of doctors being sued for malpractice?" Several students nodded. "Do you think malpractice is a good thing then?" More heads shook "no." "Then who can tell me what a 'malfunction' is?"

"Something that doesn't work right," came an exasperated answer from the second row.

"Right! Thank you. So the important point here is that I won't blame anything or anyone else if I mess up on something. I accept responsibility for my actions. And you don't blame anyone either! Not your dog, your little brother, your alarm clock, your mother, your friend, do you see what I'm saying? If you're having a problem with something in my class, you come to me and we'll figure out how to fix it."

"Miss! Someone said you were in the Army. Is that true?" Rico had recovered from his previous embarrassment.

"Yes, I was, for the past five years," Maggie answered.

"You ever kill anyone?" another boy jumped in and everyone was quiet. It was the inevitable first question raised by young people when they found out she had served in the Army.

"No, I never killed anyone," Maggie responded solemnly, "but I saw many people die." There was a brief moment of stillness in the room before Maggie regained control of the conversation.

"Now, who can tell me something about the words I've written across the top of the board?" she indicated the words in a manner mocking Vanna White, hostess of *Wheel of Fortune*. But before anyone could answer, the bell rang and she was swept to the door with the exiting class. "Notebooks and pencils tomorrow!" she shouted into the mass. With barely two minutes to catch her breath, students from the next class were at her door. She grabbed the candy bowl and prepared to hand one piece each to entering students.

Maggie's second class of 29 students was much like the first, though she avoided the seating confusion by lining students up around the classroom until she placed them in order. Having botched her first class, she found a more comfortable rhythm for her second, but still felt the need to be in close physical proximity to the more rambunctious students. An occasional hand on a student's shoulder got their attention immediately.

During her in-processing the previous week, Maggie had asked for clarification on touching restrictions. Corporal punishment was, surprisingly, still legal in over 20 states, but she had witnessed the effects of what she considered abuse of authority during her military days. She wasn't about to align herself with shady policies. She was there when one of her female sergeants removed her dying two-year-old daughter from life support tubes after the child had been beaten by her father. From her brief exposure to her new students, Maggie didn't doubt she had kids in her classes whose parents used the law to justify their physical lack of control.

Raised in a family of huggers, it was natural for Maggie to use touch for communication and bonding. But she'd heard enough war stories about teachers being escorted out of their schools by security for alleged physical contact to know she needed to be careful. The school policy was to be hands-off aside from a handshake. She took the risk of having a student report her for placing her hand on a shoulder, all the while wondering what the world had come to for this to be a concern.

The bell ending 2$^{nd}$ hour was like a blessing because she would have the next class period for planning. Maggie closed her door and was surprised by how exhausted she felt. She saw no way of ever sitting with students in the room and was glad she'd relegated her desk to the back corner. One more class before lunch, then three after, and Day One would be history. The pace of the first two classes made Maggie feel as though she'd been a performer at a child's birthday party and nothing she performed could make the children happy.

She studied the names in her next class and was relieved there were only 26 students in it, her smallest class. Ten minutes before the bell rang, the door opened and Razz stepped in.

"How ya' doin', pretty lady?" He asked, glancing around the room quickly.

# *"Miss?"*

Maggie knew it was time to say something, but she wasn't sure what. She didn't want to anger or insult the one person she might need someday, but she also didn't want to feel like she owed him anything. Everything had been so clear-cut in the military, but here she felt she was in unknown territory, and exposed.

"You know you're gonna have to stop flattering me, Razz. If any of the kids hear you, they might get the wrong idea." That felt about right.

"Aw, ain't nothin'. Jus' that you do light up a room, and haven't seen mucha that lately. Be by afta' lunch when kids get rowdy." He turned to leave. She cringed at the idea of having rowdier kids in the afternoon.

"Thanks, Razz. Glad to know I've got someone watching my back." Maggie instantly regretted her choice of words. Razz raised an eyebrow, smiled, and left.

Maggie's next class was slightly more sedate than her morning crew, probably because they were hypoglycemic, or perhaps because, like many from her morning crew, they were bored. The lunch bell liberated them all for a welcome change of pace before afternoon classes.

Instead of going to the cafeteria or eating in the teacher's lounge—a depressing little room with no windows—Maggie sunk into one of the beanbag chairs behind her desk. She was happy no one had noticed them yet and decided she'd wait to set up her special reading area. She was happy to have no visitors during the 27-minute lunch break and more than a little irked she'd have barely enough time to eat, pee, and breathe. She chuckled, thinking of the book *Eat, Pray, Love* which she hadn't yet read, and decided someday she might need to write her own version.

Maggie's 5$^{th}$ hour class was out of control and within 15 minutes, Razz was at the door. He entered the classroom, folded his arms across his massive chest and bellowed, "Who's ready to get to know me a little betta!"

The class fell silent, for which Maggie was grateful, and yet she also felt embarrassed that it took someone like the school's security guard to bring the group of 31 under control. "I hafta come back again this hour and somebody gonna take a walk with me."

As soon as Razz left the room Maggie was appalled when her students began their conversations again. It was time to assert her authority. She grabbed her unabridged Webster's Dictionary and moved to the desk of the apparent ring-leader, who was leaning over the desk of the girl behind him. Everyone had their eyes on her, but Kevin remained unaware. She slammed the dictionary on his desk, startling them all, especially Kevin.

"SHIT! What the hell, Miss?" he blurted out and everyone looked to Maggie expectantly.

"Excuse me?" Maggie asked, politely. His outburst didn't surprise her; she wasn't naïve enough to think middle school students didn't curse and she had heard far worse in her military days, but she wasn't about to tolerate inappropriate language in her classroom.

"I mean, whatcha do that for?" He was embarrassed.

Maggie removed the dictionary from his desk and returned to the front of the room, continuing her coverage of policies and expectations as if nothing had happened. Things were starting to go a little better when an unexpected question shot from the crowd.

"Why are *you* our teacher since you're not a *real* teacher?"

Maggie addressed the girl who had spoken and asked her what she meant.

"My computer teacher said you're not a *real* teacher yet, so why should we listen to you?"

Maggie was stunned by the brazen attitude with which the girl delivered this news, but she wasn't about to let it derail her. She glanced at the seating chart.

"Shareena, I can assure you I'm a real teacher and if you'd like to go talk with the principal about my qualifications, I'd be happy to call the office and have them escort you down." All eyes were on Shareena, who sulked in her seat and looked away.

Evidently Elizabeth was being vocal around more than just her peers, disparaging Maggie's licensure program and credentials in earshot of her students. Maggie knew she'd have to do something about this passive-aggressive sabotage.

Her last two classes, although not as challenging as her 5th hour class, left her completely wrung out. By the time the last student ran from her room, she felt like she might cry. One day. Her first day. *"What the hell, Miss!"* still rang in her ears. The question was legitimate. What the hell did she know about teaching a bunch of immature adolescents? They weren't soldiers. They didn't care about the theoretical classroom management techniques Maggie was learning. They didn't seem to care about much of anything.

"We missed you at the team meeting this morning!" Kirby's loud entrance startled Maggie from her stupor.

"OH! I'm so sorry! I completely forgot what day it was! It won't happen again, I promise," Maggie blabbered, mortified about having failed—on so many levels—her very first day on the job.

"Hey, chill, it's not the end of the world. I have a feeling you needed that time more than you needed to hear the report about what we've got to do to stay in business after this year. You okay?" Kirby asked.

"I dunno," Maggie responded in a way she wouldn't allow her students to respond. "I guess I'm surprised by how disrespectful and bored everyone seemed to be today. One of my kids told me her computer teacher said I wasn't a real teacher. Can you believe that? What does Queen Elizabeth have against me?" Maggie tried to add humor to the situation.

"I don't know, but that's unacceptable. I should talk to Dave about it."

Maggie picked up on the familiar name Kirby used for the principal, who wasn't yet on a first-name basis with his new teacher.

"No—please don't. The last thing I need is for people here to think I'm a tattle-tale. I'll send her an email before I leave today."

"All right, but let me know if that shit happens again. I'm taking off now and you should too. Two more days till the weekend!" Kirby added, feigning enthusiasm. Maggie was glad to know someone was on her side. She shoved the beanbag chairs into a closet and sat at her computer.

"Dear Elizabeth," she started her email. "One of my students overheard and shared a comment you made today about my teaching status. I respectfully ask that you refrain from making any further comments which could be interpreted as discrediting my authority as my intentions—like yours—are to help our students be successful. I know you have far more experience than I, and hope you might be willing to share your wisdom to help me become a more effective teacher." *Sincerely, Kiss My Ass*, Maggie thought.

She turned off the lights and left her classroom. She couldn't wait to get home.

The scene back home was a repeat from the previous day, but Maggie was unable to muster the same feeling of happiness. Harry was ready with a hug, and Maggie slumped into her chair, giving her patient friend an earful and realizing fully the magnitude of the disappointment she felt about her day's performance.

"Come now, Captain, are you telling me that you—of all people—let a bunch of snot-nosed whippersnappers get your goat?"

Despite herself, Maggie laughed at the Colonel's colorful expression. It did much to shake her from feelings of self-pity. And he was right. What was she thinking with her bowl of candy and her friendly smile at the door? She had wanted to snap the wrist of the first boy who walked into her classroom that morning, and the impulse had startled her.

"I don't know what I was expecting today, but it sure wasn't what I got." Maggie did her best to describe the prevalent attitudes throughout her classes. "I guess what really got me was the complete lack of respect. Never in a million years would I have considered mouthing off to a teacher like kids did today." For a moment, Maggie felt like an old lady talking about how things had been "back in the olden days."

"Tomorrow will be a better day now that you know what to expect," Harry suggested. "Let them know who's in charge, and why not start the year by telling them they need to write a short story. For it to be good, they need to include four elements."

Maggie had mastered the elements of a short story, but asked him to explain anyway.

"A good story needs to have religion, royalty, sex and mystery."

"Oh, Harry," Maggie said, "I don't think I should ask them to include sex."

"Well, when my teacher assigned us this task back when I was a whippersnapper, my friend little Johnny was the first to finish."

Maggie had heard of "Little Johnny jokes" before and knew she was about to hear a new one.

"Little Johnny, huh?" She raised an eyebrow.

"Yes. And our teacher had to give him an 'A' because his short story had it all. I remember it to this day," he said, drawing out the punchline.

"Do tell," Maggie egged him on.

"It was quite simple, really. He had written, 'My God! The Princess is pregnant! I wonder who did it?'"

Maggie loved the clever zinger and felt better already. She declined Harry's offer of tea, and after thanking him for taking great care of Bones, returned to her apartment to reassess her day. She had forgotten to stop at the store on her way home, so it was cereal for dinner again.

Bones was extra frisky after dinner, much like the students in her afternoon classes, and Maggie ran an extra mile that evening—for herself as well as for her pup.

But as exhausted as she felt when she crawled into bed, she was restless. Thoughts of Sam flooded her mind—she missed him more than ever—and she allowed the tears to flow. Bones nuzzled his way to her on the bed, licked her salty face, and the two finally fell asleep.

~ **4** ~

MUCH TO HER CHAGRIN, the next two days were no less frenetic despite Maggie's best efforts to impose her authority, and her students resented her candy-less greeting. Instead, she offered her hand as they entered her classroom. Although most looked at her like she was crazy—something she'd eventually get used to—they all accepted the handshake challenge.

"This isn't a contest to see who can break my hand," she warned one of her larger students. "Oh, come on, now, don't be handing me a dead fish!" she instructed most of her girls, who apparently had never been taught how to shake a hand properly.

She had gone through the mandatory professional development classes on cultural awareness and could see the necessity of specialized instruction for teaching in a school with mostly minority students from low socioeconomic neighborhoods. She appreciated there was a system in place for acclimating new teachers to the challenges they would face in their classrooms; however, Maggie also understood the realities of the world beyond school and felt an equal responsibility to teach some lessons beyond simple sentence structure. She wouldn't allow "cultural awareness" to be used as an excuse to remain ignorant of the cultural norms students would need to learn to be successful in the United States.

"Squeeze a bit harder, Linda," she instructed. "That's better!"

"Look me in the eyes, Rico, when you shake hands."

"But Miss, my dad says it's disrespectful to do that," he told her.

# *"Miss?"*

Once everyone got seated, Maggie explained why she wanted them all to feel comfortable with the handshake drill.

"In the United States, if you can't deliver a firm handshake while looking a person in the eyes, you'll be seen as being weak, or even worse, shifty. You don't want to be judged so wrongly—and so quickly!"

By Friday she'd seen the kids in action enough to realize a substantial number of her students had learning disabilities and/or behavioral disorders. Kevin had classic attention deficit hyperactivity symptoms. Just that afternoon she had to grab his arm as he lunged toward another student with a sharpened pencil in his hand. And Brad—Kevin's classroom nemesis—displayed autistic behavior. To say he was socially awkward was an understatement. Maggie frequently had to escort him back to his seat during the course of her instruction, and although she tried not to let it interfere with her lesson, it inevitably did.

Working through both her planning period and lunch for the past two days—memorizing student names and reading through countless administrative emails, each with some extra requirement attached—and feeling completely isolated, Maggie thought her first week would never end.

By the end of the day, the level of inattention in her classes had reached a peak, and she couldn't console herself by thinking it was just a Friday thing. After having intercepted a love note from Mateo—who could have been an extra in a Quentin Tarantino movie—to Rena, a special education student, Maggie decided her plan to create a "happy place in which children will *want* to learn" was just a bunch of bullshit.

All those lost hours of sleep planning the perfect classroom arrangement, all those great ideas she'd learned from her summer classes, all the money she'd spent on fun items, it all suddenly seemed worthless. Her students neither needed, nor appreciated anything she had provided so far. What they needed was a drill sergeant.

"Stop what you're doing right now and stand up!" she ordered her last hour class. Startled by the abruptness of her command, they all stood. She rolled up her psychedelic carpet, shoved it under the chalk board and proceeded to direct the rearrangement of the student desks back into forward-facing rows. The new arrangement was still crowded in the small room, but at least the desks wouldn't be touching and she'd be able to walk between the rows more easily.

Not wanting to concede defeat or let her students know they'd "gotten her goat," Maggie explained how the new arrangement would help her to learn their names faster. They grumbled, but most fell in line quickly. Just when Maggie thought she'd be able to end her day on a positive note, however, a skirmish broke out in the back corner.

"YO, muthafucka, back off!" spouted Mateo, shoving Juan. "Bitch tried to touch my balls!" He had the attention of Maggie and the entire class immediately. "Aren't homos supposed to be in jail?" He was furious, and Maggie was between the two boys in an instant. Juan appeared to shrink at the accusation.

"Saved by the bell" took on a new meaning that afternoon. Maggie held Juan back until the room had cleared and told him she'd walk him to the door. She didn't need a fight breaking out in front of her classroom and sensed the boy was fearful.

"I'll report this," Maggie told him. "You stay away from him. Can you do that?"

"Yes, Miss," he told her. "Thanks."

Exhausted, Maggie trudged to the office to see what was needed for reporting her first major disciplinary action. Cursing was one thing, but accusing another student of sexual impropriety took things to a whole new level.

Kirby and Matthew were already in the office and when they saw the expression on Maggie's face, they were all ears. The incident would require a meeting with the principal, the counselor, and the police department as soon as Mateo returned to school on Monday. Mateo had already built up a thick file since his enrollment the previous year and this was a serious offense. Maggie felt some relief knowing things hadn't ended on a worse note in her classroom. A qualified individuals would take it from there.

But she also felt angry. In every overcrowded class she had students who were grade-level appropriate, but most were not. She hadn't had time to follow up on Rico's "can't read" declaration and felt not only that he may have been telling the truth, but that there likely were others with similar inabilities. She had at least one student who was probably a felon, many without an ounce of impulse control, several with obvious mental, emotional, and intellectual disabilities and no indication she'd be getting any extra assistance in her classroom. Not a single student had returned their signed Policies and Expectations letters. Only a few students in each class had a notebook by Friday.

Grant walked into the office.

"Hey, who died?" he joked, sensing the tension in his teammates.

Kirby gave him the rundown, and he suggested they all go out for a beer; after all, it was Friday. "Come on, newbie," he looked directly at Maggie with mischief in his puppy-dog eyes, which reminded her she had obligations at home. "You're not in the Army anymore. Time for some well-deserved relaxation!"

It did sound good. She was feeling majorly stressed and this was the first invitation she had from her own peer group since moving to Colorado. The others agreed, though Kirby would have to check in with her kids and Matthew would have to pick up his girlfriend. They decided to meet at the local Hooters an hour later.

"You want me to pick you up?" Grant asked Maggie. "You know, we're all trying to be more 'green' now," he continued, as if she would buy his poorly-disguised pick-up line.

"No thanks," she countered. "I've got some shopping to do after we meet, but thanks. See you there!" Maggie had heard sad stories about workplace relationships. The year had just begun and she'd already heard rumors about the P.E. teacher's many exploits. She was looking forward to an evening out, and although she couldn't deny the physical chemistry she felt with Grant, she still held Sam close in her heart.

"Could have used you last hour today," Maggie said to Razz on her way out the door, not stopping to explain. "You'll hear all about it on Monday. Have a nice weekend!"

~~~~~

Harry was engaged in a tug-of-war with Bones when she pulled up and won the game as soon as the dog saw his owner. Maggie was exhausted, but the proposition of a casual evening with friends lightened her step. She chased Bones around the front yard before settling down for her evening report.

"You'll never believe what happened today," she said.

"Sounds like this will call for a drink," Harry offered, rising to go inside.

"You go ahead and get yours," Maggie said, "I can't stay long, but I do want to fill you in."

When Harry returned, Maggie entertained him with the highlights of her day. He shook his head while she spoke.

"I'd have every one of them by the ear if I were in your shoes," he said.

"Sadly, though," Maggie responded, "parents know there are lawyers who'd jump on a teacher who dared to touch their little angels and the kids know that too. During in-processing I was strongly encouraged to join the teacher's union for that reason alone. I'm not sure exactly when it happened, Harry, but somewhere along the line someone made the decision to hand over authority to the children and now *we're* the ones who need to watch our step. It just doesn't make any sense."

"Maybe schools like North should be shut down," Harry suggested. "That reminds me of the best advice my dad gave me before I joined the Army. He told me if I could keep my mouth shut and my bowels open, I'd be just fine."

Maggie laughed, scrunching up her face at the unavoidable image, and then mentioned her Friday evening invitation.

"Well, get going, then, young lady. You don't need to be hanging around with an old man on a Friday night!"

Although she felt a twinge of guilt leaving the first true friend she'd made since becoming a civilian, she knew he was right. Besides, she'd have the weekend to visit.

She took Bones for a quick run and contemplated what to wear for her first evening out—and then got irritated at herself for caring about something so stupid.

~~~~~

Hooters was hopping when Maggie arrived. She spotted her peers and saw a couple of pitchers on the table. Grant met her at the door and had saved the seat next to him for her. She was surprised to see Amber there too, with her arms around a nice-looking man. It was hard not to notice the Barbie-and-Ken-doll resemblance in the perfectly beautiful couple.

Grant filled her glass and then proposed a toast.

"To Maggie! She's made it through her first week of school without going insane!"

They raised their glasses and laughed when Maggie reminded them all she still had two days to go to make it a legitimate five-day week.

"There's still a chance," she cautioned them, "especially after my day today. How the heck have you guys survived there for so many years? I seriously came this close to losing it today." She shared her end-of-day highlight.

"Yep, one of North's finest," said Matthew. "He's one of our juvies on probation. Just make sure you document *everything*, and not just on him."

"Are you saying I might have kids in my classes with criminal backgrounds and no one's going to give me a heads-up?"

"You got it," said Kirby. "We have more protective measures in place for our 'challenged' kids than we do for our grade-level and advanced kids. Everyone just figures those kids will do fine regardless of where they are."

Amber—hanging onto her date as if he might try to escape—had finished her second beer and was acting uninhibited. "No Chil' Left Behind really fucked us," she drawled more heavily than ever with the alcohol, and everyone laughed.

"It's true," said Matthew, and his girlfriend nodded her agreement. "It's all about the test and I hate to say this, Maggie, but being in this bizarre transition between NCLB and whatever the Race to the Top requirements are, it sucks to be you this year."

"Go on," Maggie prompted, wondering where he was heading.

"Well, not just you. You and Amber and Kirby, and not even so much Kirby. They test English and math every year and they've just started doing science every other year. If you guys don't raise scores, you might as well update your burger-flipping résumés."

"And the knuckle-dragger gets to keep his job!" Grant raised his arms victoriously. The grouped laughed, but Maggie sensed a hint of resentment.

"It's a good thing we like you," Kirby said, throwing a handful of popcorn at him from across the table.

"So how's that supposed to work this year, since they don't test until almost spring break and they don't get the scores until the summer?" Maggie felt hopeless. "It sounds like there's a good chance we *all* might be flipping burgers this summer, even you, Popeye!"

"Hey, I am what I am, Olive," Grant defended himself, flexing his arms before draping one over the back of Maggie's chair.

His comment broke the tension and Maggie had to admit he was quick on his feet. And cute. And perhaps two beers had loosened her inhibitions. She leaned back in her seat, bumping his hand, and Grant reached in for a subtle tickle on the back of her neck.

"I wouldn't even worry about it," said Kirby. "We've been hearing this for years now and nothing's ever happened. Besides, I'm sure your students will do great this year, Miss Candy-pants!" Everyone laughed. They'd heard about Maggie's candy bowl fiasco.

"Yeah, how'd that work out for you?" Matthew asked, goading her.

"All right, all right, so I thought I might be nice the first day and let them know how happy I was to be their new teacher. I may have been in the Army for five years, but I was raised to be a social butterfly."

"Big mistake," Amber nearly shouted. "If you treat 'em like your fren', they'll treat *you* like a fren'. Like shit."

Amber was drunk. Maggie was happy to see her Ken doll pacing himself. It also reminded her that two was her limit, and there was the shopping excuse she'd made up earlier to ensure there'd be no chance for a follow-on date.

Maggie was glad when the burgers arrived, and after Grant suggested they stop talking shop, their conversation relaxed. When the food was gone and Amber mentioned a dance club, Maggie took the opportunity to leave.

Grant looked visibly dejected when Maggie announced her departure, but the rest understood. They'd been the newbies once and knew what a toll it took. No one wanted to scare her away. It was hard enough to get anyone to apply for a job at their school, let alone someone with Maggie's experience and qualifications. Grant walked her to the door.

"Doin' anything tomorrow?" he asked.

"Yeah, I kind of promised myself I'd catch up on some personal stuff and my dog has an appointment, but maybe next weekend?"

*"Miss?"*

He accepted her offer and walked back to the group, watching her over his shoulder as she departed.

"Grant and Maggie sittin' in a tree," Kirby sang and the rest of the group joined in on the chorus. "Is Mister Macho *blushing?*"

~~~~~

Back at home, Maggie enjoyed a casual stroll with her dog and fell asleep wondering how—or if—she would keep from getting involved with Grant.

# ~ 5 ~

"I'LL BE CHECKING YOUR CALL LOGS this Friday," the Monday morning principal's memo to teachers started. One more task to fit into a full schedule before parent conferences. Most of the calls would have to be made after school; she wasn't going to interrupt parents at their workplace, especially if it was to deliver bad news. She'd try her best to start her conversations with something good about their child, a common-sense tip from one of her professional development sessions. She laughed at the thought of starting a cold-call with, "Hi, I'm little Johnny's new English teacher. Your child just called me a bitch—what is *wrong* with you!"

The day began with a dictionary lesson before Maggie passed out materials for designing their portfolio covers, a task she thought they might enjoy.

"Joe, do you know what this word is?" She pointed to the challenging word before "Monday" at the top of the board.

"Mel . . . melanch . . . I give up," the young man shrugged.

"No! You're doing great! You're so close! Give it another try!" Maggie coaxed him.

"Mel . . . anch . . . oly," he finished, trying to suppress a little smile.

"Almost perfect!" Maggie praised him, then had the class repeat the word with the correct pronunciation. "But today's going to be a *good* day," she continued after having another student read the definition from the dictionary. She could always hope.

That afternoon, however, made her wonder about the prophetic nature of her word-of-the-day choice. Just about everyone was grumpy and things came to a head when she blocked Kevin's hand in mid-punch. His intended target was Shareena.

"What is going on here?" Maggie demanded an explanation.

"If she pinches me one more time, I'm gonna knock her out!" Kevin shouted, rubbing his arm. Shareena had her sweet-and-innocent look perfected, but Maggie didn't buy it. Kevin was an instigator, but he wasn't pretending to be in pain.

"You! Out in the hall!" Maggie directed the girl, "and the rest of you finish your covers." This was the first time she would step outside her classroom with a student. Maggie was determined to take care of her own classroom discipline issues whenever she could. To send a student to the office was like raising the white flag, and she wasn't about to surrender so quickly.

Shareena was waiting in the hallway, attempting to look defiant.

"Explain." Maggie's directive was calm.

"He's jus' always pickin' on me and makin' fun of me and I don't like it," Shareena blurted out, holding back real tears. "An' my momma told me to punch back an' defend myself, so I'm gonna."

Maggie listened to the girl, hearing more than just her words, and then tried to explain the difference between situations requiring physical aggression and those that could be resolved with words. Shareena agreed to get her teacher's attention if she ever felt threatened in her classroom or the school again and the two returned to the classroom. Maggie asked Jeanie, her most timid student, to exchange seats with Shareena. Even Kevin wouldn't antagonize Jeanie.

As students finished their covers, Maggie called them individually to her desk to point out something positive from their first writing assignment before handing it to them to put in their portfolio. It was time for the next social lesson.

"Naldo," Maggie called her first student.

"Whaaaat?" came the lazy response.

"Yes, Miss McCauley?" Maggie said in her sweetest voice before calling the name again.

"Naldo."

"Whaat?" His response was more abrupt this time, but he was confused.

"'Yes, Miss McCauley' is the response I should hear from you when I call your name, please. Let's try this again. Naldo."

"Yes, Miss McCauley," the boy intoned in a comical manner, making everyone laugh.

"Much better, thank you! Will you join me at my desk, please?"

This went on until the end of the day with most of the students playing along nicely and several seemingly anxious to show their teacher what they had done.

"Say my name!" Juan called out, ready to show her his cover design. It was all the prompting Maggie needed to break out into lyrics from the vocal group *Destiny's Child*.

Maggie belted out the first two lines of the song, surprising not only herself but the entire class. She could sing, and now her students knew it too.

"OH, GOD!" Bernicia interrupted. "That song's DEAD to me now."

Maggie enjoyed a little chuckle knowing she had gotten the goat of one of her more troubling students. Bernicia was beautiful, tough, obese, and seemed to have a following of less-than-stellar students attending to her all the time. Maggie hadn't figured her out yet, but sensed both a maturity beyond her years and repressed potential in the girl. She felt it would be a good thing to have this student in her court, but Bernicia hadn't provided an opening yet.

Maggie was patient. She'd eventually find out what made all her students tick; then she'd use the knowledge to make herself a better teacher.

~~~~~

Monday melted into Tuesday, and by the end of the day Maggie seriously reconsidered her word-of-the-day selection. Did the mere act of writing "Tumultuous Tuesday" on the board define how her day would go? Tomorrow would be "Windy Wednesday" and she could have some fun with the dual meaning of the word. She saw no downside to students knowing both definitions and couldn't imagine how they might translate it into bad behavior.

Trevor had just been transferred to the school and showed up in Maggie's first hour ready to take on the world—and anyone who got in his way. A chubby, freckle-faced boy, he made Kevin look sedate. Maggie received the confidential memo about how his mother refused to put him on any kind of medication despite his continual lack of success in previous schools. The mother had also been heard telling Trevor she would send him back to foster care if he didn't behave in his new school—in effect, threatening significant punishment for acting in a way he was physically unable to alter. *So much for having relatively sane mornings*, Maggie thought, and found the boy a seat where she could monitor him easily.

At least Mateo hadn't shown up for school since Friday. He'd been suspended three days for punching Kevin at the bus stop. And Mateo's love-note recipient had also been moved from Maggie's class into an English intervention class. Someone else would be responsible for keeping the amorous convict away from the special education student.

As soon as the end-of-day bell rang, Maggie started her calls to parents.

"Yes, I will do my best to provide some enrichment opportunities for Joe," Maggie promised his mother. "I do have one small concern, though, which I'd like to share with you. I've seen him banging his head on his desk—not hard—occasionally, and when I ask if he's okay, he said he's making up songs in his head when he does this."

Joe's mom had never witnessed this behavior, and Maggie suggested she purchase a small writing journal for him to write his lyrics.

When Bernicia's dad picked up the phone, he was verbally defensive and Maggie could imagine the expression on his face. "Your daughter has some unique ideas," Maggie said, "and I really enjoyed the way she expressed them in her first paragraph assignment."

There was a long pause on the other end of the line and when the girl's dad finally responded, he told her how his daughter had *never* done anything good at school. Maggie thought she heard him choke up a bit.

So perhaps there was hope, though several of her calls were greeted with animosity or disinterest. The majority of her students came from single-parent families and many of them were required to take on parenting duties for younger siblings when they got home, often until well into the night. There were also rumors of some of the kids being homeless and sleeping in shelters at night. Many were undocumented, brought to the

United States as children with parents who spoke no English at home and who were in constant fear of being discovered.

At 5:30, Grant entered Maggie's room with a "What are you still doing here?" look on his face. She was still on the phone and did her best to finish up quickly.

"I look forward to meeting you at the open house. Please bring your daughter along too. Thank you." She ended her call and sighed at the number she had yet to make. "Do you even have to do this?" she asked, hoping he would be required to take on at least some of the responsibility of involving parents in their students' school life.

"Yeah, but I usually don't have as many calls to make as you guys. When kids get rowdy in my class, I just switch it up to dodge-ball. That always has the most immediate *impact* on their behavior. Get it?" He was proud of his pun, and Maggie chuckled.

"So what brings you to my end of the hall?" she asked, secretly happy to see him and confused by the feeling.

"Just checking on you since you never come into the gym, and wondering if you still want to hang out this weekend."

"Yeah, I think so. Maybe you could join Bones and me for a run or something?"

"Sounds good. Or maybe we might do a run *and* something." He smirked.

Maggie blushed. He was smooth. And fast. And she didn't think she was ready to jump into a relationship yet, but the ball was already rolling that way. She justified her need to have a little fun based on the widely accepted work-hard-play-hard rule and if nothing else, he could be a great workout partner.

"Yes, I see what you did there, funny guy, now get outa here!" she said, shooing him away from her desk. "I've still got six more calls to make."

Grant left, suggesting she check out his class during planning period the next day, but she reminded him of their planning meeting on Wednesdays.

"So you'll be gracing us with your presence tomorrow?" he chided her.

"Yeah, yeah, rub it in!"

"I'd love to," he was quick to respond. "Maybe this weekend."

~~~~~

At Wednesday morning's staff meeting, Maggie was able to report she had contacted several parents. She was pleased when a few of them had requested more challenging work for their children and it was clear—from those parents—they weren't fans of the current classroom model which called for deliberately mixing students of differing aptitudes.

"So what happened to ability grouping in school?" Maggie asked her peers. "Do you guys remember being in classes with kids who weren't at your ability level?"

"Aside from P.E., music and art, no," said Matthew, "but you don't want to let anyone hear you question that out loud."

"Are you kidding me? Why not?" Maggie was flabbergasted.

"With Standards-based instruction," Kirby said, "the idea is, we need to allow kids to demonstrate they've mastered something at their own pace and we should give them, quote, every opportunity to succeed. It's all part of the No Child Left Behind bullshit."

"Oh, and don't forget the whole 'diversity in a classroom enriches everyone' mantra," added Amber.

"I can understand how ethnic diversity is enriching, but I don't see how it translates to mixed ability groups," said Maggie. "We have to design lesson plans for at least three different levels, and probably more like five, in every class! I think I would have dropped out of school if I'd been in classes where the teacher had to repeat something twelve times so everyone could get it. How am I supposed to—"

"Shhh! Here comes the Queen of Compliance," Amber warned the group.

Gladys, the school's stone-faced assistant principal, entered the room. Maggie sensed the woman was as clueless as most of the education instructors in the Teacher Licensure Program, who hadn't seen the inside of a classroom in years, but knew all the latest theories. Although Gladys professed to know everything about making kids behave, Maggie had watched her float through a crowd of disruptive students in the hallway as if they weren't even there. Perhaps it was the only way she could maintain her unruffled demeanor. If she had any sense of humor, she had yet to manifest it to the team.

"I'll be leading your team meeting this week, and you'll see me once a month hereafter unless there's something urgent I need to talk about with you," she told the 7th grade team.

While the assistant principal droned on about differentiated instruction, the latest academic-speak for what was expected from teachers in classrooms comprised of every learning ability from the lowest on the special needs scale to the highest on the gifted scale, Maggie suppressed a smirk when she glanced over at Kirby's notebook.

Kirby had drawn a caricature of the assistant principal with a speech bubble saying, "On your knees, minions! Heed my words!" Her cartoon was spot-on.

"Now, Ms. McCauley, would you please select one of your classes and tell me how you are differentiating for your students?" Gladys looked down her nose at Maggie as she spoke.

Maggie was completely unprepared for show-and-tell. With barely one week under her belt, she hadn't even begun to *think* about differentiation.

"Well, in my 5th hour class I've rearranged my seating chart to separate the kids who are physically aggressive with one another," she began, getting a chuckle from her teammates but not from the boss, "and I've sent a couple of kids to the library already for enrichment research, but they've come back because the library isn't set up to serve students yet. Do you know when it might be ready?" Her response wasn't what Gladys was looking for, but she wanted to throw the ball back into her supervisor's court.

Maggie had spoken with their librarian after school the previous day and soon understood new teachers weren't the only ones with little support. The woman had to manage not only the middle school's library, but the elementary school's as well, and her funding had been cut significantly over the past few years. She looked as distraught as Maggie had felt.

"I'll look into it and get back to you," Gladys sidestepped, not happy to have the spotlight shining on something negative within her purview. "But aside from that, have you given them any assignments yet, and how have you differentiated for the varying abilities?" She wasn't going to let Maggie off the hook.

"So far we've been doing group work, dictionary skills, portfolio cover design and their first paragraph. Honestly, though, I haven't even had time to speak to all of them one-on-one about their work yet."

"But you *do* understand the concept of differentiation, don't you?" The woman was relentless and made Maggie feel like a bad little girl. The rest of the team shifted uncomfortably in their chairs and then Matthew broke in.

"Gladys, we're *all* struggling with differentiation in our classrooms, especially the first few weeks when we're just figuring out who our students are and what their capabilities are."

Maggie could have hugged him.

"At least we all know most of these kids here already," he continued. "Maggie's brand new to pretty much everything."

Gladys looked at him dismissively and then addressed the group.

"You are *all* expected to utilize differentiation in your classrooms."

Maggie hated when people used the word "utilize" in casual conversation, but determined there was no "casual" with this woman.

"We have children here with many different learning styles," Gladys told the group what they already knew, "and when I come into your classroom, I want to see how you are designing your lessons in a way that maximizes their exposure to the various styles. It's the only way we can hope to have a successful year. Do you understand what I'm saying?"

Maggie understood the woman hadn't been a teacher in a classroom for the past two decades and had no idea why the current teaching philosophy—demanding lessons appealing to visual, aural, *and* hands-on learning styles—was nearly impossible to implement in a classroom with a 1:29 ratio of teacher to mostly-well-below-grade-level students. Just thinking about the logistics of creating lessons with at least three different ways for students to demonstrate proficiency was enough to have teachers reconsider the benefits of a burger-flipping job.

Gladys was the first to leave the meeting and when the door closed behind her, they were all able to breathe again.

"Now, just because her panties are always in a bind, don't you let her get all up in yours," said Amber, patting Maggie's shoulder.

Maggie was touched by the gesture and the others chimed in with similar words of encouragement. It was clear the sour-faced administrator wasn't on the Friday afternoon beer list. Only one in the group held back until he was certain Maggie wouldn't cry.

"Can we *please* leave Gladys's panties out of any future conversation we might have—ever?" Grant requested, and his question was all it took to get everyone back on track for their afternoon classes.

After lunch, Maggie had the students rearrange their desks again for a group work project—another expectation for her licensure course work and a school-wide expectation. In theory, a teacher could maximize the opportunity for differentiation by selecting individuals for each group based on their different strengths, thereby providing something for everyone to do on whatever project was assigned.

Maggie suspected it was just another ploy to have advanced students help those with lower abilities and motivation, and had a personal aversion to group work for just that reason. Throughout her public school years, she'd always been the one to do more than her fair share in any group. Always wanting to do well and knowing everyone in the group would get the same grade, she would work far longer and harder than the others who were happy to let her shoulder the burden for them.

So she would do the required groupings with her 7th graders, but she would find a way to assess the different levels of participation. After all, it just meant doing a little more work, which was something Maggie was used to.

"You okay?" Razz had come in during the commotion of the latest desk rearranging.

"Yes, just setting up for my first formal observation," she explained to him while the students clumped desks into blocks of four. "Gotta show them what they want to see."

"Well, good luck with that," he said, looking doubtful. "Seems to me they already get enough togetherness time."

Maggie had to agree.

"You jus' lemme know if you need any help, in school or out," he whispered the last part to her.

"Thanks, Razz, I'll remember that," Maggie answered without looking at him. She didn't like his suggestive tone. When he left, she tried to ignore the feeling of resentment starting to work its way into her mind over the assumption people seemed to be making about her status as a single woman. *I don't have time for this shit*, she thought, refocusing her attention on her students.

She had promised her afternoon classes she'd take them outside for their first field trip if they could complete their warm-up writing quickly; there was no money in the school's budget to take kids on legitimate away-from-school learning adventures. She'd have them complete a descriptive paragraph using all five senses. They were excited.

Fifth and sixth hour students, after finding their new seats by counting off and sorting themselves by fours, were fairly well behaved once they got outside. Maggie led them to the playing field behind the school and told them they could experience the space however they wished, within reason. Each had a 3x5 card and a pencil to jot down sensory notes.

Maggie sat in the center of the field and kept an eye on her scattered flock. The boys raced each other, tumbled, shoved and wrestled, but nothing out of bounds. The girls went off in small, chatty groups and did nothing that might make them sweat. A couple of girls sat near Maggie.

Squeals from across the field had her back on her feet quickly and moving to the group of girls backing away from two boys with something in their hands. They were happy to show Maggie the crickets they'd caught.

"Can we eat 'em?" one boy asked.

"Yeah, you said we should use all of our senses," said the other.

Although Maggie warned them against eating the crunchy critters, not knowing if they might have pesticide contamination, one boy popped his catch in his mouth, chewed it twice and opened his mouth widely for the gathering crowd to see.

"Eeewwww! Gross!" was the common reaction, and a new hero was born.

Maggie's hopes of ending the day on a positive note were dashed, however, within the first five minutes of her last class. While standing for the count-off drill for new seats, Mateo and Juan began to fight. Over what? No one knew. Maggie pushed herself between the boys, once again shoving Mateo off of his cowed adversary. She called a student nearest the door to push the office speaker button.

"Can I help you?" came the tinny reply.

"Yes. I need an escort for two boys to the office, please."

Within moments, Razz was at the door and the two boys were taken away. Maggie had wanted to say, *"Take Mateo out back,"* and she believed Razz might do it if she had asked; but even though he made her feel uncomfortable, she wasn't about to jeopardize his job. She was still new, both to the school and to civilian life, and she would be considered a probationary teacher for the next couple of years. Perhaps she had more in common with her students than she thought. Even the terminology used for new teachers implied a hint of guilt and a sense that "The Man" was watching every move. The thought left her feeling insecure and even more resentful.

Once the two boys were gone, the class was able to enjoy their field trip, and several boys looked for opportunities to outdo the cricket-eater. A couple of them captured insects, but neither was brave enough to taste their captured prey.

Gladys met the returning class—with the two miscreants on either side of her—outside of Maggie's classroom. Maggie asked her class to start their paragraphs and remained in the hall with the three. Upon Gladys's requirement for each to give their teacher a sincere apology, Mateo was the first to speak. His words sent a chill down her spine. The boy was a gifted schmoozer. The words were just right, but Maggie believed this troubled young man could charm the scales off a snake. And the way he looked her dead in the eyes made her feel his little show was more an affront than an apology.

Juan could barely look at her when he delivered his meek apology. They all knew he had been the victim.

Gladys left the boys and their teacher with a smug look on her face that said, "See what I did? They're little angels now." Maggie had no time to waste on feeling resentful, but realized, without a doubt this time, it was more than just "The Man" who was breathing down her neck.

"Where'd my sunshine go?" Razz shouted across the entryway to Maggie as she left the building that afternoon.

"It's gotta rain sometime." Her reply was flat.

*Two more days*, she thought, *and then I can breathe again.* As much as she was looking forward to the weekend and a chance to get to know Grant better outside of school, she also felt anxious. It would be the first time she'd go on what might be considered a date since Sam had been killed.

~~~~~

*"Come closer, Babe."*
*Maggie could feel herself being cuddled from behind, a strong arm wrapping around her waist and pulling her closer, the warm glow from the fireplace casting a romantic light on the lovely room in the European Bed and Breakfast.*
*"Say 'yes,'" he whispered in her ear, the heat of his body pressing against hers, her ache for him growing with each soft caress of his fingers along her thigh.*
*"Yes!" she whispered, turning to take in all he had to offer. She would be his wife.*

~~~~~

Startled awake by her morning alarm, Maggie was disoriented by her surroundings. She was not in a cozy B&B. Sam was not holding her in his arms. And even though Bones stood with his tail wagging, looking to her expectantly, she felt horribly alone.

~~~~~

Maggie's first formal observation from her certification program advisor went well. She had her groups working on creating a visual representation of the different words on the growing word wall.

"One person from each group, please, pick up a sheet of butcher paper and some markers," Maggie directed her students. "You all have a different word from our wall. As a group, I'd like you to define the word, use it in a sentence, come up with one synonym and one antonym and then represent the word with a picture of some sort."

There was a flurry of activity as students decided who would do what.

"When you're finished, you'll present your chart to the class. I expect everyone to participate in the presentation."

She had grouped her students randomly, and hoped a leader might emerge in each group. She wasn't about to confess to her evaluator she hadn't hand-selected each group based on their diverse talents. She had yet to see *any* legitimate display of true talent, but it was still early.

Most classes completed their charts with minimal bickering, though many students didn't pitch in. She'd have each of the students determine— on a secret ballot—which percentage of work they believed each person in the group had contributed. Of course, she'd roam around the classroom and record her own observations and would learn quickly which of her slackers were liars too.

~~~~~

Friday morning, Maggie had a request from the principal to meet with him in his office during her planning period. She suspected he'd be checking her record of calls to parents, but she was jittery. She was a professional who'd worked with military superiors for years with ease, but still she reacted to the principal's summoning the same way she reacted to being followed by a police car. Even when she knew she wasn't doing anything wrong, the suspicion of guilt was enough to have her question her innocence.

It was test day and Maggie wanted to put some decent marks in her grade book.

"For this assessment," she told her students, "select five new vocabulary words, any you can remember since the first day of school, spell them correctly and use them in a meaningful sentence. And I'll give you all two bonus points for spelling my name correctly at the bottom of the page!"

"What do you mean by a meaningful sentence?" one student asked.

"Good question! A meaningful sentence is one in which a reader could figure out the meaning of the word based on how you use it in the sentence. For example, if the word is 'melancholy,' then your sentence would be something like this." Maggie went to the board and spoke as she wrote:

"I'm feeling melancholy today because my beautiful dog ran away. Do you see how someone could probably figure out you mean 'really sad' because that's how they'd feel if their dog ran away?" Most of her students nodded their understanding.

"You can't use my example," she told her class as she erased what she had written, "but if you want to use that word, come up with another meaningful sentence."

Sadly, scores across the board in all classes were horrible. Even more tragic, in Maggie's mind, was how few students were able to spell "Miss McCauley" correctly—despite her name being on the top border of the test sheet, over the front door and hanging on a name badge she wore every day.

But it was Friday and she was still alive.

"So tell me, honestly, how are you doing?" David asked her once she settled into the guest chair in his office. She liked his sincerity and the way he didn't beat around the bush.

"Honestly? I don't feel like I've been able to teach them anything yet. I just gave them their first test on words we've been discussing all week and based on the results, I may as well have been speaking in Swahili."

He smiled when she told him about the bonus-points question.

"I think you're being too hard on yourself," he said, and Maggie knew this wouldn't be an interrogation. "Believe it or not, I've had new hires run from this building screaming before their first week was over."

They both laughed which—from Maggie's perspective—was better than crying.

"Remember," he continued, "there are people here to help, so don't be too proud to ask."

They talked briefly about parent calls, a formality on his part, and she was on track with expectations.

"Recharge this weekend and we'll see you on Monday. Hang in there," he said, shaking her hand.

Maggie thanked her boss and left, secretly hoping she might get to the point where he'd tell her to call him Dave. Perhaps he was waiting to see how long she'd last.

When the Friday afternoon bell rang, it sounded like a choir from heaven. Maggie flew out of the building.

"Hey!"

Maggie turned when she heard the shout.

"I thought we weren't running until tomorrow?" Grant caught up to her in the parking lot.

"I'm pretty much always running," Maggie said. "So do you really want to come along tomorrow morning? Bones sleeps in until seven with me on the weekends, so no need to rush over."

"See you at seven-oh-five then. But I might want to take you for breakfast after, if that's okay."

*I'm sure you would,* she thought. But the memory of Sam's body against hers was still fresh. She would need to be careful tomorrow.

"It's my favorite meal," she answered, getting into her Jeep. She was glad no one had suggested Friday beers as she was feeling like she hadn't had a moment to herself all week and was looking forward to relaxing with her next-door buddy. "See ya!" she called out the window. Driving away, she saw him in her rearview mirror, standing there like an abandoned puppy and watching her leave.

~~~~~

Maggie stopped at the liquor store on the way home and bought a bottle of Dewar's for Harry; it was the least she could do to show her appreciation for his expert dog-sitting. Bones had never been so well-adjusted and she suspected Harry was spending more time with him during the day than just a lunchtime walk. She was ready to share a drink with him when she got home.

"Eight days! I've been a teacher for only eight days so far," she blurted out after her first few sips of the mellow beverage, "and I've already broken up two fights, stopped a kid from smashing his head into the lockers, rearranged my seating charts twice, physically grabbed a kid who threatened to throw himself out a window, kept kids from eating crickets—oh, and I failed on that one, kept my mouth shut when an administrator treated me like a child and talked to way too many disgruntled parents." She sighed heavily.

"But you're hanging in there and you know things will get better," Harry offered with encouragement.

"I don't know," Maggie confessed. "I gave them the easiest test in the world today on words we've used all week and they completely blew it. And the worst part is they didn't seem to care!" She was getting worked up and Harry could see her chin start to quiver.

"Do they know what the word 'fascinate' means?" Harry asked. Maggie could see a little glint in his eyes.

"I haven't used that word yet, so probably not."

"Well, when I was in school, our teacher asked little Johnny to use the word in a sentence and within moments he came up with an answer she'd never forget." Maggie raised her eyebrows, knowing she was about to be had.

"He was a smart one, that little Johnny. He looked right at the teacher and proudly told her how his older sister was given a new sweater for her $16^{th}$ birthday. It was blue and had twelve buttons, but because her tits were so big, she could only 'fasten eight'!"

Maggie burst into laughter and tried to imagine how her students would react if she shared the joke with them. Based on the past week and a half, she didn't think they'd get it.

"Harry, I can't thank you enough for all you've done for me. I hope you know how much I appreciate you."

"What else do I have to do besides keep my young Captain in line?"

Maggie decided not to mention her running date the following morning. There was no need to share everything and she didn't even know how the day would turn out. They shared a see-you-tomorrow hug and Maggie went home to tidy up for her first visitor—besides Harry—to her apartment.

Although anxious about seeing Grant the next morning, she slept soundly, exhausted from the trials of her new job and just a little tipsy from her Friday evening indulgence.

~ **6** ~

---

"SO WHERE DID 'BONES' COME FROM?" Grant asked, petting the dog and looking uncomfortable in Maggie's living room.

"I got him at the shelter when I moved in at the beginning of the summer," Maggie told him while tying her laces.

"No, I mean the name," he said, "is it because he likes bones?"

Maggie could tell he was trying to make conversation. He seemed embarrassed to be alone with her in the personal space of her small apartment.

"I named him after the T.V. series. Have you seen it? It's pretty gory, but the character development is great," Maggie answered. There was no way she was going to share the truth about the genesis of her dog's name with Grant. Not yet. Maybe not ever. She wondered if he even knew what she meant by character development. She hoped so.

"I've heard of it, but I haven't watched it. I try not to watch too much T.V. It makes you soft," he said.

Maggie raised an eyebrow at him.

"Not that I'm calling you soft," he said too quickly, his embarrassment becoming more obvious.

"Just wait till we get on the road and you'll see how soft I am," Maggie said, shoving him playfully.

"So how far are we going today? I mean distance, ah, miles," he stammered.

Maggie laughed. "How far can you handle?" she taunted him. "I wouldn't want to incapacitate you or anything."

"Oh, you're on! Bring it!" he said, finally back on comfortable territory.

They stepped outside with Bones ready for his run and excited to have two buddies for company. Harry opened his door just in time to see them disappear around a corner, then went back inside to clean up his breakfast dishes.

"Hey, your legs are way longer than mine! This isn't a race, you know!" Maggie complained as soon as they left the neighborhood, and Grant backed off his pace.

"Sorry! In my world *everything's* a competition. And Bones doesn't seem to be having a hard time keeping up!" he teased.

Maggie could see Grant was regaining his self-confidence. She laughed at the comparison, and once their running paces meshed, they could carry on a conversation.

"So how have you managed to dodge the scorn of the Wicked Witch of the North?" Maggie asked him.

"How do you know I have?"

"Well, I've never seen her get on your case. I think she hates me."

"Nah, don't take it so personally," he said, "she doesn't really like anyone, except maybe herself, and I'm not even sure if she likes herself. She's probably jealous of you because you're getting all the attention now."

"It's not good to have a boss who's jealous of you," Maggie said. "She could decide whether or not I have a job next year."

"Don't give her that much credit. Dave's the one you need to impress and I'm pretty sure you already have."

"How do you know?" She was curious about what was being said behind closed doors.

"Let's just say I've heard things. We've seriously had new teachers quit before their first week was over. He respects newbies who can take the heat and you've already been through a few fires. Plus, you're a veteran. How could he *not* think you were awesome."

"Well, thanks," said Maggie, "but I sure wouldn't call myself that." It was her turn to feel embarrassed by the obvious compliment. "I swear I've already been so angry I've wanted to hurt somebody. Honestly? I think it was easier being in the Army. When you tell someone to do something, they do it. They don't come up with a million reasons why they can't."

The two continued to discuss school challenges and Maggie enjoyed the easy pace of both the run and the dialogue. As they passed what Maggie knew was the four mile mark of a 10K loop she had set up, they were both covered in sweat.

"So, I know I told you to 'bring it,' but could you give me a clue about how far you plan to run us boys today?" he ruffled Bones' head without breaking stride. "Not that this is any big deal or anything, but your little guy seems to be panting a lot."

"Just a couple more miles!" Maggie told him. "He's used to this course and he'll be good as gold the rest of the day."

"You should take some of my classes out for a run sometime. I think they'd be amazed!"

Maggie appreciated the compliment. "Only if you teach some of *my* classes someday. I think having you teach English might amaze them more!"

"What! Are you saying I couldn't handle it?" he goaded her. "See Dick run. Run, Dick, run. Look, Jane, look. See Dick run. Piece of cake."

"Yeah, that's about all I'll be able to get through this year, I'm afraid. But you just gave me a great idea. I actually own the Dick and Jane book series. I think I'll bring them in sometime and show the kids I expect their sentences to be more complex than what they should've learned in first grade."

"Glad to be of service, Ma'am," he said.

"I don't know which is worse, Ma'am or 'Miss?' They can't even be bothered to learn my name."

"Yeah, they can be self-centered little brats sometimes."

Maggie slowed to a walk the last 2/10ths of the 10K loop and Grant let out a sigh of relief.

"I think I need to start running more. Can't have the kids talking about how their English teacher can whoop my ass."

"So dodge ball doesn't keep you in top shape?"

"I think I'm in pretty good shape for an old guy!" Grant puffed out his chest.

"Speaking of older men, I want to introduce you to my neighbor if he's home when we get back. I absolutely love him." Maggie noticed a perplexed expression on Grant's face. "I think you'll love him too."

"Hey, I don't fly that way," he said, stopping in his tracks.

Maggie just laughed and continued walking. When she rounded the corner she could see Harry walking back from dropping off his trash. Grant caught up with her.

"Good morning, Colonel!" Maggie called from across the parking area. "My lovable neighbor," she said to Grant.

Maggie took Bones off his leash and he ran to his familiar friend, who seemed just as happy to see the shaggy dog.

"Good morning to you too!" he replied, waiting for the two to approach.

"Harry, I'd like to introduce my friend Grant. He's the P.E. teacher at my school."

"Pleased to meet you," Grant said, and apologized for his sweaty hand.

"That's a good, strong handshake you've got there, young fellow. Were you able to keep up with my new best friend here?" Harry asked, indicating the panting dog lying at his feet.

"Just about," he said. "When Maggie invited me for a run with her dog, I thought we'd be doing a couple laps around the neighborhood, not a 10K."

"Good thing this wasn't my *long* run day! Harry, would you like to join us for breakfast?" Maggie offered. She didn't catch the dismayed expression on Grant's face, but Harry didn't miss it.

"No, but thanks just the same. I've already had my poached egg on toast. I'm heading to the supermarket in a bit—is there anything you need?"

"No thanks, I'll probably go out tomorrow. We'll see you later!" she gave him a quick hug and headed back to her apartment.

Harry shook Grant's hand once more, whispering, "She's a special lady right there," before letting go of his hand.

Grant just nodded.

Back in the apartment, he asked, "So, can I take you out for breakfast? I'm not sure I'll be seeing you again after today, so you can name the place."

"What do you mean?" Maggie was confused.

"I mean your commanding officer! I have a feeling he doesn't approve of me."

"NOW who's feeling picked on?" Maggie laughed. "I think it's sweet how he watches out for me. And I don't know what I'd do without him. Do you know he watches Bones for me every day while I'm at work? I think Bones likes being with him more than with me sometimes!"

"So, where would you like to eat?" he asked.

"How about right here," she offered. "I can make a pretty decent omelet. I've got bagels, cream cheese, coffee . . ."

"Sounds great! What can I do to help?"

"You make the coffee. I'll get the eggs going."

The two worked together in the small kitchen, unavoidably bumping into one another. Bones lapped up his water and flopped on the cool linoleum floor by the door. By the time Grant got the coffee brewing, Maggie was at the stove adjusting the heat under the eggs. He stood behind her and watched over her shoulder as she flipped the cheesy egg mixture in the pan, and then couldn't stop himself. He placed his hands on her shoulders and when Maggie didn't protest, he rubbed them gently.

"That feels great." Her voice was soft. "I guess I didn't know how stressed I was." She turned off the burner, closed her eyes and felt herself leaning back into him. He stiffened, caught his breath and continued to massage her shoulders more intensely. She trembled, her body tingling, wanting to surrender to his touch.

Bones jumped up and woofed quietly at the sound of Harry's front door closing, jolting Maggie back from the edge of losing control.

"Oh! Wow, thanks for that," Maggie stammered breathlessly, trying to regain her composure as she stepped away from the stove, and from Grant. "Hungry?" She busied herself at the kitchen table.

"Starving," he said, his voice husky, his eyes searching for hers. "Hey, did I do something wrong?"

Maggie saw the confusion in his expression and realized she'd given him mixed signals. He had no real knowledge about her past.

"No, no," said Maggie, putting down the plates, her crisis of conscience averted for the moment. "I'm sorry, Grant. I honestly thought I might be ready to start a new relationship, but I just don't think I can right now."

"Is it because we work together?" he asked.

"That's part of it, but it's more because I'm still working through things with my past relationship. I was engaged to be married this year," she said, hoping she wouldn't have to answer any more questions about Sam, but Grant persisted.

"Where is he now? What did he do to you?"

"He was killed during our last deployment," she said, still not wanting to believe it was true and trying not to cry.

"Oh, my God, Maggie, I'm so sorry," he said, moving to her with open arms. "I didn't know."

Maggie accepted his embrace. "I know you didn't. Thank you," she whispered as he held her gently in his arms. She wouldn't tell him the whole story of how Sam had died. Those details were still too painful.

# ~ 7 ~

MAGGIE WAS READY to take on the world and her students after her weekend away and her time with Grant. He wanted more than just friendship with her, yet he had been completely respectful of her need for time to heal once he understood the tragedy of her recent past.

Her new challenge would be to keep her personal life separate from school. She was too busy on most days to contemplate a serious relationship, but wanted to make time for Grant. She tried not to overanalyze the hunger he had unleashed in her, knowing how physical intimacy can complicate matters, so she'd slow things down and get to know him better before committing her heart.

Her students seemed to sense her renewed levity when she welcomed them at the door and, as if resentful of her happiness, refused to play along. They squirmed and complained and accomplished little on their sensory paragraphs despite Maggie's attempt at bribing them with more fun field trips.

During her planning period she made more calls home to parents and had a depressing talk with Brad's mother.

"I'm concerned no one in the school is helping him," the woman said. "He told me he's thought about going into the boys' room to kill himself and he doesn't want to go to school ever again. He's tired of being left out and made fun of."

Maggie was upset by this revelation and did her best to be a sympathetic listener. She could only imagine what it would be like to live with a child who was so needy and unstable; she saw him only 55 minutes each day. She wasn't sure about bringing up the topic of autism.

"I'll speak with the counselor before the end of the day and we'll do our best to come up with a plan to make Brad feel more a part of his class," she told the mother. The counselor would know how to proceed.

In her heart, though, Maggie believed the child had needs that went beyond her ability as his teacher to take on. She doubted there was much she could do to change his feelings of alienation. His classmates didn't like him because he was irritating, anti-social, at times violent, and "weird." She was just an English teacher. She emailed Anne to let her know she'd come to her guidance office to talk at lunch, and included the gist of the conversation.

Her students continued to wear her down throughout the day and by the time Maggie intercepted a note between Kyle and Ebony—with mostly illegible suggestions about liking to suck on hotdogs with lots of mayo—her buoyant mood was completely deflated. Masters of nasty note-sending, the kids had no time for perfecting paragraph construction. Both students denied the writing and the artwork claiming they had found the note on the floor. Maggie was too tired to confront either of them on their mischief.

After releasing class at the end of the day and sitting glassy-eyed in her classroom trying to figure out what to do next, a little surprise walked through the door. Dashay, one of her good-girl-bad-girl students, was as likely to help a classmate as she was to punch him in the face. She was more than happy to tell her teacher what she needed to do next.

"But the groups of four didn't work," Maggie told her, sounding like one of her own petulant students. The girl had a brilliant response.

"If you put people together who don't really like each other, there won't be much talking," she said.

For the next hour, the two rearranged the desks again and Dashay went through each class putting kids where she believed they'd be least inclined to chat. Then the girl discussed new classroom rules.

"There's gum under these tables you don't even know about," she told Maggie bluntly, adding the sassy black-girl-with-an-attitude head-joggle. Maggie thought she should try it the next time she needed to set a student straight.

Dashay then told her she shouldn't allow food in the room because "they've already made a mess in your room and they don't clean up after themselves, so just say no."

Maggie had been lax about allowing food in the room, partly because she knew many of her students weren't eating well at home and low blood sugar would make them less open to learning. Based on what she'd experienced since her first day in the classroom, however, allowing them to eat in class hadn't translated into better attitudes or learning.

"And you need to tell them your name is Miss McCauley, not 'Miss,' not 'Hey,' not 'Dude.' Give them lunch detention when they're bad."

Her students' seeming inability to learn her name drove Maggie crazy. Dashay made it all sound so simple. She thanked her wise and generous student and opened her arms for a hug. She was both surprised and relieved when the 170ish-pound girl accepted the gesture. Maggie thought the girl might not let go.

"Wait! Here," Maggie opened her closet and gave the girl a bright pink squish-ball she had purchased for a word-game activity and Dashay smiled as if she'd been handed a diamond ring.

After Dashay left, Maggie made one more phone call to a parent who told Maggie if her daughter got into trouble again, she'd have to use the belt. More notes to take to Anne later, so many reports to write, so much time devoted to covering her ass on everything. If she could spend the time she lost—calling parents and writing up disciplinary forms—on lesson plans, she might actually have a chance to attempt legitimate differentiation. As it was, she barely had time to create basic plans for her classes each day.

Grant stepped into her room to check on her and see if there was anything he could do to help.

"Another bad day?" he asked, noting the expression on her face.

"Ugh. That's all I can say. Check out this note." She handed him the obscene correspondence.

"Damn. I don't think I could've come up with this when I was 12. Did anyone get credit for descriptive writing?"

"Ha! You're funny. But no. Hey, I've gotta run! Class is in an hour and I need to check on my pooch."

# "Miss?"

"I really enjoyed our run this weekend." He sounded unsure of himself. "Maybe next time I'll make breakfast for you. My place isn't too far away."

"I'd like that," she said, although she was still nervous about how intensely she had reacted to their first physical contact. "You heading out now?"

The two walked out together. Grant looked like he wanted to kiss her goodbye, but he held back. He opened the Jeep door for her and she tossed in her backpack.

"See you tomorrow," she said. He stood in the parking lot until she drove away.

Razz stood in the window of Maggie's classroom and watched the two. He crossed his arms and frowned.

~~~~~

The next morning everyone was irritated at the new arrangement and the new rules. Maggie reviewed them with her students in each class, letting them know the time for foolishness was over.

"It doesn't mean we can't have fun in class, but if you don't shape up and start focusing on what we need to learn this year, some of you may be in my class again next year." It was an idle threat and Maggie knew it. Her students knew it too. No one was ever held back, especially after the elementary school years.

"I want to talk about this last rule because it's important to me and I'll bet it's important to you too. Your name is something you should be proud of. It identifies you and makes you special. I've learned over 100 names so far these past few weeks and you only have to learn a couple new teachers' names each year. So when you want my attention, I'd appreciate it if you'd stop yelling out 'Miss!' 'Dude!' 'Hey!' or 'Biatch!' and I know the last one's not on this chart." Students in every class gasped when she said the "B" word.

"How come teachers get to cuss and we don't?" The question came up in most classes. Maggie had to explain she wasn't cussing; she was simply giving them an example of what they shouldn't call her.

"Oh, stop looking so shocked!" she told her students. "Like I don't hear what you guys are saying in the hallways?" She added a head-joggle, which elicited smirks from many of her students. She talked about how they might come across inappropriate language in literature, but it didn't mean they could use profanity in their classroom.

"And don't even try cursing in Spanish because I *know* what you're saying."

"You speak Spanish, Miss?"

"Miss? Mistake? Misunderstanding? Miscommunication?" Maggie acted confused, looking around the classroom as if she hadn't heard the question.

"Miss McCauley, you speak Spanish?"

"Enough to understand enough!" she answered her student.

"So will we get to read things with the 'F' word in it this year?"

Maggie thought about how to proceed. It was the first time since the first day of school she had every student's attention. She decided to take a risk.

"Okay. How many of you have *never* cursed in school before?" She was amazed to see a decent number of hands go up in every class. "And how many of you would love to be able to curse in school?" Many more hands went up, but not all. "Okay. What if I said you could go ahead and curse right now?" She looked around to see startled expressions everywhere.

"You crazy, Miss?"

"I've been called worse." They didn't know what to say or do. Maggie finally felt like she was in control.

"Go ahead," she coaxed them, "Trust me. Say whatever curse word you want."

"Anything?"

"Seriously?"

"We won't get in trouble?"

"Anything. Seriously. You won't get in trouble." Maggie waited a moment before it began.

"Shit!"

"Asshole!"

"Puta!"

"Pendejo!"

## *"Miss?"*

"Fuck!"

There was nervous giggling followed by silence.

Maggie waited, looking around to see if anyone else wanted to join in.

"So tell me, was anyone in here struck by lightning?"

When she got no response, she continued.

"Good. The reason I let you all curse in class today is because I believe there's a time and a place for everything, including curse words. You'll read curse words in literature, if not this year then sometime. They're a normal part of some people's dialogue. I even curse sometimes when I'm frustrated or hurt, and for whatever reason, yelling out something bad can make you feel a little better. Not always, but sometimes."

"But are you gonna report us?" asked the student who was daring enough to voice the "F" word.

"I said you could trust me. No one's getting reported. I could probably get fired if you all go home and tell your parents Miss McCauley made you curse in school today, but I'd like to think you're mature enough to understand I'm trying to teach you something important."

They were still paying attention.

"As I said before, there's a time and a place for everything. Cursing is a way of communicating, but it's at the bottom of the scale for people with brains. Can anyone tell me what would be a higher form of communicating?"

"Talking on the phone?" one student guessed.

"Writing a paragraph?" asked another.

"Yes and yes," Maggie encouraged them. "How about poetry?"

"It's hard."

"I don't get it."

"It's stupid."

Maggie wasn't surprised by the responses.

"Has anyone heard of 'Hip-hop'?" she asked, already knowing the answer. Heads nodded and she went on. "Even though most old people like me don't think it's music, it's definitely poetry. Pretty much every song you hear is just a poem put to music." Maggie could see light bulbs going off over heads around the classroom.

~ 69 ~

"So what I'm saying is, cursing is *not* an appropriate way to communicate in my classroom, even though you may see it in your reading, and the reason you take English classes is so you'll be able to communicate more effectively and so people won't think you're an idiot when you graduate." Yup. She said idiot.

"Are you calling us idiots?" protested more than one student.

"No. I'm saying that if you cannot speak well, and without profanity, then people will think you're an idiot. How many of you have been around people who are talking about something and using big words and you have no idea what they're saying?" She saw heads nodding. "How did it make you feel?"

"Stupid," confessed one girl.

"My goal is to help you so you won't feel stupid around anyone. I won't be successful, though, if you don't want to learn. I know I keep putting up new words on the board, but honestly, speaking well is one of the most important things you can learn in school. No, it's THE most important. Don't tell your math teacher I said that." They all chuckled.

Maggie wondered if she'd have a job the next day.

*"Miss?"*

$S$HE WALKED INTO SCHOOL the next morning ready to be reprimanded for her previous day's lesson on effective communication skills, but the first person she saw was Razz. He was standing in his signature arms-crossed-brick-wall stance, but something was different.

"Morning, Razz!" Maggie offered her standard greeting. One of her goals was to start every morning with a smile and a positive outlook. More often than not, walking into school was the happiest part of her day.

"That it is," Razz responded without even a hint of a smile.

She wanted to hear his standard *sunshine* remark and be on her way, or even nothing at all, but she felt obliged to ask what was wrong, which would cut into the precious few moments she had to collect her thoughts in her classroom before the morning stampede.

"Is something wrong, Razz?"

"I jus' think you makin' a bad decision, thas all," he replied, pouting.

"Oh, no, were my students talking about what happened yesterday?" Maggie was nervous, wondering if someone had reported her for the lesson on curse words.

"No, I don't think they know yet," he said, and she was truly confused. "I jus' know more 'bout him than you probably know, an' he ain't right for you."

It finally dawned on her what he was talking about, but she had no idea how Razz would have put two and two together. She and Grant were in the early stages of getting to know one another; they had agreed to keep things professional at school. Kids sniffed out budding romances quickly, but as far as she knew, no one had picked up on any their "togetherness" signals. Maggie felt her privacy had been violated, but didn't know how. She wasn't about to discuss it with the security guard in the entryway of the school, however, and abruptly ended the conversation.

"Don't worry about me," she said as she continued down the hallway. "I'm smarter than you think!" She didn't look back.

*Great,* she thought, *a jealous overseer.* She had no time to wonder how he knew about her extracurricular habits, but it was creepy.

~~~~~

Maggie's first e-mail of the day told her she'd been assigned to the Writing Goals Team. She would meet once a month until the administration of the yearly state tests to determine ways to ensure the school—or rather, the English teachers—would raise writing proficiency scores from 29% to 70%.

*Yeah, sure,* she thought, *piece of cake.* It didn't matter that her students had been pushed along from year to year with no consequences for their failure to master even the basics of reading, writing, and arithmetic, victims of a system favoring statistics over real learning. The viability of the school rested in her hands and those of the other English and math teachers.

Maggie refused to contemplate how the school might close if her students failed to improve their writing by 41% in the next five months. The expectation was simply ridiculous.

She started class with a quick, easy quiz on the Six Traits of Writing, something they'd been drilling since the first week of school and which she knew they would need to apply—brilliantly—on the state test to ensure *any* improvement in scores, let alone a 41% jump. Despite their routine practice, however, no one seemed to know any of the answers and acted as if the quiz had been written in a foreign language.

Wanting to kick and scream and throw herself down on the floor, Maggie instead pulled out one of her Dick and Jane books. It was time to talk more about sentence structure, one of the traits, and she figured the books—showing scenes of the perfect white family with the perfect little dog in the perfect little white-picket-fence neighborhood—would at least be entertaining. Perfect little white students were the minority at North and even those students would be surprised to see the *Father Knows Best* story line Maggie would present to them.

"These are the books my aunts learned to read with in the first grade," she said. "I know that was a long time ago, but the Dick and Jane stories are classics and some of you may even have seen the movie *Fun with Dick and Jane.*"

"Dick!" several of her students giggled.

"Yeah, yeah, try to get over the name. It used to be a pretty common nickname for Richard," she said, trying to downplay their reaction.

"I want you to listen to the sentences and think about how short and simple they are. My expectation for your writing this year is for your sentences to be more advanced than what I'll read in this book and what I've been reading in the notes you continue to pass to one another." There were snickers throughout the class.

"This chapter is called Big and Little." Maggie read the first page.

"Come, come. Come and see. See Father and Mother. Father is big. Mother is little." She showed her students the illustration of mom and dad, then turned the page. "Look, Father. Dick is big."

As soon as the words left her lips, the snickers escalated to hilarity.

"Calm down, everyone," Maggie said, looking at the next page and wondering why she hadn't previewed her selection. Nevertheless, she decided to push on. "Sally is little. Big, big Dick."

The students howled, several boys held their stomachs and one rolled on the floor in laughter. And as hard as she tried, even Maggie couldn't suppress her amusement.

"I think maybe we should stop here," she said, trying to control herself but knowing it was too late.

"No, Miss, No! Keep reading!" her students pleaded. It was a teacher's dream.

"Okay, but just a little more," she said, still laughing, "and then we need to get back to your writing." She flipped to the front of the book, hoping for simpler, less suggestive material.

"Look, Jane. Look, look. See Dick. See, see. Oh, see. See Dick. Oh, see Dick. Oh, oh, oh. Funny, funny Dick."

By the time Maggie had finished, there were tears in her eyes and her students were laughing harder than ever. Maggie hadn't laughed so hard in weeks and it felt wonderful to let down her defenses and share the hilarity with her class.

When she could talk again, she tried to get them to refocus on their assignment, but it was a lost cause. She accepted her role in getting off track from the lesson she had planned, but felt what she had gained as a teacher from this experience was far more valuable.

~~~~~

Maggie brought the inappropriate lesson to her 7th grade team meeting the next day and within minutes, changed all of their opinions about her. All of them—except Grant—thought she was a "goody-two-shoes." By the time she finished reading the rest of the book to them, however, with her extra-sultry reading of the "Oh, oh, OH!" parts, she knew she was one of the team.

Grant shifted in his seat while Maggie embellished her delivery of the simple stories, and although Kirby noticed her teammate's discomfort, she kept her focus on Maggie.

"Oh my God you have to give me those," Kirby demanded once she got her laughter under control. Maggie was happy to remove them from her classroom as they had become a fun distraction for her students.

"If only I could get them as interested in 7th grade books," said Maggie, still laughing.

"I'm going to go through all of these and come up with a condensed reader for staff meetings," Kirby continued, and they all laughed at her contagious enthusiasm. The seasoned science teacher was generally pretty matter-of-fact, and her excitement was refreshing.

Since Gladys wasn't there, the meeting ended early and everyone went back to their classroom for a few peaceful moments—except Kirby, who told Maggie she needed to do a mentor thing.

"Holy shit, are you and Grant hooking up?" Kirby asked as soon as the others had departed.

"Ahhhhh," Maggie stalled.

"You ARE!" Kirby yelled. "You little hussy!" She pushed Maggie playfully.

"We're not exactly 'dating' yet," Maggie protested, "but we are spending some time together."

"Well, I think it's great. He's had his moments, and some of his past dates have been morons, but I can definitely see the two of you together. Does anyone else know?"

"Ah, yeah, and I need to talk to you about that. I was going to tell you, honestly, but I've just been so ridiculously busy lately, and I don't want to make a big deal out of it."

"Go on," Kirby asked, looking at the clock and realizing they didn't have much time before the next class started.

"Remember how I told you I felt a little uncomfortable around Razz?" asked Maggie.

"Yeah, what happened?"

"Well, he evidently saw me with Grant somewhere, and I don't even know where, but he told me this morning he didn't approve and it really creeped me out."

"Wow," said Kirby. "That's definitely weird. Do you think you should talk to Dave about it?"

"I don't know. I don't want to get Razz in trouble, but I also don't think it's appropriate for him to be meddling in my private life. What would you do?"

"Maybe you should just tell him what you told me, that it's not appropriate. Maybe he's just feeling like he needs to protect the newbie."

"I suppose. Hey, thanks, and maybe the next time we go out for a beer we'll let everyone know. I really want to take it slow and I'm just not ready to make anything official yet, okay?"

"Your secret's safe with me. Now I've got to go add my own drawings to this new story line. I can't believe you read that to the kids!"

"Well, I didn't exactly read it the way I read it to you guys, but it was still hilarious. Thanks for listening. I appreciate it," said Maggie, and the two departed for their next classes.

~~~~~

Since the reading of the Dick and Jane stories had been such a big hit, Maggie thought it might be a good idea to prove to her students she was a real person and brought in several family photos. They all loved the pictures of Bones and asked her countless questions about him. She encouraged them to bring in their own photos of themselves, their families and pets, and she would post them on one of the back boards.

Maggie used their enthusiasm about her dog and their own pets or favorite animals to have them do a spontaneous descriptive paragraph. They could illustrate their work too.

Rico had been hesitant to participate in much since the first day of school and Maggie learned he was one of the many students identified as being low on the academic performance scale. But she sensed he wanted to please her. She knelt down by his desk and asked if he had any pets.

"Yeah, I got a pit," he said. Many of her students talked about their pit bulls and she had heard rumors of dog fights.

"Is he nice?" she asked, trying to get him to open up.

"He's all right. He's not mean like a lot of 'em."

"Great! How about starting your description with his name and what he looks like, and then you can say something about his personality! That's all you need to do, okay?"

"Yeah, okay, I'll try," he said. He still couldn't look her in the eyes.

*One step forward*, Maggie thought.

Her students were doing somewhat better with the latest seating arrangement, and the breakthrough she'd made with them on a personal level had made the atmosphere in the classroom more bearable. Still, Maggie learned not everyone would be happy—ever. Even when she decided to allow music in the background occasionally, someone would hate what was selected, so she eventually stored her iPod player away with the beanbag chairs.

"While you're working on your descriptions, I'd like to talk to you about your performance on the quiz." She tried to ignore the snickering.

"I want you all to be successful, but as I've already told you, I can't do the learning for you. I can, however, be here before and after school to help you. So I'm going to give you all until the end of the week to arrange a time to come in and re-take the quiz if you'd like to get a better grade."

"Can we come in at lunch?" one girl asked.

"Absolutely. If you want to do better, I'll help you. But here's the deal. I don't want you to think it's okay to fail your assignments because you think you can just come in anytime later and fix what you've messed up. You need to do your best the first time. Once you leave school, your boss isn't going to keep giving you chances to do well, he's just going to fire you."

"That's cold, Miss," said one boy.

"That's reality, kiddo," Maggie responded. "So who thinks I'm here to fail you this year?" She was truly pleased when not one of them raised a hand.

Since Brad was in detention for punching someone in another class—while the principal was present—Maggie enjoyed a reprieve from having to monitor his every move. She'd spoken with Anne about her conversation with Brad's mother, but even the counselor knew there wasn't much they could do to socialize the boy. It seemed clear to Maggie his behavior patterns fell somewhere on the Autistic Rating Scale, but his mother had yet to see it.

"Has anyone been honest with his mother about what we're seeing at school, Anne, or have you suggested getting special help for his condition? I can't be the only one who's seeing signs." Maggie then learned about another kink in the system.

"Well, we've talked with his mom about his behavior, but we can't suggest he be evaluated for autism," Anne said.

"But why not?"

"Because if the school suggests he needs a special evaluation, then it becomes the school's responsibility to foot the bill for any special treatment that might come from the suggestion. You should know by now that our district barely has enough money to keep toilet paper stocked in our bathrooms."

Maggie couldn't believe what she was hearing. Anne warned her not to say anything that might put the school in jeopardy. Maggie wondered how many other children were being passed along, or worse, ignored, until they became someone else's problem.

~~~~~

By the end of the week Maggie might as well have been a brand new teacher again. Her students became combative once more. They had also worn out the liberty to use the restroom and to get water whenever they felt the need. Her classroom entrance had become a revolving door and she was finding her students loitering in the hallway.

"That's it!" she hollered. "No more passes to the bathroom or the water fountain."

"But I'm thirsty," several complained.

"But I'll pee my pants," admitted another.

The wailing and gnashing of teeth was unbearable, and finally Maggie let out a blaring "WHAAAAAAA!" which startled most of them. She was blatantly mocking their sniveling. And it was time to prepare them for reading Anne Frank's *The Diary of a Young Girl*.

"Listen up, snivelers! If I can't pee until lunchtime, then you can hold it for 55 minutes. And just so you know I'm serious, you can't honestly complain about being hungry or thirsty until you've gone without food or water for a full day. We'll be starting a story soon about a girl your age who truly knew the meaning of hunger and thirst." She wasn't sure if any of them caught the snivelers part, but no one called her on it, most likely because they weren't sure about the meaning of the word.

"But I'll die!" said Linda, who looked seriously irked.

"If you die during my class from starvation or thirst, I'll personally call your parents and let them know it was my fault." The grumbling continued, but her students seemed to sense she was serious.

"What if I really really really have to go?" asked one of the smaller boys in her class.

"I'll be able to tell if it's 'really really really' an emergency, so just make sure you go before you come to my class. There's a bathroom on the way and you have plenty of time between bells."

During what would have been her morning planning period, Gladys called a special team meeting and brought to the 7th grade team a new list of meeting goals. Maggie kept her mouth shut while her teammates asked about the possibility of extra support for the additional requirements they were being asked to fit into their schedules.

*Just let it go*, Maggie told herself as she watched her teammates get cut down by the boss. She would try to make this her new mantra, even though she was ready to fight alongside her peers. She needed to watch her words; they were tenured, she wasn't. And although she recognized the intentions from higher up were good—they all wanted to save the school and their jobs—there was only so much one teacher could do with over 100 students in one day.

That afternoon, Kevin was on the brink of mischief with his pencil again, waving it in his neighbor's face.

"Let's put your pencil to good work, Kevin," Maggie said. She grabbed a journal from the stash she had purchased for kids who, for whatever reason, failed to bring one to school. "I know you're a good artist, so use this for your drawings during class and if a question pops into your head, write it down first. Then when I ask if anyone has questions, you'll be ready!"

Most of her students struggled with impulse control and it was a daily battle to remind them to raise their hands rather than blurt out answers or questions. Maggie remembered classes about the frontal lobe development in the brains of boys happening later than in girls. For her students, it wouldn't happen for another eight years, if it happened at all for some of them. There was absolutely no filtering happening between brains and mouths in her classes. If she could get Kevin to concentrate on doing something she knew he loved, at least one class would be less disruptive.

Kevin smiled and constructed an elaborate pattern on the first page. He didn't make a peep for the remainder of the class.

With 20 minutes remaining until the weekend bell, Maggie picked up on an increase in volume in the center of the class. Mateo was cursing at Kyle, and when she saw the expression on Mateo's face, she quickly moved between the two. Maggie didn't know they had issues with one another and thought that by standing between the two and telling them to knock it off, she could defuse the situation.

But the dagger-filled glare coming from Mateo frightened her, and as Kyle stared at his desk—silently and looking fearful—Mateo clenched and unclenched his fists while continuing to spew forth invectives.

"You're gay! I'm gonna kill you! Pussy! You're a homo," Mateo ranted, and before Maggie could react, Kyle bolted up and screamed, "Let's go then!" nearly pushing Maggie out of his way.

"Shut up! Just shut up!" Maggie screamed, pushing Kyle back into his seat and grabbing Mateo by his sleeve.

She had lost control and was shaking. The whole class was as quiet as a dead man and she registered fear on several faces. Although she should have called security immediately, she chose instead to escort Mateo personally to the counseling office, both so he could get help and so she could cool off.

"Shareena, you're in charge," she said, and dragged the furious boy down the hall.

After dropping him off at the office, Maggie met Gladys on the way back to class. The assistant principal chastised her for leaving the class unattended and asked why she hadn't used the office call button.

"I thought the situation demanded a speedy removal and did what I believed was best for everyone." Maggie defended her decision.

"Well, let's just hope everyone's okay in there," Gladys shot back authoritatively, acting as if Maggie had left her students alone in a room filled with vipers, which may not have been an unfair analogy.

Maggie opened her classroom door slowly, fully expecting to see monkey-like behavior and general mayhem, and instead saw Shareena standing in front of the class and everyone else in their seats quietly paying full attention to her. She had no idea what Shareena had been telling them and for all she knew, the girl was threatening them with pinches, but she didn't care what Shareena had said to them. She whispered a quiet "Thank you, God."

"Don't leave your classroom unattended again," was all Gladys said before turning and walking away.

Maggie walked up to Shareena, who remained at the front of the class, and gave her a huge hug. The rest of the class erupted into applause.

*"Miss?"*

"**D**ID YOU SAY ANYTHING to Razz about us?" Maggie asked Grant over a burger that evening. "Because somehow he figured out we're seeing each other."

She and Grant had started meeting occasionally for a quick dinner before her evening classes and Maggie hoped Grant wasn't bragging about it with anyone.

"Are you kidding? The guy's had a serious attitude toward me since my first year at North. No, we're not exactly on friendly terms."

"Well he's also pretty opinionated and told me he thinks I'm making a mistake by being on friendly terms with you."

"You let me take care of that, okay? What a pompous asshole. I know everybody thinks he's all scary and the kids are afraid of him, but he's all bark. I can't believe he's still working there after what he did last year."

"What did he do?"

"Supposedly, and I guess that's why he's still working—nothing was proven—but a couple of 8th grade boys were caught with weed and they said they got it from him. They did an investigation but didn't find any evidence on him, so it came down to his word against two of our stellar students', and you know how that ended up. I still can't believe they couldn't find some other reason to fire him, though. He's more shifty than most of our juvies. Did you feel like he was threatening you?"

"I wouldn't exactly call it threatening, but it definitely felt inappropriate and I still don't know how he knew anything. I don't think feeling creeped out is enough of a reason to get someone fired, though."

"I'm definitely going to have a little chat with him on Monday, but if you feel even the slightest bit intimidated by him, I want you to report it, okay? Maybe they'll listen to you."

"Okay." Maggie wasn't sure how she felt about having Grant fight this battle for her, but she had felt uncomfortable around Razz since she'd first met him and wanted it to stop. "So what are you going to say?"

"Don't worry, I'll be appropriate, even though I'd really like to use something other than my words. I'll just let him know he has no business getting into anyone's personal relationship."

Despite Grant's bravado, Maggie remained unsure of his plan, but decided she'd let it play out. Her new life—which was supposed to be a breeze—was getting more complicated with each passing day.

~~~~~

*"I've got you!" said Sam, his right hand grasping Maggie's outstretched arm. She had been falling into a bottomless abyss, cold and dark. She knew she was about to die and wondered why everyone was laughing. Sam had saved her. They were together. She knew they would always be together.*

Maggie didn't want to wake up.

~~~~~

"So, am I fired yet?" Maggie asked her boss first thing Monday morning.

She'd gone to school earlier than usual specifically to see David about leaving her classroom the previous week. She also wanted to get to her classroom before Razz showed up for work. She was surprised and pleased to see Kirby was already in his office discussing the latest list of requirements dropped on her team. *Good,* she thought, *backup.*

"Sorry, there's no way out," he replied with a smile. Maggie couldn't understand why he'd have an assistant principal, Gladys, who was so cold and out-of-touch with interpersonal relationships between members of the same staff, but perhaps there were no other applicants. Perhaps previous assistants had already run from the building screaming.

"Um, I seem to recall that when we asked you if you had any questions for us during your interview, your first question was, 'May I have the job?'" Kirby and David laughed.

Maggie had forgotten about Kirby being on the interview team; with her move and her certification classes and her interviews at other schools, summer was a surreal blur.

She felt great comfort in knowing that—aside from Gladys, the tight-lipped assistant principal and Elizabeth, the snarky computer teacher—the rest of the people in her peer group were supportive. She tried not to think about Razz.

"I know you did what you thought was best last week, and I probably would have done the same thing. Hopefully you won't run into a situation like that again, but if you do, definitely call the office first and let someone know if you're leaving your classroom."

Maggie nodded.

"We have a meeting scheduled with Mateo and his parents on Thursday," David continued. "Until then, he's suspended. The kid's had troubles since his family moved here from Guam last year and things seem to be getting worse. He was already kicked out of one school."

Maggie wondered why he hadn't been kicked out of North yet. She had certainly done her fair share of administrative documentation already and had heard he wasn't being an angel in any of his other classes. From her perspective, the things he'd already said and done should have been enough to have him transferred to a school for special boys just like him, but she also knew the administrative wheel rolled slowly and was mired in muck. She kept quiet, and after thanking David for his understanding and patience with her, retured to her classroom.

The day was filled with more required standardized testing for math and English and because the tests took up the entire class period, Maggie enjoyed a break from the usual hour-after-hour stage show she needed to perform to keep the attention of even a fraction of her students.

"Hey, if you all convince me you're actually trying and not just rushing through and making pretty bubbled patterns, we'll have a chips and candy party tomorrow," Maggie bribed her students. The response from every class was positive, and the hours passed quickly.

Maggie didn't see Razz the entire day and was feeling a little nervous about the talk Grant would have with him. Since she had classes that evening, she wouldn't talk with Grant until later. It was time to get advice from someone she knew—without a doubt—she could trust.

~~~~~

"So, how're things going with that clearly infatuated young man of yours?" Harry asked Maggie after the two of them settled into their visiting routine. He knew she didn't have much time before she'd need to leave for her teacher certification classes.

"I hope he knows he'd better be good to you, or he'll have me to deal with," he added, not altogether joking.

"Oh, he knows all right. He knew you'd be keeping an eye on him from the first time you shook his sweaty hand!" She laughed, remembering how embarrassed Grant had been to meet the Colonel in his scruffy running clothes.

"So what's on your mind, young lady? Have I been underperforming in my doggie day care duties?"

"Are you kidding me? The only concern I have there is I think he loves you more than he loves me! No, it's not that at all. I'm just wondering if I could ask you for some advice on a school issue."

"Certainly! I'm not sure how much help I'll be, but I'll be honest with you," he said. Maggie had no question about his sincerity.

"I know I've told you about our security guard Razz, but I haven't told you I think he may be snooping into my personal business. I've always felt like I needed to be careful around him—he's made some questionably suggestive comments to me since I started there—but he crossed the line last week with an inappropriate comment about Grant, and Grant was going to talk with him today about it."

"And how'd it go?" Harry asked. He looked concerned.

"I don't know. I didn't see either of them today. It's just that I'm new there and I think Razz may be involved with other things and I'm not sure what I should do about it."

"Well, find out how Grant's meeting went. Maybe if this Razz fellow knows you're on to him, he'll back off. I know you know how to defend yourself, but I'd say if you continue to feel uneasy, take it to your boss. Shouldn't be like that in school, but then again, a lot of what's going on now shouldn't be going on."

"Thanks, Harry. I agree with you, so it sure helps to hear you say it. And just so you know, Grant's been wonderful. You don't need to worry about him."

"Is he Irish?" Harry asked, raising an eyebrow.

"I think he may have some Irish blood. Why do you ask?"

"Well I had this friend once, an Irishman. I remember he took his wife to Ireland for their 25th anniversary."

"How lovely!" Maggie said. "I'd like to go there someday."

"So, then I remember asking him how he'd top that trip for their upcoming 50th anniversary."

"Yeah?" Maggie waited for his response.

"Well, for our 50th, he told me, I'll go back and pick her up!"

Maggie laughed out loud, both at the joke and because she hadn't seen it coming. She never failed to feel uplifted after spending even a little time with her trusted friend. She wished she didn't have to go to her classes, but skipping was never an option.

"Let me know how it goes, Maggie. And don't take any chances. And no back-talk to your teachers tonight, you hear?"

"Yes sir, I'll be a good girl," Maggie promised. "See you later!"

~~~~~

"He wasn't too happy when I got finished with him," Grant told her on the phone that night, "but let's just say he shouldn't be bothering you anymore."

"What did he say?" Maggie asked, even more nervous than she'd been earlier. She believed Razz could be dangerous, but didn't know him well enough to predict how he'd react to a confrontation.

"He said he'd leave you alone and that's all he said. Don't worry, Maggie," he said tenderly. "I've got your back."

For a moment she considered how Grant reminded her of Sam. Something in the way he said her name just then made her feel special. She considered asking him to come over, but needed her sleep to make it through the rest of the week. She also wasn't ready to take their growing friendship to the next level.

~~~~~

The next morning Maggie brought in a bunch of wildflowers to class. Before she'd start the promised post-test-party, they'd have to complete a fun writing assignment. At least she thought it would be fun, and there was no way she'd be able to justify an entire day of parties to her bosses should any of them decide to check in on her. A fifteen minute end-of-class celebration, yes, but her kids would have to do something standards-based first.

She showed them the beautiful bunch of wildflowers and then walked around the classroom with a scissors, ruthlessly snipping off pieces of the flowers onto each student's desk.

"Oh! Miss! What are you doing?" several protested.

"I don't know, what am I doing? Am I doing something wrong?" she asked, happy to be getting an emotional response from them.

"You're trashing the flowers!" some said.

"Does that bother you?"

Some said yes, others, no.

"Before we open the chips and candy"—she had their full attention— "I want you to write down anything that comes to your mind about these flowers or about the way I just shared them with you all. My requirement is for you to write for fifteen minutes straight. No talking, no walking around, no squirming, no shenanigans. Remember what we did with the five senses writing if you get stuck. Oh, and you can draw pictures too, but do your writing first." Maggie's students would have to sit and write for far longer than fifteen minutes on the state tests. She wanted to believe they could.

"Is it okay if we eat them?" asked one boy, and before she could answer him, another boy popped the flower top into his mouth and chewed.

*What is it with boys and eating everything?* Maggie wondered. She walked nearer to the hungry boy who was smiling and patting his stomach while the rest of the class watched his antics.

"Well, I suppose it won't kill you, but I did get these flowers from my back yard and I can't be sure my dog didn't lift his leg on them before I picked them!"

The class erupted into hysterics, all of them pointing and laughing at the student who had acted too soon, and it took a while before they settled down and got to their writing. Maggie reassured the flower-eater he'd be fine, whispering in his ear how she was just teasing about the possible watering his flower may have received, and she even got him to write about his surprise classroom experience.

Although the party at the end of each class left her room a wreck by the end of the day, Maggie was pleased by what her students had achieved. It was one more tiny step forward.

# ~ 10 ~

THURSDAY'S MEETING WITH MATEO and his parents was rescheduled for the next day and began as Maggie expected, with the family arriving a half-hour late. After uncomfortable introductions, the Child Action Team—comprising the principal, the counselor, Maggie, Kirby, and much to Maggie's surprise, Elizabeth—found out that after moving here, Mateo had made no friends. This revelation didn't surprise his teachers.

"I'd like to include you in my boys' group, Mateo," offered Anne. "We meet every Wednesday during lunch in the counseling office and I think you'd fit in nicely."

"I don't need anyone," he said, pointing a finger at her and smirking maliciously.

"Get that smile off your face, son—and I'll break that finger off if I see you point it again." Mateo's father spoke just as Maggie was about to say something to her disrespectful student. The father was small and meek-looking, but it was obvious that although he wanted to appear to be in control, he needed help with his son.

"Mr. Mendoza, we'd like to keep our conversation here civil," David joined the conversation. "Mateo has had significant trouble adapting to our school since he joined us and we'd like to see him succeed, but he needs to want to succeed as well."

"What kind of program do you have for getting him to stop making excuses and blaming other people for everything?" There was a note of belligerence in the father's tone.

*"Miss?"*

There was no way Maggie was going to speak up, especially being the newest member of the team. She had witnessed Mateo's refusal to accept responsibility for his actions.

"Aside from the boys' group I mentioned," said Anne, "I do meet with a group of students a couple of times a week to concentrate on making good decisions. Mateo would be welcome to join us."

Mateo sneered. His mother, red-eyed and visibly anxious, fidgeted with her hands before speaking up.

"I don't know why he does what he does, but we're doing the best we can. Things aren't too good at home. We have six children and only two bedrooms and he doesn't come home sometimes. If he gets expelled again, he wouldn't be able to go to any other schools in Colorado. I don't know what we'd do if this happens." She finished her confession and broke into tears.

Elizabeth was seated next to her. She patted the tearful woman on the shoulder, but said nothing. She looked bored. An awkward silence filled the small room and the smirk returned to Mateo's face. His father pointed a finger at him with his eyebrows furrowed.

Maggie had never been one to label people—especially children—as evil, but her military experiences had destroyed her Pollyanna world view. She sensed nothing virtuous in her young student. Everything about him spelled bad news.

"The bottom line is, we need to move forward from here, and unless everyone is on board, that won't happen," said David. "I've brought some of Mateo's teachers to the meeting because they're the ones who've been having significant difficulty with your son in class."

Maggie was surprised to hear Elizabeth would have admitted to having difficulty with anything.

"I'd like for each of them to tell you what they're seeing in class so you have a better idea of why we brought you in. Kirby? Would you start?"

"Well, in science class Mateo has been extremely disruptive, particularly with some of his female classmates, who have complained about him making inappropriate comments. I've moved his seat away from them, but then he's combative with his male classmates. He pretty much refuses to complete any work in class and claimed it was an accident when two of the beakers on his desk broke. If he stays on this path, he most likely won't pass my class." Kirby's presentation of her experiences with him was unemotional.

Mateo's mother continued to fidget with her hands and his father was becoming increasingly agitated.

"I've seen similar things in my class," Maggie followed. "He's been particularly aggressive with a couple of boys in class and has openly accused more than one of them of being gay. That kind of language is completely unacceptable. I'm running out of places to seat him as he's been inappropriate with both the girls and the boys. He currently has a 'D' in English."

Mateo and his father were engaged in a staring contest, Mateo with a half-smirk, his father with daggers in his eyes.

"Elizabeth, what's the issue in computer class?" the principal asked.

"Mateo's computer privileges were revoked today." She shifted uncomfortably in her seat. "Despite our safety filters, he somehow got to a site with pornographic images when he was supposed to be working on a typing program and was showing his classmates. When I made my way to his station, he just looked at me and smiled."

Maggie almost felt sorry for the woman, who looked completely flustered by the situation.

Mateo's father pounded the table and stood, bringing David to his feet too.

"Let's take it easy," David said to the man, gesturing for him to sit back down, which he eventually did.

Anne took over; the bell was about to ring, and everyone needed to get back to work.

"We have a contract here outlining the type of behavior we expect to see from Mateo effective immediately."

She read through the expectations. Maggie was stunned that things like "refraining from making sexually explicit comments to his peers," "refraining from physical aggression against his peers," "staying away from pornographic materials," and "focusing on the requirements in his classes" were things to be agreed upon by a middle school student and his parents.

Forms were signed and the meeting was concluded with no one truly believing anything would change. The bell rang, there was another round of hand shaking and the group dispersed.

~~~~~

Maggie was pleased her classes were shorter because of an end-of-day music assembly. Students throughout the school were already checked out for the weekend. She conducted a short in-class exercise on letter writing, and hoped it would keep her kids occupied.

She wrote on the board, "Dear Miss McCauley," then scribbled several lines of nonsense and spelled out "Sincerely" at the bottom of the board.

"You will write a letter to me and you may write anything you want between the salutation and your signature, which goes here," she pointed below the "Sincerely."

"Will you be reading these to the class?" asked students in every class. They knew if she ever intercepted a note, she might read it to the entire class, and they had already experienced many embarrassing moments. It had also cut down on, but didn't completely eliminate, the distracting activity.

"No. These letters will be completely between you and me."

"Will our parents see them?"

"No, not unless you want me to show them to your parents."

"Miss McCauley, how do you spell 'manure'?"

"S.H.I.T.," another student answered, and everyone laughed.

"Just remember our discussion a while ago about appropriate language, though," Maggie reminded them, "and know your audience for this writing assignment is me. You can write whatever you'd like, but I'll be much more inclined to pay attention to something written intelligently over something purposefully offensive. Got it?"

They nodded.

At the assembly, which was a sad performance of what the band class had learned so far, Maggie skimmed through the stack of letters. Some kids claimed the after-test-party was the best they'd ever had. Some apologized for "trashing the place," but thanked her for letting them play loud music. She was surprised by the number of students—including Rico—who expressed thanks for how she had helped them so far. Although Rico had done little academically, Maggie believed he wanted to learn and sensed he wanted to please her. There were several requests for more parties, but a few suggested she shouldn't ever have one again because of the mess some made of the room. Many shared personal stories of relationships and friendships.

The assignment was a good one for getting to know her students on a more personal level and for providing an impromptu gauge of her effectiveness. Even if one student thought she was making a positive impact, she could smile on her way home.

She looked up between the second and third painful musical numbers and caught the eye of Razz, who had been watching her from across the gymnasium. His stony expression startled her and she felt vulnerable. Maggie hadn't run into him all week, which still surprised her, even though she had purposefully arrived and departed when she knew he wouldn't be around.

She forced a weak smile, but there was no change in his composure. Feeling guilty about taking the coward's way out of confronting him herself earlier, Maggie had to suppress the anger she felt toward him for making her feel uncomfortable in the first place. Before the end of the assembly, Razz disappeared out the side door.

For reasons making no sense to any of the teachers—perhaps the principal couldn't take it anymore—the assembly ended with 15 minutes to spare before the end of the day dismissal, so students were sent back to their last hour classrooms. By the time Maggie got her kids back to the room, there were only ten minutes left to kill. Everyone was more than ready to escape for the weekend.

"Go ahead and chat in small groups if you'd like, as long as you keep the volume down, or you can play hangman or draw on the front board. Here's some colored chalk." Maggie hoped to keep her rowdiest class under control until the bell rang.

It seemed to work. She worked her way around the classroom to the different groups to ask what they planned to do over the weekend.

"I'm gonna beat up kids in my neighborhood," said Mateo, who had sulked since the start of class and hadn't started his letter.

"You don't need to tell me that." Maggie's eyes delivered a subtle warning.

"But it's what you think I'm gonna do," he continued, staring her down as he had his father that same morning.

"Well, the decision of what you're going to do is up to you, but I'm going to hope you make some smart ones this weekend." Maggie stared right back, challenging him, before moving on to another group.

Five minutes left.

In the middle of a much more pleasant conversation with a couple of her girlie-girls in the back corner, Maggie's attention was diverted back to where Mateo was performing an unmistakable jerk-off gesture toward another male student, who was backing away from him. Maggie called him over.

"What you were just doing is completely inappropriate and unacceptable," she told him, not wanting to say any more.

He feigned ignorance, but Maggie could see she'd caught him completely off-guard. She stepped uncomfortably close to him, told him what she'd seen and said his actions warranted a write-up.

"Yes, Miss," was his only response just as the bell rang.

She'd made it through another week and couldn't pack up fast enough to get home. She didn't even care she'd have to pass by Razz on her way out by leaving so quickly. And then her classroom door opened and Shareena entered in tears.

"What's wrong, Shareena?" Maggie asked, opening her arms to the sobbing girl.

"Mateo pulled my hair in the hall and then I shoved him 'cause that's what I'm supposed to do," she choked and caught her breath, "and then when I asked him why he did it, he pulled up my skirt and grabbed me here," she pointed to her bottom, "and ran away."

*Shit*, Maggie thought. *Shit, shit, shit.*

"Shareena, I need to report this, but I also need to know if it's what you want me to do."

"I want to report it," she answered, sniffling and still holding onto her teacher. "He's a dirty pig!"

"Okay then. Do you need me to call someone to pick you up? Did you miss your bus?"

"No, Miss, I walk home. I'll be okay," she said, wiping her eyes. "Thanks for being here still."

Maggie wasn't sure if Shareena meant still today or still as a teacher, but gave her another hug and told her to be careful over the weekend.

So she wouldn't be flying out of the school early.

Maggie sat back at her desk and looked up Shareena's contact information.

"What did she do now?" Shareena's mother sounded angry.

"It wasn't what *she* did," Maggie said, defending her student before explaining the incident. Although the mother didn't want Maggie to report it since her own daughter's history of discipline was shaky, she understood why it was necessary.

"I wish I could tell you she's over her predisposition for pinching," Maggie told the mother, trying to turn the conversation to something more pleasant. "But I've also got to tell you how proud I am of the way she took charge of the class when I had to take care of an emergency last week." She ended her conversation on a positive note.

She didn't tell her the emergency was created by the same boy whose academic fate was now sealed by what he had just done.

After hanging up, Maggie realized she'd been spending more time doing intervention and social work since the beginning of the school year than she'd spent teaching. She'd be shopping tomorrow for more necessary classroom items, spending a good chunk of her own meager pay with no expectation of reimbursement. She pulled a referral form from the stack in her desk.

This was Mateo's third major disciplinary referral, the very same day as the worthless meeting with his parents. Maggie felt hopeless. The child, Mateo, had probably never truly been a child. He would never have the opportunity to be a child. He was lost.

~~~~~

She remained seated, elbows on her desk, head in her hands, and tried not to cry. Even the momentary joy she experienced while reading snippets of her students' letters during the assembly wasn't enough to overcome the feeling of failure she felt. She had failed to influence a troubled student positively. The paperwork she had just completed would guarantee he would never step foot in a Colorado public school again.

Her door opened.

*What now,* she thought, looking up to see the concerned expression on Grant's face; he was by her side in an instant, and she stood to let him hug her. The full circle of a comforting embrace that afternoon wasn't lost on her. She let herself disappear for a moment in his arms until she was ready to explain the unfolding of events that day.

"I'm so sorry, Maggie," he said, holding her gently. "Man, I sure wish I didn't have to add to this shit-storm."

"What do you mean? What's wrong?" She pulled back.

"Well, I went out to throw my stuff in my car before coming back to see if we could get together sometime this weekend and the sidewalls on my two rear tires are slashed. I'm gonna need a ride to the Goodyear store on Pine."

"Are you kidding me?" Maggie was on high alert. "Who? Do you think it was Mateo?"

"No, not Mateo, he's never been a problem in P.E., but I have another idea."

"Razz," Maggie guessed. "I had a bad feeling about him during the assembly this afternoon, and I don't know if you noticed, but he disappeared before everyone was released. Please tell me we have security cameras on the parking lot." She had never thought about that before.

"Nope. And it's funny you should mention that, because I've been asking for them for a couple years. There's been a lot of vandalism out there, but I've never been targeted. Believe it or not, I actually think Elizabeth has security cameras in her stash back in the computer lab and I've even mentioned it before, but no one's been interested in looking into it. Her budget's bigger than anyone's and she's got all kinds of equipment back there, but I've never seen how any of it's been used for the school or the kids."

The information didn't surprise Maggie at all, but it did reignite her animosity toward the woman.

"Have you called the police yet? And did you tell them who you thought did it?"

"Yeah, I filed a report with them before I came back in, but I don't think they'll do anything with it. This stuff happens all the time and since I can't prove anything, they suggested I don't accuse anyone. I *will* talk to

Dave about it on Monday, though, because I think we all should be watching what Mr. Razzle-Dazzle's up to. And hey, if it's too much for you today, I understand. Matthew said he'd give me a lift."

"No way—I'll take you there. Hey, it's Friday afternoon," she said with a hint of humor in her voice, "and I can't think of a better way to start the weekend than by helping you change some tires! You'll seriously owe me for this, though." She grabbed her backpack.

"Name your price, woman!" he challenged her.

"I'll have to think about it over a little tire iron action," she teased, "and no, that is not a euphemism."

"You and your big words. After you, warrior princess." He opened the door for her, and the two left the bad vibes of the school day behind.

# ~ **11** ~

WITH TWO NEW TIRES on his vehicle, Grant followed Maggie back to her apartment. Harry was just returning from a walk with Bones when they pulled up. Maggie couldn't stay depressed with the frisky pup around, and both she and Harry enjoyed the show Grant put on chasing the dog in circles around the yard.

*One puppy chasing another*, Maggie thought. Grant was fun to have around and wanted more time with her. In her heart, however, she felt he just didn't measure up to the kind of guy she had fallen in love with not so long ago. Her fear was that no one ever would.

"Thanks for your call," Harry addressed Maggie, "and I'm so sorry to hear about the vandalism, Grant. Maggie told me about your suspicions and I just can't imagine working with people who are out to sabotage you."

"Yeah, and to have to battle both the students and your workmates really sucks." Maggie had more experience than Grant with both of those challenges since the start of school and felt a twinge of resentment toward him once more.

*What is wrong with me!* Grant was attractive, employed, and panting after her. Perhaps it was the puppy-dog correlation which disturbed her most. He was always ready to do whatever she wanted to do, and in her mind, that indicated weakness.

"So I've taken the liberty of ordering far more Chinese food than I could possibly eat by myself tonight," said Harry. "Would you two join me? Looks like you both could use a break from thinking about everything right now."

"Absolutely." Maggie answered without considering Grant's response and then felt guilty. "Does that work for you?"

"Sure, sounds great."

Maggie noted a flash of disappointment.

"You a scotch man, Grant?" Harry asked.

"Well, not so much. I'm more of a beer drinker, but don't let it stop you two from enjoying one. Maggie's been telling me about your cocktail hours and I must admit I'm a little jealous of you, Colonel." His tone was good-hearted, but Maggie suspected there was some truth in his statement.

"Sam Adams okay?" Harry offered, and Grant was happy to help him retrieve the drinks.

"So what's the next step with this Razz character?" Harry asked. "I've been concerned about him ever since Maggie first mentioned his attentiveness. Sounds to me like his motives aren't exactly noble."

"I'll be talking with the principal on Monday, and I think if Maggie tells him about her concerns too, then something might be done. The tricky part, though, as Maggie knows, is that no one's caught him in the act yet and you can't really do much on a hunch."

"Maybe none of it will matter soon anyway," Maggie said. "We're hearing more and more talk about the school possibly closing and even though my friend Kirby said they've heard it before, our principal seems to be taking it pretty seriously lately."

"So do you think it would be a bad thing?" Harry asked.

"It would be bad for us teachers, for sure," Grant said. "We'd all need to look for an open position someplace. We've been told employees in the district would get first consideration, but that doesn't mean much when everyone's already hanging on to their jobs."

The food arrived and conversation continued over the dinner table. Bones lay quietly by Harry's chair; Harry had already fed him his dinner before Maggie got home.

"I'm just not sure how I feel. Sometimes I think I'm making progress," Maggie said, "like the other day when one of the new kids who was just moved into my class offered to teach the other kids what it's like to have dyslexia. I couldn't believe it! This kid's almost halfway through his 7th grade year and he's *just now* been diagnosed. I wrote a sentence on the board and asked him to write down underneath it what he was seeing. We were amazed when we saw his translation. He said he was finally getting help with making sense of words, but not from anyone at our school. He's so far behind in his reading and writing, but because he's a good kid and hasn't caused any problems, he's been pushed through each year with passing grades."

"He must trust you, Maggie. You should feel proud of that," said Harry.

"Well yes, but more often than not I have days like I had this past week. I had to get right in one girl's face the other day—I think I told you about Linda telling me she'd 'die' if she couldn't go to the water fountain during class—after she got all pissy at me when I asked her to focus on her paper instead of on her neighbor. I saw her in the cafeteria with a couple friends the next day and went over to suggest we get a fresh start, and you know what she did?" The men waited for her to continue. "She dismissed me with a wave of her hand, as if she were shooing away a fly! Can you believe that little shit?"

Maggie was starting to feel the effects of her drink. Harry and Grant exchanged raised eyebrows and waited for her to continue.

"And then our literacy resource teacher came to our planning meeting and identified about fifteen more kids who needed additional, additional, additional literacy support." Maggie was on a rant.

"They're already in two pull-out classes and now I'll have to come up with *extra*-extra special plans for them. It takes me so much time to read through all the e-mails piled up by the end of each day, let alone act on any of them, and then to have to come up with new lesson plans in addition to getting done the basics for my routine classes every day and pass all my certification classes. It's just too much."

"Oh, now," Harry patted her arm gently, "I know you've been through a lot this year, but you've been through worse. You'll make it through the rest of the year just fine."

"I know I'll make it through, but there's so much that doesn't make sense to me, even in my teaching classes. It's like our instructors—you know, the people who are supposed to help us become great teachers—resent us. Two of my classmates were in tears last week. One hates her school and gets no support from her administration and the other was already asked to leave by her principal. We're asked questions like, 'So what are you going to do with the handful of students who STILL don't get it despite re-teaching and giving them multiple opportunities to succeed?' and they expect us to give them an answer, but there isn't one. At least not a legal one."

"Things were different in my day," Harry said. "Not everyone made it through high school, but then again, there was a World War going on and there were different expectations. The world's a different place for kids today. I don't think I'd want to be a youngster in this new world."

"My last hour class was so ridiculous one day that I just thought, screw it, and I sat down at my desk," Maggie continued. "It was minutes before anyone realized I'd stopped teaching. One of my non-stop talkers asked why I wasn't doing anything, and when I told her it was because I was done with trying to talk over her, instead of apologizing, she told me she could continue to talk while I was teaching because she could multi-task. When I explained how she was disrupting everyone else too, and needed to stop, she had the balls to growl at me, 'Who says you can tell us what to do?' Can you believe that?"

Grant just listened, his eyebrows still raised.

None of the teachers had it easy at North, but at least a P.E. teacher could keep his students moving—something they needed to do—and relatively focused on whatever physical challenge he presented them with. None of them wanted a dodge ball upside the head.

"And she's just one of so many students who don't seem to give a damn about learning anything. I've had it up to here with one of my 'special' kids. Autistic or not, this boy needs to be out of my class or given an aide. The law is all about providing the least restrictive environment for the benefit of the student with special needs, but who's looking out for the benefit of all the other students? This kid's completely disruptive, throws things, walks across students' desks and I've had to physically restrain him more than once. And I'm supposed to differentiate for that? What a bunch of bullshit."

When Maggie took a breath, Harry addressed Grant.

"So when will they know for sure about the fate of the school?"

"That's the thing," said Grant, "everyone's still pretending things are just fine, but we've got another professional development class coming up from a group that's supposed to help turn around troubled schools."

"Yeah," said Maggie, "and the program's called 'Let's Fly.' Seriously? They might as well call it 'Take a Hike.' I can practically hear the remarks now."

Although her inhibitions were already unchecked, Maggie got up to refill their drinks. She sat on the living room floor with her second scotch. Bones trotted over to her, licked her chin and settled by her side.

"It'll be just another program we'll have to schedule into our days and one more thing to suck away time we should be spending on teaching these kids the basics, which the majority of them clearly haven't learned yet. It's not just the good kids getting pushed through school either. It's all of them. They're in $7^{th}$ grade—they're 12 and 13-years-old and they don't even know how to use a period at the end of a sentence, and I'm not exaggerating!" She was feeling drunk, but didn't care.

"It sure does make me sad," said Harry.

After more talk about the possible fate of the school, Harry stood to clear the table and Grant gave Maggie a secretive time-to-go signal. Maggie wasn't about to leave her host with a mess. She rose unsteadily to help him in the kitchen, and when everything was back in order, gave Harry a big hug and thanked him for always being there to help out.

"Sorry for the tirade," she said, slurring her words.

"Don't you worry about a thing, young lady. It's got to come out sometime. You two go have yourselves a nice weekend. I'll be heading to Vail for the weekend to visit my little sister, but I'll be back for duty on Monday."

Maggie had never considered Harry might have other family nearby; she didn't like to pry and it was the first time he'd offered personal information. She felt bad she'd never asked.

"Drive carefully," she warned. "I've heard those mountain drivers aren't much better than the ones in my neck of the woods. And if you need to stay longer, just give me a buzz." She chuckled at the thought she was already buzzed. It was her first two-scotch night.

Grant followed Maggie and Bones back to her apartment.

"Hey, are you gonna be all right?" he asked, pulling her into his arms once they were inside.

"Maybe," she said, trying to convince herself.

"You sure knew what you were doing with that tire iron this afternoon," he said.

"You don't even know how many tools I can handle," she teased, feeling playful—and hot. She was tired of ranting. She raised her face to him, wanting him to kiss her and sweep her off her feet, and then the dizziness hit her.

"Hey, now, cowgirl, I think maybe it's time you got some sleep." Grant lifted her easily and carried her to the bedroom.

"Wanna sleep over with me?" she asked, giggling.

"You have no idea how much I'd like to, but I don't think that would be such a great idea right now." He set her gently on her bed and covered her with a blanket, kissed her on the forehead, said goodbye to Bones and left.

Maggie was sound asleep before her front door closed. Not long after, she dreamt.

~~~~~

*"We'll live in Colorado and have a dog and a big garden and go fishing every weekend!"*

*Maggie could feel Sam's arms around her and she laughed as he bit her neck playfully. The warmth of his skin as he pressed against hers stirred the fire in her belly. She adored him, she ached for him, and when he lowered himself upon her, devouring her lips, she rose to meet him, keeping pace with his desire until neither could breathe.*

~~~~~

"How're you feeling today, Annie Oakley?" Grant asked Maggie as she approached him in the Denny's parking lot.

"Like I've been in a rodeo and lost," she said, squinting in the too-bright morning light and chuckling at his greeting.

"A little strong coffee will get you back on that bull," he suggested, holding the door for her.

"Sounds like a lot of bull to me," she said, and they both laughed.

"You were on a roll last night," he said once they were seated. "I think you had Harry worried."

"Yeah, I know. I saw him this morning before he left so he knows I'm okay. And hey, I'm sorry about how I acted with you. I shouldn't have. It wasn't fair."

"If you mean almost passing out in my arms, I think I can forgive you for that," he said, and Maggie could tell he was feeling uncomfortable.

"That, yeah, and you know, I think I was leading you on and I didn't mean to." She felt horrible. Her dream of Sam still lingered like a water mirage on a rolling road under a sweltering August sun. She could still feel the heat.

"Listen, Maggie, I know you're still dealing with things from your past that I can't even imagine. You know I want to be with you, but until you're ready, well, I'll do my best to be patient."

"Thank you," she said, her eyes cast downward.

"Now finish your coffee and let's get our grub on!" he said, and Maggie could think of no words to express her gratitude to him.

GGIE AND GRANT were the first ones in David's office Monday
morning.

"I know I can't prove it," Grant said after recapping the recent issues
both he and Maggie were experiencing with Razz, "but I think he's up to no
good and I know you've heard the past accusations against him."

"You know I'm not easily intimidated, David," added Maggie, "but
the look he gave me last Friday before he disappeared from the assembly
was openly hostile and his behavior is so different from how we started the
year off. I'm a little worried about his mental health."

"I'll need you both to write up what you've shared with me today so I
can send it to the D.A.'s office, and be as specific as you can. I don't think
you'll need to worry about Razz anymore. It's still hard for me to believe.
He's been such a great asset to our school, but there were allegations last
year and evidently they were valid. I let him go this weekend after the police
contacted me. They caught him selling to minors, so he'll be tied up in the
court system for a while. I'm sorry you both ended up as his victims. I guess
I just didn't want to believe he'd do something so destructive. You'll meet
Gary, his replacement, at lunch today. I've sent out the message to everyone
about this last minute get-together."

"Wow," said Grant. "How will the students be told?"

"Good question. At first I thought we'd just say he's had a family
emergency and that it's unlikely he'll be coming back, but with the rumor
mill around here, the truth would come out quickly and that would make us
look foolish. I'm going to tell them the truth and maybe it'll scare a few of

them. I'm just thankful none of our students was involved. Oh, and Maggie, most everyone calls me Dave, so unless you're uncomfortable with that . . . and I'm glad you got over calling me 'Sir.' It always made me feel so old!"

Maggie smiled, happy with the implied acceptance as a member of the more permanent staff. She and Grant left the office.

"Kinda freaky, huh?" Maggie said to Grant, looking at the kids gathering outside the door and wondering how they'd fare with Razz's replacement, a trained Resource Officer.

"Can't say I'll miss him. Maybe things will be better now. At least we won't have to worry about him snooping in our business. Have a great day, Maggie, and hey—you should come to one of my classes during your planning period. I'll let you lead P.T.!"

Maggie just smiled and headed to her own classroom. She didn't need any more demands on her time and wasn't as optimistic as Grant that things would get any better.

The arrest was all the kids could talk about, but Maggie still managed to enjoy her day. While her students pretended to work on their vocabulary and sentence structure skills, she met with them individually about the letters they'd written to her. Many were surprised she was able to laugh at what they'd written, especially one boy who had drawn comical before and after pictures of her as nice teacher/evil teacher. If they had expected her to get upset by what they'd written, they were disappointed, but the overall result provided one more step forward in the teacher/student relationship.

The staff meeting went well. Gary came across as a stand-up guy and Maggie discovered she wasn't the only one who had felt uneasy around Razz in the past. Over lunch, members of the seventh grade team thanked her for the part she played in getting Mateo expelled from the school, but their words brought no sense of joy. Yes, it would be nice to have one less student in her classroom to worry about, but he'd likely end up being one more criminal on the streets.

Although Mateo's parents, among others, would come to the conclusion the system had failed their son—didn't they have a program to "fix" him?—Maggie was beginning to believe some children were well beyond the capabilities of any school system to save.

~~~~~

The Wednesday before Thanksgiving break was nerve-wracking; Maggie and her peers suffered through the most intense team meeting with Gladys yet. Even mild-mannered Matthew expressed his frustration when the assistant principal demanded to know what was being done to prepare students for the high-stakes spring testing.

"You want us to achieve 70% proficiency yet no one will fund even the most minimal supplies for the Positive Behavior Support program we're supposed to be running." His voice quavered.

"We can't even promise a field trip for deserving students because of the 'no exclusions' policy we have," Kirby jumped in, voicing the disgust they all felt about the take-all-or-none policy, "and you expect us to get families on board with student behavior, but how the heck can we do that when families expect *us* to fix their kids while they're working two jobs—or are unemployed—and don't have the time or inclination to be involved in anything more, which is a big reason why these students are the way they are to begin with!" She was uncharacteristically livid.

"Honestly," said Maggie, "most of my students still can't write a decent complete sentence and their reading skills are horrible. I can read a paragraph to them from the overhead with them reading along, and then ask a simple question about what's in the paragraph, and they either truly don't know the answers or they don't care. They sure don't care about the state test and they're already irritated with all the pre-test testing we're doing."

"I can count the number of kids who have their times tables memorized on the fingers of one hand," Amber added, "and the rest of them have to use their fingers for addition problems."

Grant had nothing to contribute, and for once, didn't offer a wise-crack to make them all laugh. Maggie had never experienced such unanimous disgust at the state of their students' behavior and learning. By the end of the meeting, even Gladys looked deflated. But she rebounded before leaving the group.

"I'm hopeful this Friday's professional development on the 'Let's Fly' program will give us the tools we'll need to turn things around here. I've heard it's brought great results to lots of schools just like ours. So let's move forward and start giving a little more than 100% when you stand up in front of those kids and we'll turn this school around." She departed brusquely.

"More than 100%?" several of them said in unison.

"Are you kidding me?" asked Amber. "I'm never out of here before five and I'm tutoring kids almost every day during my planning period!"

"I just had a couple kids ask if they could come to my room during lunch," Maggie said, "and I felt so guilty when I told them no. I think I'd lose my mind if I didn't have my 27-minute break. We're halfway through *The Diary of Anne Frank* unit, something I thought they might relate to, but because her vocabulary in the book is so far beyond what these kids know, I practically had to translate everything! It was a drag, and I never felt like they had any compassion at all. I'm so depressed."

"It'll be okay." Grant placed his hand on her shoulder. "No kids this Friday and then a whole week off and we're almost through with the semester."

"Let the countdown begin," Kirby announced, "and we all better start updating our résumés."

The bell rang, and Grant gave Maggie a quick hug before heading back to class. No one on the team was surprised Maggie and Grant had been spending time together.

"I wish you didn't have class tonight," he told her.

"You and me both," she sighed.

~~~~~~

Grading journals on Thursday, Maggie had to remind her students the journals were for English lessons, not for passing "Wassup, homie?" notes to neighbors. Trevor ended up with lunch detention, which made Maggie feel horrible. He was trying so very hard to behave—she could see it and feel it—but the task was beyond his ability.

Document, document, document. Most teachers at North didn't have enough hours in the day to write up every infraction from every student and without adequate proof of misbehavior, no administrative action would take place. She made calls home during lunch break concerning continual verbal outbursts from several students and hung up from the calls wondering what would be in store for her students when they went home. She'd struggled with coming up with something positive to say about the kids before being truthful with their parents. It made her feel like a complete failure.

"Did you ever think maybe children should just stay home between the ages of six and twenty-six to give their frontal lobes time to kick in?" she asked Kirby at the end of the day.

"If only!" Kirby said, happy to see her friend's sense of humor return. "Let's bring that up as a suggestion during 'Let's Fly' tomorrow!"

"You going to the track meet this afternoon?" Maggie asked.

"Naa. I feel like I get more than enough face-time during the day. I'm not a masochist like you!" Kirby punched Maggie playfully on the arm and left.

~~~~~

"So you just come here to cheer on the team?" David asked Maggie, surprised to see her at the track meet.

"Yeah. Since seven of my kids are on the team, I feel like it's important they know I'm supporting them outside of class too. I figure any kind of encouragement we can give might help, even if it just makes them feel obligated to try a little harder later. I know this might sound arrogant, but I think if a kid likes you, he's going to want to try to please you."

"You may be right. And if it makes you feel any better, I saw a few faces light up when they saw you sitting up here. Thanks for coming out, Maggie, but don't forget to take care of yourself."

"I will," she told her boss before he left to greet other parents and supporters. She appreciated his caring and candor and that he showed up for extracurricular events too.

~~~~~

"Let's Fly" Friday training was exactly what the team had expected: ten posters intended to fix all the ills of the school. Each poster represented a metaphor for some aspect of life and provided a visual reminder for overcoming challenges. It was designed to target small groups of troubled students, but North was directed to implement the program school-wide.

"So much for differentiated instruction, eh?" Matthew whispered to his teammates during the lecture. "I'm sure my advanced students will really get a lot out of this." He was disgusted.

"Check out the roller coaster chart." Kirby pointed to it. "It makes me dizzy, but I'm sure if Mateo had been able to see it, it would've motivated him to make different decisions." She giggled, which set them all to giggling.

"Yeah," Amber joined in, "he would've been just like the crab trying to get out of that pot of boiling water in the peer pressure poster! Or maybe he'd be the one trying to drag the escapee back in!"

Noticing they were attracting attention, Matthew shushed the group.

"God, we're just as bad as our kids," Maggie whispered, and the suppressed giggling continued. "Why weren't we issued these posters in August when we still thought we might have a chance?"

"This is awesome!" It was Grant's turn. "They'll finally learn they can make *good* choices instead of bad ones. Why didn't we think of telling them that?"

Maggie suspected the program would cost the school district several arms and legs and would use funds that could have gone to purchasing more state-of-the-art equipment. She couldn't believe how in a 21$^{st}$ Century classroom, teachers were still stuck using early 19$^{th}$ Century chalkboard "technology" and a lab with second-hand computers.

But what did she know about teaching? With so many helpful tools available for teachers, it was impossible to sort through it all, let alone determine how to inject it all into multi-differentiated lesson plans. And now there'd be even fewer hours to work on basic material in the core courses that would be tested.

*Let's Fly . . . away from here*, her sarcastic inner voice said, and then she scolded herself for being negative.

~~~~~

"You're sure you want to take the little guy to New England?" Harry asked Maggie while watching her pack her Jeep for Thanksgiving vacation. Bones was running around the yard, excited by all the commotion.

"Yes, and I wish you'd come along too!"

She'd gotten used to visiting with her neighbor several times each week and realized just how helpful he'd been in allowing her to decompress when things got stressful. The school district had uncharacteristically scheduled a full week off, though, and Maggie loved to drive. Passing the miles with her quiet companion would be blissful.

"My little sister wouldn't be too happy with me if I disappeared, although your offer does sound appealing. Can't remember the last road trip I went on," he said, scratching the top of his head. "What's your suitor up to this week? I imagined he might be in one of those suitcases!"

"No, he's got some college buddies he hasn't seen for a while coming here for the week and I know my folks will want me all to themselves." She wasn't completely truthful; Grant did have friends visiting, but he would have left them in a heartbeat if Maggie had asked.

"Ten days will go by fast. Bones and I sure will miss you." She was almost done packing. "I hope I can forget about my kids, though, and maybe even sleep a night without dreaming about trying to teach."

"Talking about your kids reminds me of a friend of mine a long time ago," Harry said. Maggie knew she was being set up for a laugh. "He was in the supermarket and he noticed an attractive woman waving at him. When they got closer, she said, 'Hello.' Well, he was somewhat taken aback because he couldn't place how he knew her."

Maggie smiled in anticipation of the build-up.

"So he asked her, 'Do you know me, Miss?' and he didn't like her answer. She said, 'Yes, I think you're the father of one of my kids.'"

"Oh dear!" said Maggie, anxious for the ending.

"So his mind traveled back to the only time he had ever been unfaithful to his wife, and he asked her, 'Are you the stripper I made love to on the pool table back in '98 at my friend's bachelor party?' And then she looked into his eyes, calmly, and said, 'No, Sir. I was your son's teacher.'"

"Ha! Oh, Harry, what'll I do without you this week?" Maggie hugged her friend.

"Oh, I think you'll manage just fine. Now be safe, have a rest, and we'll see you soon."

Harry helped Bones get settled in the passenger seat and closed the Jeep door. As Maggie pulled away, he waved and walked back to his apartment. Maggie never saw the tear threatening to spill down his cheek.

# ~ 13 ~

THANKSGIVING BREAK PASSED like a falling star leaving Maggie feeling no less burned out and wondering how she'd muster the enthusiasm to finish the semester on a positive note. In addition to making it through three more weeks of lessons and creating final exams for her students, she'd have to complete her own exams for her certification classes. Most of her students still failed to earn the bonus points by spelling her name correctly on routine quizzes, so she wasn't anticipating stellar results on the semester's summative assessments.

"I don't know, Harry," Maggie said over her welcome-back drink. "This silly poster program is supposed to save our school, but they won't have any state testing results until well into the summer. Does that mean they won't make a decision on the school until then?"

"I suppose if they were serious about seeing if their investment will work they'll wait, but I'd say you don't have to worry about your job next year. It doesn't make sense to bring in expensive new programs unless they have faith in the results."

"I hope you're right. I just wish I felt more optimistic about starting up again tomorrow. I'd say I'm afraid they'll have lost everything they've learned this semester over the break, but then I remember most of them haven't shown me they've learned much anyway." She laughed, but not because she was happy.

At least Bones was joyful to be reunited with his caretaker, and Harry welcomed the exuberance of his fluffy side-kick. Maggie wished for a moment to be in their world, where all appeared to be just right.

~~~~~~

Melodramatic Monday began with a flexible plastic ruler duel between two rambunctious boys which started innocently enough, but escalated to the point where Maggie felt the necessity to confiscating the flimsy weapons.

"Oh, Miss! That's mine!" one boy complained, though the other gave his up without argument.

"OH! Whatever shall I do? Unarmed and defenseless am I!" Maggie bellowed, putting the back of her hand to her forehead and pretending to swoon against the blackboard. The room became quiet instantly and all eyes were on her.

"Oh! Woe is me!" she continued, milking the moment. "'Tis melodramatic Monday, and monstrous Miss McCauley demands my attention!" Some of the students chuckled.

"Might there be a learn-ed one here who would'st enlighten the masses on the meaning of this magical word?"

"I dunno," one brave soul said, "waaaaay dramatic?"

"Bravo! Bravo, kind sir!" Maggie worked her way down from her melodramatic state and felt—for just a moment—the day might be wonderful. Halfway through class, however, she was brought back to earth.

Trevor, who sat in front of the overhead Maggie was working from, snuck his hand behind him and onto the overhead to make shadows on the screen. Maggie, in possession of the flexible rulers, playfully smacked his hand with one. Trevor responded melodramatically and everyone laughed— except Linda.

"You have no right to hit a student!" Linda stood and shouted at her teacher. "I'm going to report you, and you could get sued!"

Maggie simply rolled her eyes and asked her politely to sit down. Everyone else enjoyed the antics between Maggie and Trevor, which continued a couple more times, and Maggie was able to get through the information she needed her kids to know.

Maggie continued to find a reason to start each class that day with a moment of melodrama. Despite the early morning lawsuit threat, she ended her day with no further incident.

~~~~~~

Wistful Wednesday's staff meeting with Gladys left the team feeling even more overwhelmed than they already were. In addition to the ramp-up for implementing the "Let's Fly" program, Gladys had been to a Continuous Quality Improvement (CQI) seminar—yet another corporate model for improving efficiency and buy-in from the work force, and she expected all her teachers to run their classes with the Plan-Do-Study-Act model she presented.

"I want to see your bulletin boards up by Friday. Start using this cycle with your lessons. Corporations are using this model to get buy-in from their employees, and when employees feel their input is valued, it's been shown they are happier and will work harder."

Gladys handed out packets of the PowerPoint presentation and expected compliance. The team sat, dumbfounded, until she finished going over the most important slides in the packet.

"Oh, and Maggie, I think you might be right about Brad having Asperger Syndrome. I had a long chat with his mother this morning and she's considering putting him in another school. Don't say anything, obviously, and it might not happen, but I just wanted to give you all a heads-up. Remember we have parent-teacher conferences next Thursday, so make sure you've made calls to everyone you think should attend. Questions?" Gladys looked at each teacher, and if she could tell her presentation had completely demoralized them all, she didn't let on.

"Oh . . . My . . . God," Kirby said after Gladys departed, looking for a moment as if she might burst.

"Buy-in? We have to have buy-in from our students?" Matthew stood abruptly and his chair tipped over behind him.

"Can't we just leave a few of these boneheads behind, or at least leave them in the hallway during class?" Maggie asked.

They had all previously discussed the problems created by the *No Child Left Behind* edict which made it impossible to work on the things most teachers felt would be valuable, and the *Race to the Top* agenda wasn't yet clear to any of them.

"Can you believe I can't even do public speaking skills because they're not evaluated on the state test?" she continued. "We have kids who are physically incapable of controlling their mouths and bodies, and they're the ones whose scores we have to raise. I handed out duct tape this morning in literacy class to a few of my boys who knew they couldn't stop chatting, and they were happy to put it over their mouths."

They all laughed.

"Unfortunately, some of them were even noisier with the tape on! Go figure."

"I've decided to address my instruction to those I know will listen," Amber confessed quietly. "I'm done with having to repeat my instructions a million times and I'm tired of not being able to move forward with the kids who want to learn because I'm constantly having to redirect the trouble-makers."

Maggie was surprised Amber seemed to be having as much difficulty as she was in her classes. She considered trying Amber's approach.

"Dinner tonight?" Grant asked her on the way back to class.

"Only if you'll finish one of my term-end projects and make about 75 calls to parents who really need to show up for conferences." Maggie was irritated Grant still didn't seem to understand how much more burdensome her year was than his.

"Sorry. I just thought you might like a break," he said, dejected.

"No, no, you're right, I do, but I just can't." Her tone was apologetic.

"You know, you're doing a great job," he said, more upbeat, "and the kids honestly do like you. I hear them talking sometimes and they think you're cool."

Maggie was surprised by his announcement.

"Thanks, I needed that. I know it'll be okay, but I just still feel like I'm a newbie and can't get through to most of them."

"You will. Hang in there, okay?" He moved in for a hug, but stopped himself.

"Yeah," she replied, unconvincingly. She dreaded the long nights of homework and home phone calls awaiting her.

~~~~~

*"Miss?"*

Trevor gave Maggie a big bear-hug at the start of class on Thoughtful Thursday—Maggie wanted to test her word-of-the-day theory—and told her he'd do his best to behave. Sadly, his best was far from successful and during a session of "pair and share," one of many group activities Maggie was expected to incorporate as a teaching tool, Trevor shoved his partner and became belligerent.

"Yo, Dude!" Trevor yelled in Maggie's direction, trying to get her attention. "I need a pencil!" He was tipping his chair precariously backward.

Maggie walked to the front of his desk after finishing with the group she was assisting.

"Please set your chair back down," she told him calmly, "and I know you know the proper way to get my attention."

"You better stand back or I'll slam this down on your foot," he announced, goading her, a mischievous smile on his face.

Although Maggie understood her student truly had no impulse control, she had run out of patience; with so many students needing attention, she simply didn't have the extra endurance this child demanded.

"I'll ask you one more time to lower your chair, and if you refuse, I'll call for security to escort you to the office" Maggie warned her rambunctious student.

Unfortunately, this was just what he wanted and he expressed his excitement about having security come to get him. Maggie called his bluff and pushed the office button. She feared she might do something that would get her fired.

The visual she had of herself slamming his chair down forcefully and then grabbing him by the ear and dragging him out the door frightened her. Her student's blatant disrespect appalled and infuriated her.

"May I help you?" came the voice from the office, startling Maggie from her daydream. She was shaking.

"Please send someone to escort a student." She managed to control her voice, staring at Trevor, who had become visibly distressed by his own lack of control. She felt sorry for him.

*Why the hell am I doing this?* she wondered, but was unable to come up with a satisfactory answer.

Her afternoon classes fared no better with Bernicia starting to make random ear-piercing screeches for no apparent reason. The large girl, who had made some earlier progress with trusting Maggie enough to share her feelings in her journal, was more interested in constantly fiddling with and displaying her newly-pierced tongue. Maggie wondered how many of her students had absolutely no adult or parental control when they were outside of school.

When the school day ended, she pulled out her referral binder. It was growing thicker with each passing day. She prioritized her phone call list. She questioned what good any of it would do.

~~~~~

"Now, I have something I need to tell you and I don't want you to say anything at all in response. Just listen," David told Maggie in an uncharacteristically stern tone after calling her into his office first thing Friday morning.

Maggie felt, for the first time, that she was truly in trouble, but didn't know why.

"I received a phone call last night from a parent who claimed you struck a student earlier this week with a ruler and with an open palm."

Maggie sat stunned as David continued.

"If you know anything about this, or say it's true, I'm obligated to contact the authorities and start the procedure for administrative leave."

"Dave, I . . .," Maggie said, not sure how to proceed but feeling the fury rise in her throat.

"Don't say anything to me if this is true," David reminded her with a look of both disbelief and anger.

"I have to tell you what happened and no, I did NOT strike a student with an open palm." Maggie could feel the blood rise in her face as she defended herself and explained the genesis of the ruler game with Trevor on Monday.

David wasn't smiling.

"And what about duct taping students' mouths shut?" he asked, though it appeared he didn't want to hear the answer to this charge.

Maggie laughed.

"Oh, brother! I *offered* tape to certain students who claimed they'd be quiet if their mouths were taped. This was all done in good humor. Several kids asked for the tape, which I stuck to the front of their desks, and they promptly put it over their own mouths."

By the time Maggie described the resultant muffled noisiness and the eventual removal of the tape by her unruly students, David was visibly relieved.

"Listen," he sounded apologetic, "this is one of the hardest parts of my job. If the phone call had come from a reliable source, or from the boy's mother, this would've been ugly, but it came from someone else, and I can't tell you who."

Maggie didn't need for him to tell her.

"I just need you to know the environment we're working in and remind you that you have to be really cautious about what you do in your classroom."

"So, and I hate to keep asking this question, but are you thinking about firing me yet?" Based on his demeanor, she knew the answer, but still felt the need to hear it from his mouth.

"I'd hire you again if I could do it over and I'll expect you back next year—if the school's still open and I'm still the principal."

Maggie shook his hand and headed to her classroom, shaking off the jitters on the way down the hall. She did her best to overcome the revulsion she felt over the position both she and her boss had been put in, and by an "unreliable" source. And there was still the lingering question of the school's fate.

*No wonder everyone's complaining about teacher turnover*, Maggie thought. There was no way she'd put herself through the hassles of certification and the daily preponderance of administrative crap if she really didn't want to teach. In her heart, she knew she was already helping some kids who'd never accepted help before.

*Two more weeks till Christmas break*, she reminded herself, and enjoyed a legitimate feeling of happiness the rest of the day.

# ~ 14 ~

*H*UNDREDS OF YOUNG CHILDREN *looked up at her from the bottom of a pool with desperation in their eyes. Maggie jumped in to save them, but there were too many. She didn't know where to start. They were swimming toward her, grabbing at her, and she knew if she didn't breathe soon, she would die too.*

Maggie awoke early Saturday morning with a startled scream, her heart still racing from the nightmare, and Bones was instantly on alert.

The Army provided counseling on the possibility of Post-Traumatic Stress Disorder during her out-processing from the military, but she never thought it would affect her. She was wrong.

~~~~~

Harry was at the door just as Maggie was about to leave Monday morning. She hadn't kept up her practice of running with Bones before school lately, opting instead for an extra hour of sleep whenever she could grab it, and Harry was happy to take over the morning routine. Bones seemed fine with his new routine, and waited at the door in anticipation of his friend's arrival.

"Let's hope today doesn't leave you feeling like a fruity dog," he joked with Maggie as she climbed into her Jeep.

"A fruity dog?" She wasn't sure where this one was going.

"You know," his face lit up, "a melon Collie?"

"Oh, that's *horrible*," Maggie laughed, "but I like it! Wish I'd heard that one before my first Monday on the job!"

They waved goodbye and Harry was successful once more at sending off his struggling young friend with a smile.

~~~~~

The day started with an unscheduled team meeting with Trevor's mom, who finally agreed to put her son back on medication. Maggie did her best to assure the group she believed the boy was capable of doing well if he could maintain some control over his impulses, but the others weren't as convinced. He was basically a good kid, unlike the gut feeling she had had about Mateo.

That afternoon Maggie had a surprise observation from the Teachers Training Teachers organization, an asset the district had for assisting new hires. Never one to turn down help, she was eager for any suggestions the seasoned instructor might offer.

Bernicia, whose behavior had continued to decline, was completely inappropriate while the older woman was in the room, acting petulant and openly disrespectful. Instead of getting angry at her or hoping she'd behave, however, Maggie was happy the observer would get an accurate picture of her daily experience.

At the end of the day, the woman left Maggie with a folder full of more helpful tips on classroom management, more than Maggie could ever digest.

"Could you please highlight just a couple of your best suggestions?" Maggie asked after thanking the woman for her observation. "That would be really helpful."

"Well, I think you should engage your students more with decision-making about the lesson," she said.

Maggie had no idea what decisions students could have made about the process of putting an essay together, and wasn't about to ask. She was completely fed-up with being told students should be making more decisions, but she *had* asked for the advice. She just nodded.

"And you might also try having your unruly students call home— right during class—and have them explain why their teacher had to stop the lesson because of their actions. That's been one of my most effective tools and it's one they'll remember."

Maggie thanked the woman again for her time and promised to try her suggestions. She was already trudging through the Continuous Quality Improvement process with her classes with no noticeable results other than the increased reluctance of students to participate in a procedure that had no relevance to their lives. She wasn't about to search for other ways to engage them in decision-making.

But she would try the calls home during class. She was willing to try anything to relieve the burden of having to make so many of the after-school calls herself.

Still, she had about ten calls to make before heading to her evening classes. Although Christmas vacation was right around the corner, it felt a million years away.

~~~~~

On Tumultuous Tuesday Maggie implemented the call-during-class suggestion, hoping the embarrassment students would feel by having to do this in front of their classmates would be just the deterrent they'd need to finally stop acting out in class.

Two of her morning students—visibly appalled by their teacher's request—made calls home but had to leave messages when no one answered. Maggie was pleased by the reaction of the miscreants and felt momentarily elated thinking a disciplinary tool might actually work.

Then it was Ebony's turn. She had been a pain in Maggie's side since the first week of school; but Maggie had forgotten about the comment the girl's mother had made about "using the belt" earlier in the year and regarded the palpable fear in the girl's face as just another manipulative ploy.

The room was quiet as Ebony dialed her mother. With no answer, however, and evidently no messaging capability, the girl hung up, looking relieved. Maggie told the girl to call her Dad.

"But he doesn't live here," she told Maggie, who told the girl to call him regardless.

## *"Miss?"*

Maggie instantly noticed her student—typically a tough girl—was working hard to hold back legitimate tears. This was no act, and in a moment of compassion, Maggie asked her to finish calling in the hallway. Every student appeared somber and most just stared at their desks. She was beginning to feel she was making a mistake, but if this tactic worked, perhaps she'd never have to use it again.

"Please use your Table of Contents to find the poetry section in the back of your books and begin reading. I'll be right back," Maggie told her students and stepped into the hallway to monitor Ebony.

The door closed just in time to hear her sobbing student say, "But Mom doesn't want me either."

The statement took Maggie's breath away. She took the phone from Ebony.

"Sir, this is Ebony's teacher, and I've asked her—and several other students—to call home just to let parents know there have been some on-going issues in class which are slowing down my ability to teach, but Ebony's done nothing major. I'd just like to have your support in encouraging your daughter to try harder to pay better attention when she's in class."

Maggie then listened, incredulously, to the barrage of words from an abusive man who had no interest in either his daughter or Maggie's classroom issues.

"I'm truly sorry you feel that way, sir, and I'll do my best not to disturb you again." She ended the conversation and turned to her student, placing her hands gently on her shoulders.

"Ebony, I'm so sorry. I'd like you to go and talk with the counselor, okay?"

"What did I do *now?*" the girl responded, shrugging off Maggie's hands and storming down the hallway. She didn't realize Maggie had simply wanted her to get help processing what had just happened.

Maggie wanted to chase after her student to explain her request, but the bell was close to ringing and she needed to get back to her other students—who were still stone quiet when she returned. She made a quick call to the counselor to let her know what to expect when Ebony arrived.

*"But mom doesn't want me either."* Maggie struggled to keep it together until the bell.

Class ended and Maggie fled to her team meeting, breaking into tears the moment she entered the room. How could she have let that happen to a 12-year-old girl? She couldn't stop crying, despite the best efforts of Kirby and Matthew to convince her it wasn't so bad. Amber and Grant couldn't make the meeting. For that, Maggie was grateful.

"We're signing you out for lunch early today," Kirby decided, and sent Matthew to the office to let them know they'd be letting their classes go to lunch earlier than normal.

Maggie pulled herself together for her next class and then the three friends walked across the street to a local diner and found a corner booth where Maggie could hide her misery.

"I thought I was doing the right thing," Maggie explained to her peers, telling them the idea had come from her surprise visitor.

"I know you did, and stop beating yourself up about it," said Kirby. "What you didn't know, though, was that the expert advice you got was from a woman who teaches in an affluent school district east of here. She might have to deal with one or two ethnic students in each class, and even they're not like our kids."

"But what do I do now?" Maggie asked, still trying to hold back tears. "I've just completely alienated everyone! They think I'm a monster. I could see it in their faces."

"Oh, now who's being melodramatic?" Matthew teased, putting a comforting arm around her shoulder. "We've all made mistakes, but the kids forget pretty quickly. They might hold a grudge against a friend, but we get off the hook pretty easily, probably because they don't think about us as much."

Matthew and Kirby must have warned their remaining classes about their English teacher's tough day because students in her afternoon classes offered more hugs than she could handle, making her feel both encouraged and embarrassed.

A couple of her model students asked what her favorite color, flower, animals were, as if feeling the need to catch up on lost opportunities to bond with their teacher as a real person. Little Juan, her brush-you-off do-nothing student with a huge attitude who had claimed teachers would never help him, thanked her for giving him a chance to make up work.

## *"Miss?"*

Maggie cried herself to sleep that night thinking of the little girl nobody wanted.

~~~~~

Maggie wrote up a "Dear Abby" letter for her students to read on Wednesday. It was time to allow her students to vent and she felt it was a much more relevant way to get the required buy-in from them than by using some artificial cycle chart.

Ebony was significantly subdued, refusing to make eye contact with anyone, and Maggie gave her some space.

She handed out the letter to all her classes:

> *Dear Abby,*
>
> *I'm writing about a serious situation. I'm a 7th grade teacher, but I haven't been able to teach yet. My students don't seem to want to learn. All they want to do is ignore me and talk to their friends about dating and who they love and who they hate. They openly disrespect each other and me. I try not to yell, I try to respect them as people, I try to show them I want to help them to be successful later in life, but nothing seems to work with many of them. So what do I do now? Do I:*
>
> *1. Quit teaching and get a burger-flipping job?*
> *2. Keep doing what I'm doing and hope they figure it out?*
> *3. Yell and scream and be someone I'm not in order to get their attention?*
>
> *I need help! Please tell me what to do!*
> *Signed,*
> *Exasperated English Teacher!*

"Pretend you're Abby," she instructed her class, "and give your personal advice on what you think this exasperated teacher should do. And does anyone know what 'exasperated' might mean?"

"Probably mad," most students guessed, "or tired."

"Good guesses! Now get to work, and be honest!"

When she read her kids' responses at the end of the day, she was surprised they had covered the range from "Go flip burgers" to "They'll figure it out," but none suggested option #3.

*"Give us time, we're going to be talkative, and we'll eventually figure it out."*

*"I want to thank you for not giving up on us students. You are a great person, don't change! Please don't let any of these students get to you!"*

*"I found out this was your first year teaching and wanted to let you know your doing gret! After having a class like us other people would run, but not you! Don't worry, it will get better."*

Spelling and punctuation continued to thwart most of her students, but she couldn't complain about the sentiment.

*"Have me slap them. Will you let me yell too?"* Maggie suspected that one was from Shareena and chuckled.

*"Never loose your cool. Don't try to let your instincks to take over a nice person like you. Please try to fix somethings up but not all to show you are still in charge. You need to become strick."*

But how "strick" could she be without being called on the carpet for child abuse? The *Catch-22* she had experienced with being reported for what she considered discipline with humor earlier had backfired on her frighteningly; teachers were truly at the mercy of a system that favored believing students over teachers, and the students knew it.

*"I'm very sorry I have been so obnictious (I don't know if I spelt right)."*

Maggie appreciated the student's attempt at using a difficult word, and the honesty.

The most incredible letter, however, came from a boy who wrote how he had contemplated suicide earlier in the year, but his thoughts were gone now because Maggie had made him feel good about himself.

No one had ever mentioned to her how teaching would deliver a roller coaster of emotions that would often leave her breathless.

~~~~~

The next morning Maggie entered a classroom filled with streamers and balloons, and there were encouraging messages of "Don't Give Up!" stapled to her bulletin board. A small group of her students had convinced Kirby to let them into her room and she had stayed to supervise the surprise party. Maggie was visibly moved by the spectacle, and her party planners gathered around her for hugs.

Since school was on a half-day schedule because of conferences, Maggie decided to give in to the festive atmosphere and allowed her students to continue decorating the classroom for the holiday break with paper snowflakes and individual artwork. At least the place would look nice when parents arrived, and she was too emotionally exhausted to try to keep everyone focused on the day's grammar lesson.

Two of her girls had made cakes to share with their classmates and Maggie was able to ensure everyone would get a treat by taking candy bars from the stash she'd purchased as rewards for her after-school athletes.

During the day several kids apologized for behaving badly, though not the most troublesome ones, and Maggie's peers came in sporadically to check out the party and see how she was doing. Word of her breakdown had circulated quickly and the support she felt from most of her fellow teachers was inspirational.

"Hey, Amber," Kirby said to the math teacher in a voice meant for all to hear, "I think maybe I'm going to have myself a hissy-fit sometime soon!"

The students were oblivious to Kirby's remark. Maggie laughed out loud, feeling once again she just might make it till the end of the year.

~~~~~

Parent-teacher conferences were a complete disappointment. The only parents who showed up were those of students who never made it on the trouble radar. Maggie was saddened by the wasted hours of phone calls, but she did appreciate the opportunity to speak with the handful of parents whose students were a delight in class. At the end of the event, she wrote a note to herself to find ways of advancing these students' learning experiences the following semester.

Before heading out, Maggie was surprised to find three letters stuck in the side pocket of her backpack, but decided to save them for when she got home. Over a bowl of cereal—she was too tired to cook anything— Maggie read the letters. The first one was from Kirby, explaining how she had asked some students if they would write something encouraging for their English teacher. The next letter made Maggie feel like she had fallen into and episode of *The Twilight Zone*. It was from Linda.

> *What I like about North Middle School is the teachers. Exposaly one teacher she is nice except when you get on her nerves. She will send you to the office (not for a good thing) with a refuel after she gives you 3 warnings. She has so much fun when you do not mess aroun in her class. Her name is Miss McCauley. SHE IS THE GRATERS TEACHER. She helps people with there problems. Today we decorated her room. We used steremers, bloons, colored paper. We made her happy, an when she walked in her room she was happy, she almost cried. We also made her a crown. She war it all day. That is what I like about North.*

Maggie couldn't believe her eyes. Why would this outspoken little student-rights-lawyer care a whit about a teacher she'd reported not so long ago? She didn't dwell on the question. The next letter was a group effort from Dashay, Rico, and—unbelievably—Bernicia.

> *Miss McCauley, you are a fantastic teacher. You try to solve problems, but seem no one cared but few of us. Students make you burst into an ocean of tears. They make you feel like an abandoned car's wants to quit. Most of us get on your nerves. I think the reason everybody mean to you is because you new and they try to take advantage of you. If we want respect we have to give twice as much. She might think of us as the worst gang of kids ever except a cupple of us. She prepares for her class. She makes us laugh our heads off. She loves to put a smile on our face, so why should we take advantage of her just because she is new. We should show her the same respect we show our parents and friends. Do you treat your mom and dad like crap? I don't think so so why treat another teacher like that? We should be ashamed of ourselves to let the teacher drown in an ocean of tears. If your dad or mom were drowning would you not help them? Of course you would help them faster than a bullet could kill some one. So why not help a teacher. She is here to help you so why don't you help her.*

Maggie chose not to focus on the mistakes, the shift in audience, the nearly illegible handwriting, but instead on the message and on the numerous inclusions of figurative language. No, her students would likely bomb the state tests in March, but yes, there was hope many of them, ultimately, would be okay.

~~~~~

And then came another Friday dashing any hopes the school could drag itself out of the crab-pot. Why the administration would decide to have a kick-off assembly for "Let's Fly" a week before Christmas vacation and on a Friday afternoon, no one knew.

To top it off, Gladys would run a Town Hall meeting for all 7$^{th}$ graders after the assembly and would set them straight on expectations for future behavior. Evidently, referrals were at an all-time high and not just from Maggie's classes.

It took a while for Maggie to get her students to the assembly because they couldn't get quiet while in line in the classroom. Kyle, at the head of the line, was the ring-leader of the disruption. Unaware Maggie was watching, he acted out an elaborate love-making scene against the room door. Students behind him, who were looking at the expression on their teacher's face as she watched Kyle, laughed even louder, although Kyle thought it was all about him.

"Kyle, do you need to hump anything else in the room before we head to the assembly?" Maggie asked innocently.

"Ah, no Miss," the embarrassed boy replied.

"Then let's get to where we should have been five minutes ago, please."

The "Let's Fly" assembly was a debacle. School administrators performed a skit in which they acted like bad students and then pretended to learn how to act appropriately. Maggie and the other teachers could see the students were focused on the fun antics of their typically staid overseers, laughing through what should have been the serious messages. They definitely didn't get it.

When the other grades were dismissed, Gladys attempted to give her Town Hall meeting, which was more a one-sided lecture than anything else. Students paid no attention to her, despite having the whole team of 7$^{th}$ grade teachers patrolling the aisles and pulling out students to sit in a "time out" section while she talked. Maggie wondered if the woman had any idea how completely unproductive her presentation was, or if it had given her a taste of what her teachers had been experiencing all year.

The only fortunate thing about the meeting was her lecture continued until the dismissal bell.

Maggie returned to her room to the sound of her desk phone ringing.

"Before you leave this afternoon," the counselor said, "would you please go through samples of your students' writing and bring down any with neat handwriting and open-circle dots over the i's? I'll explain when you come down."

It took Maggie 30 minutes to flip through her students' folders, and it would've taken longer if she had included her male students' work. She came up with three examples, one from Bernicia, who had surprisingly lovely handwriting, and brought them to the office where Anne, David, and Kirby stood waiting.

"What's this all about?" Maggie asked, and was handed a beautifully written note addressed to a boy which read, "I want to fuck you and put whip cream on your dick and lick it off." The note was signed, "Linda." Maggie sighed.

"Well, I can tell you for sure Linda didn't write this. Her handwriting is *almost* as good as a second-grader's."

The teachers were dismissed—administration would handle the situation—and Kirby followed Maggie to her room.

"With these kinds of notes being passed around, scoring 70% on the state test really becomes irrelevant, don't you think?" Kirby laughed sarcastically.

"We're doomed," Maggie said matter-of-factly, but it was Friday and she wasn't going to start the weekend off on a gloomy note.

"I think we're going to start bringing kids into our planning meetings," Kirby said. "It's time they start taking responsibility for being dicks in class. Maybe if we start next week it'll give them time to think about things over the break."

"Sounds good," Maggie said. "I'd love to have a night where they're not showing up in my dreams. I hate waking up exhausted."

"I hear you," said Kirby. "Hey, have a nice weekend. One more week and we'll all be able to recharge. And OH! It's been decided. Brad will be moving next week!"

"Is it horrible I feel happy about that?" Maggie asked.

"Not at all. Maybe he'll finally get the help he needs. You and Grant doing anything *fun* this weekend?" she teased.

"Actually, he's on a team competing in some weekend basketball tournament in the city. I'm going to try to make it to one of his games before finishing up my papers for my instruction classes." Maggie had a mound of work she needed to complete.

"Hang in there, friend. You're almost not a newbie anymore!"

The comment *almost* convinced her.

# ~ 15 ~

"SO WHY DO I FEEL like you're already pulling away from me," Grant asked as they finished their pizza in town Sunday evening. His team had won their championship, and Maggie had made it to the last game.

"It's not that," Maggie said. "It's just that I've got my finals this week and then we're going to be apart for two weeks and there's so much up in the air right now and I'm having a hard time concentrating."

Everything she said was true. She had been trying all semester to convince herself Grant might be someone who could take her into the future and away from her painful past. She had never been one to rush into decisions of such magnitude, though, and also sensed something was missing. Perhaps Grant's reputation as a "playah" gave her reason to question his fidelity. She had never questioned for a moment Sam would be faithful to her forever.

With each new boyfriend Maggie brought home before joining the Army, her mother would tell her she was just "in love with love," but Maggie never saw what was wrong with that. Still, she hadn't yet thought about bringing Grant home to meet her family.

"So, is everyone going on the cruise?" he asked, trying to believe things would be better after the holidays.

"Yes! My Dad has always wanted to go to Bermuda and the cruise ship leaves right from Boston, so we decided to make the trip our Christmas gift to ourselves."

"What about Bones?" he asked.

"Harry practically begged me to let him stay with him. I honestly can't believe how lucky I've been to have such a great friend. Ugh! I'm so stuffed." Maggie rubbed her stomach, trying to lighten the mood.

Before Maggie could get into her Jeep for the drive home, Grant pulled her close, lifted her chin, and kissed her lips for the first time.

"Dessert," he said.

Maggie caught her breath. He knew how to kiss. He let her go and turned to walk away.

"I'll see you tomorrow," she told him. "And *nothing* will stop me from being in a good mood this week!"

Her lips tingled as she drove home, but that wasn't enough to erase the uncertainty she felt about a future with the handsome P.E. teacher.

~~~~~

"Good day!" Maggie greeted her students at the beginning of finals week. They were all used to her handshake-at-the-door routine and most were now able to look her in the eyes when they returned their greeting. Maggie was prepared for her own final exams and was feeling on top of the world.

"So, Miss, I gotta ask," Rico said after everyone was seated. "Why you always wear those big ol' belts?"

Maggie had continued to visit the local Goodwill and prided herself in her funky retro wardrobe. She had the best collection of fat, colorful belts in town.

"To hold up my underwear, of course!" she replied. Most students just shook their heads, trying to suppress their amusement, but not surprised by their teacher's silly response. Even on her worst days, Maggie did her best to interject humor in her lessons.

In class that day Rico volunteered to read the directions on the project assignment for the week.

Maggie was thrilled to find out later he would be one of twelve students she would meet with weekly for "Let's Fly" sessions the following semester. Although she hated how the meetings would take time away from curricular requirements, she'd enjoy working on problem solving skills with a small group of kids she might be able to help.

But she also had Ebony and Dashay in her group, and earlier in the semester Maggie had broken up a hall fight between the hefty girls, inserting herself between the two and physically moving Dashay away. She remembered thinking if Dashay had truly wanted to hurt her nemesis, there would have been no way she could have stopped her. So perhaps the rivalry could be resolved.

"Thanks, Rico!" Maggie said when he had finished his halting read-aloud. She didn't want to make a big deal over his participation, but could tell by the expression on his face he was pleased with his performance.

Tiny steps.

"The only thing we'll be working on this week is an essay on respect." Most of her students had little experience with the topic and she hoped it might send them into their vacation with something to reflect upon before returning for a semester that could determine the fate of the school.

"We've been working on writing good sentences and putting them together to make focused paragraphs, and now you have the tools to create a cohesive essay. Who remembers what cohesive means?"

No one raised their hand.

"Have you heard of cohesive, or adhesive, some kind of 'hesive' tape?" she prompted, and got some nods. "What do the 'hesive' tapes do?"

"They stick to something," Rico mumbled. Maggie smiled.

"Yes! And so a cohesive essay is one that sticks together because it's focused on one thing, and the thing for this essay will be the idea of respect. I want you to spend the next 30 seconds brainstorming people you respect. Just jot down anyone that comes to mind."

"Can it be my dog?"

"Well, I'd rather you pick a person, but go ahead and put him on your list."

"Can it be myself?"

"Absolutely."

"Can it be more than one person?"

"Put down everyone who comes to mind, but your essay will focus on only one person."

"Can it be dirt?"

"No, Trevor, it can't be 'dirt,' but I applaud your attempt at creativity. Now focus on making your list. GO!"

# *"Miss?"*

Her students struggled to jot down names of people—and probably things—they respected.

"Now circle the one *name* on your list you know the most about."

When they had completed the task, she continued.

"For the remaining time, you'll be brainstorming everything you know about this person. Don't leave anything out, and don't question anything that comes to mind, just write it *all* down. The more things you can write about your person, the better your essay will be, and you could all use a good grade on this."

She ignored the scattered groans and did her best to ask leading questions to get her kids to consider various character traits as she circulated the room to spend one-on-one time with each of them.

When Maggie got to Ebony's desk, the girl was writing diligently. She had been the embodiment of perfect comportment since the phone call fiasco, but Maggie knew her student didn't trust her anymore. Regaining her trust would take time.

"It looks like you have a great start on the list about your sister. How about adding some specific things like how she lets you do things. Maybe she sacrificed something she wanted to do so you could do what you wanted?"

"Miss McCauley," the morose girl responded, "I just made this stuff up. My sister's really mean to me."

*Damn,* Maggie thought. She felt there was nothing she could say that would be appropriate.

"Well, maybe since you've already made up this much, you could make up the rest by adding details about how a sister you'd really respect would act."

Surprisingly, Ebony nodded in agreement and went back to work.

"Remember, everyone," Maggie announced to the class, "when you're given a writing prompt on the state test, the people grading you don't know you. If you feel like you don't have the experiences they're asking about, go ahead and make stuff up! Just be sure to answer the question they're asking and to include some of the figurative language elements we've been working on this year." She hated having to talk about how to do well on a canned test, but it was a necessity.

Her day went well until Kyle made it clear he wasn't having anything to do with the assignment. Instead, he chose to walk around the room and chat with his buddies. Since wrestling season had ended, he had become increasingly inappropriate in class and didn't seem to be able to focus on anything.

"Please take your seat, Kyle," Maggie asked politely.

He ignored her.

"Kyle," Maggie intoned more forcefully this time and he looked over his shoulder at her. "I asked you to sit down."

The boy sauntered to his desk, put one knee on his seat and bellowed, "I am sitting down!"

Maggie could tell by the expectant looks on his classmates' faces that even they knew he'd stepped over the line.

"Now you may go sit in the office," she said, unfazed, "and take your work with you."

He stared at her in disbelief until she won the staring contest. She called the office to let them know he was on his way. Nothing would rattle her this week, and Kyle would be her first invitee to the team meeting on Wednesday.

~~~~~

All her peers agreed Kyle should be first on the list. He'd been the school's star wrestler, but the class-clown role he'd previously adopted had morphed into a more cynical can't-touch-me attitude and everyone was tired of his antics.

He entered the meeting room full of himself, with an air of defiance completely inappropriate for the situation.

"Hey, I've never even been in ISD yet, so what's the big deal?" He slouched in his seat.

And then Matthew shut him down with a voice Maggie—and the others—had never before heard from the benevolent brown-eyed teacher. He assured the startled boy he would experience his first in-school detention the following day, and the team would expect him to stop his disruptive behavior immediately.

"I just like to make people laugh, that's all," he mumbled.

"Laughter is one thing," Maggie said, "but impudence is quite another, and you need to go look up the meaning of that word when we dismiss you."

Everyone on the team spoke to him about their expectations and walked him through writing up a Personal Action Plan—the school had administrative paperwork for everything—for future success. One of his responses for action was his request for teachers to treat him like they treat other students because he was feeling picked on.

"Poor little white boy," Amber said after Kyle departed.

"Yeah, must be rough to be cute and athletic and funny and actually smart in this school," Matthew played along, having regained his composure.

Trevor and Shareena were next on the list and each was respectfully compliant. Trevor was back on his medications, but it would take him a while to readjust to acceptable behavior patterns. Shareena continued to walk the line between wanting to behave and being overly aggressive when provoked even slightly.

"So, what do you think?" Kirby asked her teammates when the meetings had ended.

"I think this will be effective," said Grant. He rarely had a complaint against a student, but wanted to support the process and his peers.

"I agree," said Amber. "It's time our kids started believing we're the ones in charge."

Word of the kangaroo court proceedings got around quickly and the 6th and 8th grade teams decided they'd adopt the disciplinary technique the following semester.

By the end of the week, and despite the increasing restlessness anticipated before a holiday break, all but a few of Maggie's students had completed an essay worth grading. The end-of-year vacation was a joyful milestone for everyone and as students said their goodbyes to teachers and classmates, Maggie thought back to her own grade school days. She remembered the piles of cards and gifts on favorite teachers' desks and how she'd been blessed with so many great role models.

Her own desk sat barren in the back corner of the room.

At the end of the day two girls walked up to Maggie in the hallway.

"We figured out who you reminded us of," one girl said.

Maggie looked at her quizzically.

"Miss Frizzle from *The Magic School Bus* show!"

Maggie hugged them both. She'd just been awarded the best gift ever.

~~~~~

"Now, don't you spend one moment worrying about us," Harry told Maggie Saturday morning after she had arranged the doggie items Bones would need for the next two weeks in Harry's apartment.

"Thanks, Harry," she said, giving the man one more bear-hug before heading home for the holidays. "Tell your sister thanks too, and I hope he doesn't get into mischief there."

Harry planned to take Bones with him to visit family in Vail on Christmas day.

Grant, who had just arrived to see Maggie off, entered Harry's apartment and waited for Maggie to finish her goodbyes.

"Have a Merry Christmas, Harry," Grant extended his hand.

"How about a hug for an old man?" Harry offered, and the two men shared a quick embrace.

"And what are your plans for the holidays?" Harry asked Grant.

"Oh, not much," Grant said. "I'll probably just catch up on some sleep and hit the gym more. My mom's cooking dinner on Christmas, so I'll spend a couple of days in Grand Junction with her and my aunt and uncle."

Grant was an only child. His parents had divorced when he was nine and his mother had never remarried. Maggie had never pressured Grant for more about his family, and he had never offered to talk about them.

"You kids take care of yourselves, and I'll see you next year," Harry said, seeing them out. "And I don't want to hear about you swimming with any sharks, young lady!" Harry warned, smiling as he waved goodbye.

Grant walked Maggie to her Jeep.

"It feels like I'm always saying goodbye to you," he said, looking sad.

"I'll be back," she said, wrapping her arms around him.

He kissed her again, hesitantly.

"Bring me back a sea shell?" he asked, closing her door.

Even though Maggie knew how Grant was feeling about her departure, she was too excited about the prospect of two weeks away from the stresses of the school year to feel sad. She couldn't wait to see the city of Denver from the airplane window.

*Free at last!* she thought as she drove to the airport, her "Charlie Brown Christmas" CD playing loudly and transporting her to another world.

# ~ 16 ~

"HEY, BEAUTIFUL, how's the Wild West treating my girl since Thanksgiving?" Maggie's father met her with open arms at Logan International Airport.

"Not bad, Daddy-O, and it looks like Mum's still taking good care of you!" she replied cheerfully, patting his belly. Ever since she was a child, her father had made her feel special and called her "beautiful," even throughout her scrawny, pimply years.

"Yes," he chuckled, "and she's got a nice beef stew waiting for us at home."

Maggie's mother never failed to have "enough food to feed an army," as was the joke in the family, and Maggie was happy to know there would be no smashed peanut butter sandwiches while she was home.

"So how many new outfits from Marshall's will I have to try on when we get home?" Maggie asked her father.

"Oh, a few." He chuckled again.

In addition to being the best cook on the east coast, Maggie's mother was also an expert bargain-hunter. Maggie and her sisters would tease their mother about her purchases, which she would generally either give away to her daughters or return to the store after discovering they weren't "quite right." The girls all decided she shopped like some people hunted animals, for the thrill of the prize, even though her capture was often a catch-and-release.

The aroma of a home-cooked meal welcomed Maggie and her father, and her younger sister, Kathy, was there to greet her too.

## "Miss?"

"So glad we'll have time to catch up now," said her mother, squeezing her tightly. "We barely had time to say hello at Thanksgiving! Crazy girl, driving across the country for a turkey dinner!"

~~~~~

Maggie leaned against the rail of the cruise ship—eyes closed and breathing in the salty air—as it increased speed in the open waters.

"So how are you, honestly?" asked Kathy. She was aware of how devastated her Army sister had been when she returned home without Sam.

"Honestly? I just can't stop thinking about him."

"Why do you feel like you need to stop thinking about him?" Kathy's question was one no one had asked before.

"I think everyone expects me to move on." Maggie paused. "And there's this guy at work, Grant, who's more anxious than anyone."

Maggie hadn't mentioned Grant to anyone during her brief visit home the previous month.

"Well?" Kathy coaxed her sister. "Is there a chance you might fall in love again someday?"

Maggie thought about the question for a long time before answering.

"I think that's the real problem. I'm still in love."

# ~ 17 ~

AFTER TWO WEEKS of relaxation and heartfelt talks with her family—all who cautioned her not to rush anything in her new life— Maggie returned to Colorado ready to take on whatever challenges would threaten to thwart the success of her students. Bones had made himself at home with Harry while she was gone and greeted her as if she'd never left. He was such a comfort to have around. She wasn't surprised her neighbor had enjoyed his short-term roommate.

She looked forward to seeing Grant and giving him the sea shell he had asked for, but she was also anxious about their reunion. Maggie's family had helped her realize she was still grieving her loss. It would be unfair to keep Grant on a string until she healed.

"Miss! You came back!" several students from different classes exclaimed while she positioned herself for Happy-New-Year-handshakes.

During classes that day she felt a palpable shift in their attitude toward her, perhaps because they finally believed she was there for the long run. She hadn't yet run away screaming. Whether they liked it or not, Maggie was determined they'd learn a thing or two by the end of the year.

The air was charged with gossip and Maggie decided to capitalize on the energy.

"Today you will all give a three-minute verbal presentation on anything you'd like to share with the group about what you did these past two weeks. You now have five minutes to jot down some notes before I call on you!"

The next three months before administration of the state test would be all about prepping for it, and Maggie was taking a chance that an administrator might inquire about the focus of her teaching objective for the day. But public speaking—a "non-essential" 7<sup>th</sup> grade skill—was important.

Although a handful of students were happy to brag about the fun they had during vacation, for most, the break was too long. The reality of their home lives would never compare with what Maggie had shared with them in the Dick and Jane books. Still, many of Maggie's more loquacious presenters were able to entertain their classmates with something amusing, even if it was a story about a scuffle they'd witnessed or a movie they'd seen.

Jack, however, a new student to the school, asked if he could put on a skit. He had a story he wanted to act out. With permission from the class—because his skit would take longer than three minutes—he asked for several volunteers to play different roles. Maggie was pleasantly surprised by the number of students who did the "OH! PICK ME!" dance.

When he had selected his actors, he then directed an elaborate story about an angry young boy whose mother had no time to take him to a baseball game, so he died from a broken heart, but remained a ghost in his own house.

"Now, you're my new little brother, okay?" he gave a non-speaking role to the boy who would play the sibling from his mother's new boyfriend.

"You're my mother's new boyfriend, so you have to act like you're falling out a window, then you'll die and go into the light."

Maggie was starting to feel uneasy with where the boy's plot was heading. She understood the old precept about writing what we know. There was a glimmer of hope, however, for the story to have a happy ending, macabre though it was.

"You're my mom, Linda, and you decide that if you take my ghost to a game, then I'll be able to go into the light and not bother you anymore."

Maggie was frankly amazed at Jack's ability to direct his classmates in their acting of his questionable story. After the applause had ended, while the next presenter prepared to speak, Maggie whispered, "Is your story based on your real life?"

"Yeah," he whispered back.

Maggie found out later from Anne that the boy's mother was a drug addict and was both physically and verbally abusive to him. He was currently being raised by his grandparents. Maggie was incensed, and an abrupt surge of what could only be described as a maternal instinct lit a fire in her chest and made her want to scream.

*Happy Freakin' New Year,* she thought. She felt completely unqualified to help her students.

~~~~~

During Wednesday's staff meeting Gladys informed the teachers one of their underperforming females had been feeling nauseous in the morning for the past three weeks. It troubled Maggie that the news of one of her 13-year-olds being pregnant no longer surprised her.

But the good news didn't stop there. One of the 6th grade teachers had been threatened just that morning by a student who told her he could sue her and hurt her after she had demanded he take his seat.

Maggie remembered numerous seating incidents with Kyle and other students and the threat Linda had made earlier in the year. Gladys left the meeting early after delivering the news and letting them all know she'd be checking on the progress of their test preparation.

"How do these kids even know about how the legal system works in schools?" Maggie asked no one in particular.

"Because a lot of them live in it," replied Matthew.

"The real question is, who gave them the balls to be spouting off threats to teachers whenever they feel like it?" Amber crossed her arms and slouched in her chair.

There were no good answers.

Maggie had started the semester off as she had started the year, with high hopes and a belief she could change the world one classroom at a time. In reality, she and her peers worked in a world in which obstacles were thrown at them every day. There might be answers in the stacks of files the school kept on each student, but she had no time to dig for those answers.

She was starting to wonder if the time had come to abandon her idealism.

Nevertheless, she wasn't a quitter and would continue to give her all, at least until the end of the school year. Rumors of closure were on the rise, though no one wanted to believe it might actually happen.

"So, when am I going to see all those family movies someone must have shot on your cruise?" Grant asked Maggie when the staff meeting ended. He was more than eager to rekindle their interrupted relationship.

"There aren't any movies, but I'll put some photos on my Facebook page this weekend. Here," she said, handing him the shell. "There were so many on the beach, but this one was perfect."

"It's beautiful." He turned it over and ran his fingers over the pearlescent shell. "But seriously, will I see you this weekend? I miss you." He gazed down at her with his best sad puppy-dog eyes.

"Sure," she hesitated, knowing how difficult her revelation to him would be. "Let's have dinner Friday night. I've got a whole new batch of classes to prep for and more hours this semester than last. It's really gonna suck," she said, hoping that would prepare him for seeing her less frequently.

"Dinner it is, then. Call you later. And thanks for remembering." He held up the shell and then walked away.

Maggie returned to her classroom with heaviness in her heart. Grant was a nice guy. But he wasn't Sam.

~~~~~

The following day David visited Maggie's last hour class to see her teaching to only ten students—whom she had separated from the rest of the class.

"I noticed Bernicia reading in the hallway," he said, looking around the colorful room and wondering why only a select group of students appeared to be doing anything academic.

"Yes," Maggie responded, embarrassed by what her boss must have thought. "She refused to stop her ear-piercing shrieks. I think half the dogs in town might be deaf by now."

Maggie had written disciplinary referrals on Bernicia's inappropriate behavior before, so she knew David would understand her decision to isolate the girl.

"Might I ask what those students are doing?" he pointed to one half of the class.

"Well, since I couldn't send half my class into the hall and because they refused to settle down and focus on their project, I asked who wanted to get their work done. I moved those kids over here so at least they could learn something today."

To Maggie's great surprise, David said, simply, "I understand," and then proceeded to reprimand the rest of the class. Although they listened to him half-heartedly, it was clear to Maggie they still didn't care. At least they acted like they didn't care. The kids she had separated, however, looked truly grateful.

*Poor guy*, Maggie thought when David left her classroom. The fatigue of captaining a sinking ship was visibly wearing on him, but still he did his best to encourage his new employee.

As frustrating as her first week back had been, however, Maggie resolved to end the week on a positive note and told her classes on Friday that once they finished their figurative language study sheets—which they could complete in pairs on the track field—they could play Frisbee or ball or run on the track. It was an unseasonably warm day and Maggie needed the fresh air as much as she supposed her kids did.

The change of atmosphere boosted everyone's morale and with the promise of some fun time, everyone finished their work quickly, though perhaps not comprehensively. Soon, students were all over the field playing ball and Frisbee and rolling in the grass. Maggie noticed shy little Jeanie attempting to do a headstand, but failing miserably.

"Here! Watch how I do it and then I'll help you," Maggie offered, explaining how to make a strong triangular support with head and hands, and the girl was delighted her teacher could do with ease what she was struggling to do.

"Look at Miss McCauley!" she heard from other students who had stopped what they were doing to watch the unusual scene. They were even more enthralled when she followed up with a handstand. Maggie believed it was a good thing to be able to surprise her students every once in a while by doing something un-teacher-like and she was pleased to see Jeanie persist with her effort to complete her first headstand.

Every class appreciated the unexpected outing and things went relatively smoothly until Maggie experienced a fearful moment in the afternoon. One of her new boys, who attended her class with an aide because of the severity of his autism, was curled up on his side on the field. Maggie ran to where he lay.

"What happened? Do I need to call 911?" Maggie asked the aide in a panic.

"No, I don't think so," the meek young girl replied. "I think there's something wrong with his hand, but I can't see anything."

The boy was unable to communicate verbally.

"Danny, may I see your hand?" Maggie asked the boy. He hesitated a moment, then held out his hand, which she took in her own. She could see nothing but a smooth, slightly dirty little palm.

"Show me where it hurts, Danny."

He stopped rocking and crying. He pointed to a spot in the center of his hand, but Maggie could see nothing unusual.

There was only one cure she could think of, so without hesitation, she bent over, kissed his palm with an exaggerated smooch, smiled and said in her most convincing voice, "All better!"

The look on Danny's face was one of surprise and delight. As soon as Maggie stood up, he was ready to play again. The dumbfounded aide was equally pleased.

Maggie recognized the multitude of lessons learned that day. None of them was an "essential 7$^{th}$ grade skill," but they were lessons that would likely be remembered for a lifetime. Inundated as they all were with whatever method the psychology-du-jour insisted upon, she wanted to remember her students were just children trying to impress those who mattered to them.

And despite the overly fearful must-be-politically-correct-hands-off atmosphere, she decided she'd continue to provide a kiss to a dirty hand, or a hug, whenever needed.

~~~~~

Maggie asked Grant to meet her for dinner at a local Italian restaurant. They served full glasses of wine there and she'd need two to get through what she felt she must say. They caught up on their weekly highlights over dinner and their first glass of wine, and Grant was impressed with her handstand story.

"It's about time we went someplace fancy," Grant said, unaware of Maggie's true reason for selecting the place. "You look beautiful tonight."

She felt horrible.

"Grant, I need to be honest with you."

He stared into her eyes for several moments before looking down at his plate. "So you *were* pulling away. I'm such an idiot. Why, Maggie?"

"Everything is such a whirlwind right now, Grant. I mean, we might both be unemployed next year, but I still have to finish these ridiculous certification requirements. I hardly even have time to take care of my dog. But the real truth is I haven't been able to get over what happened with Sam yet, and I finally realized that when I was home. It's not fair to you right now that I'm not ready to make any commitments, and I really, really, really don't want to string you along until I'm ready."

"But what if I don't mind being strung along? What if I'm just fine with seeing you whenever I can?" He met her eyes again.

"Seriously?" Maggie said, sipping her second glass of wine. "We could be looking for new jobs in a few months! You should find someone more stable. You deserve better than what I can give you."

"I'm not interested in anyone more stable, so you can forget about that. Why don't we just take it slow and see how the year turns out, okay? I'm not ready to quit on you. Don't quit on me. Not yet. Please."

By the end of dinner Maggie told Grant she wouldn't abandon him, but asked him to be understanding of her struggles. She wondered if she'd ever truly be able to move away from her past—and love another man as much as she loved Sam.

# ~ 18 ~

---

**"P**LEASE ENSURE YOU have plenty of student exemplars posted around your room ASAP," came the directive near the end of January. State evaluators were expected to be swarming the building and teachers needed to simulate a façade of exceptional accomplishment. Maggie stayed at school until 7 p.m. that evening hanging up the completed essays on respect from the previous semester. Some of them were surprisingly acceptable.

Instead of allowing teachers to focus on the basic requirements of their subject areas for the short time remaining before the state test in March, the district decided instead to bring in still more outside help.

A woman from higher headquarters who'd never heard of the "Let's Fly" program showed up with the latest method for addressing troublesome students. Response to Intervention (RTI), like "Let's Fly," was supposed to be the miracle cure for every challenging classroom situation. It would save the school.

Beverly, prim and proper and far-removed from the inner city teaching environment, attended a staff meeting with the 7th grade team and gushed with enthusiasm. She had a magical book with "thousands of ideas" for dealing with every imaginable scenario. She was paid well for the hours she spent pushing the new process.

"May I be honest with you?" asked Maggie when the woman paused to breathe. Beverly seemed startled by the question, but allowed Maggie to continue.

"As a first year teacher I'm finding it difficult to assimilate all of the routine tasks I have to do in each class, and the idea that I might have to look at another thousand techniques makes me want to jump out my window."

Maggie had expressed her feeling of being overwhelmed by the sheer quantity of resources she was expected to digest earlier in the year. It seemed everyone was expected to become a Master Teacher quickly.

"Well, certainly I'm not saying you have to use all one thousand ideas, but you should expect to try as many approaches as you can until you find ones that work."

Maggie gazed around at her teammates and saw the look of resignation in their faces. Even Matthew looked like he was ready to quit. No one wanted another bandage for the gaping wound draining the school of its viability. They were spending as much time as she was trying to find ways to work one-on-one with needy students, doing paperwork every night to document infractions, updating Individualized Education Plans (IEPs) and arranging phone time or meetings with parents who had no more control over their children than the school had.

"Are there tips in there to tell us how to engage our students who just want to learn what they're supposed to learn, but can't because of all the other kids we're busy RTI-ing?" Kirby asked. She didn't even try to hide the disgust she was feeling.

"I wish I had more time to spend with you," Beverly said, avoiding the question, "but I've got to get across town for my next meeting. I'll leave a copy of the book in your principal's office. I think you'll find everything you need in it and you can contact me by email if you have any other questions. Thank you for your time." The woman flew out the door.

"When will we get the cattle prod training?" Amber tried to lighten the mood.

They all felt numb.

Maggie suggested to the group that even though their situation seemed bleak, their new challenge should be to find something good to focus on each day. She talked about how her ability to take control of her reactions had saved her many times before in situations far more dire than this one. They all could rely on a student or two each day to say or ask something to make them smile or realize the connections they were making were significant.

"Yes, ma'am," said Kirby, feigning submission. "Leave it to the newbie to remind us all why we're here!"

~~~~~~

"Does anyone remember any of our Monday words similar to this word in the paragraph?" Maggie asked, pointing to the word "mundane" in one of the reading comprehension drills on the overhead.

"Melancholy!" was the instantaneous response from several students in each class. She was looking for "monotonous," but it tickled her nonetheless to think they remembered a word from early in the school year. Maggie continued to feel she wasn't doing much real teaching; however, she sensed a tidbit of hope for many of her struggling kids.

"Kyle, would you *please* take your seat," Maggie implored the progressively more unruly student that afternoon. Since bringing him in for the team meeting before the holidays, his disruptive behavior had resumed insidiously.

Kyle simply laughed in her face and looked victorious as he left her room for the office before she had the chance to respond. His inappropriate behavior seemed to set the stage for what turned into a troublesome afternoon, and by the last hour, she felt as if she were back in the first week of school.

"Everybody OUT!" she commanded, startling her students from their chatter. They looked at her with confusion. "Out, I said, and line up in the hall."

The class grumbled and dragged their feet, but eventually ended up standing in a pack in the hallway.

"One line, facing me," Maggie continued, and was startled to see Rico walking up and down the line and physically moving some of his classmates, trying to get them in order even while several shoved him away.

Rico had been an asset in her weekly "Let's Fly" group and Maggie knew how hard the young man was trying to please her. She had to be careful with how she acknowledged his positive behavior as his walk along the right path was always tenuous.

"I wish our 'Let's Fly' group could be my regular English class," he had told her during their last session.

Earlier in the year, several teachers had suggested he would probably end up being a gang leader, but Maggie hoped like hell they'd be wrong. What he was doing at the moment inspired hope for his future.

"You'll stand here until you're quiet, and then we'll finish our lesson." Maggie saw Gladys coming down the hallway, but when the woman saw the group, she turned and headed back toward the office. *Coward*, she thought.

It took ten minutes for everyone to settle down and stare at her quietly, some with anger in their eyes, most with disbelief.

"As long as you continue to act like first graders, I'll treat you like first graders. Now let's get back to work."

She made the best of the remaining class, having her students finish the sentence, "If I were only one inch tall." There were giggles as they wrote. Somehow, their previous behavior didn't make her want to jump off a cliff.

Perhaps it was because she realized she could line them up again and again in the hallway until they got it right, knowing ultimately they would, and praying it just might happen before the end of the year. Perhaps it was because she knew they'd continue to sabotage themselves. Most had no previous model for success.

If only for the kids who came to rely on a hug from her each day, she would continue to believe in them even though they didn't believe in themselves. She was feeling more and more each day her internal conflict between wanting to toss most of her students out the window and wanting to adopt them all.

~~~~~

"What am I going to do, Harry?" Maggie asked her friend when she got home that evening. Harry and Bones were watching the five o'clock news when she arrived.

"Now, what kind of question is that, Captain? It looks to me like you've got a bad case of exhaustipation." He said this with his typical hint of mischief.

"I'm too tired to even try to figure out what that means." Maggie smiled despite her mood.

"Close!" said Harry. "It means you're too tired to give a shit, but I know you still do."

"I know, I do, and that's a good one, by the way, but it just feels like every time I take one step forward, I get knocked on my ass. I know they don't know they're doing it, but my kids keep dragging themselves and their classmates down."

Maggie slumped on the couch and was happy to have Bones join her. He nuzzled into her lap and she stroked his soft fur as she unfolded the day's events.

"I believe you're making more progress than you think. You're just being hard on yourself. Obviously your students have faith in you, and they must know you're looking out for them."

Maggie knew he was right, but she still felt the progress she had made, if any, would never be enough to prepare her students for their next year—or their next potential school.

"At least we don't have a principal who tells us we need to override 'Fs' on report cards from last semester," Maggie said, perking up. "Matthew's girlfriend works at the high school and her boss told her to give a bunch of students another few weeks to make up the work they blew off from last semester. Can you believe that?" Bones cocked his head at her.

"Sadly, yes, based on what you've been telling me this year. Seems there are no consequences anymore. Just plain sad." He shook his head. "Just remember, though, you can't fix everything, so keep your focus on what you *can* influence, even if it's just making one kid feel a little better about himself at the end of the day."

Maggie felt uplifted already. He was right. There was little she could do to change a system spiraling out of control. All she could do was ensure her students remained grounded despite the surrounding storm.

~~~~~

That weekend Maggie had to write a Career Goals paper for one of her classes, which was ironic since many of her peers in the program were already reconsidering their chosen profession. The licensure program, being run concurrently with their first year of teaching, was worse than boot camp. At least in boot camp you got to sleep, and soundly, because of the physical exhaustion.

Even Maggie was uncertain from one day to the next if she'd be terminated, and for a probationary teacher, the administration didn't even have to show cause. She felt she had already provided plenty of cause for her boss to start looking for someone else, but as long as the doors were still open when she arrived, she'd continue to show up prepared for another day of attempting to teach.

Maggie started her paper by talking about her decision to return to the work force as a teacher of secondary school English, a decision that thrilled her mother. Although proud of her daring young daughter, her mom wasn't shy about expressing her concern over the dangerous lifestyle that being in the Army imposed on her child.

"Someday you'll know," her mom would tell her, "when you have kids of your own."

Maggie supposed her mom was right, but still wouldn't have traded anything for her Army experiences. Well, all the experiences except the one that took away the man she loved.

"My philosophy of education parallels my philosophy of life and can be summed up in two words: Never stop! Never stop learning, and never stop living each day in a complete and fulfilling way," she wrote.

It sounded so simple. But while Maggie had lived by her never stop philosophy, the majority of her students had never even started. So where was the 'on' switch?

She ended her paper by coming back to her philosophy of life and how she would inspire her students to live each day in a fulfilling way.

*Yup*, she thought, knowing how to tie together a satisfactory essay. *It's all about presenting neat little packages.* But her students were not neat little packages.

They were a mess.

~~~~~

*Confusion filled the scene. The signal station where Maggie arrived for repair work had been bombed. There were body parts everywhere and hands rose from bloody masses to grab at her. She saw the faces of several students, all screaming for help, and in the middle of the cluster, Sam. He was silent.*

*"NO!" she screamed, trying to get to him, trying to save him, but the hands held her back . . .*

"NO!" Maggie screamed aloud, bolting upright and startling Bones. She wondered when the tears would stop.

# ~ 19 ~

"**A**TTENTION NORTH: this is a lockdown, internal lockdown immediately, lockdown immediately!"

The uncharacteristically harried tone of the principal's voice over the tinny intercom system startled Maggie and her students from their post-lunch writing assignment.

Her students looked at one another and then at Maggie without budging. Knowing about Columbine and Virginia Tech and other school massacres, they were used to having lockdown drills each semester and were unfazed. Nothing would ever happen to them, of course; it was always *other places*. But Maggie knew this was different.

"NOW! In the corner, leave your stuff, let's go, quickly!" she barked without hesitation, finally getting the response she expected.

She ran to the door to lock it and turn out the lights. The blinds were already down since she'd been using the overhead projector. She grabbed her laptop from her desk and a pair of scissors from her drawer and joined the students in the far corner of the room, away from windows and barely out of sight from the glass pane next to the door, a piece of glass that could be smashed easily by someone motivated to get into the room.

"Quiet!" Maggie demanded in the sternest whisper she could muster.

"What's wrong, Miss? We do this all the time," said one of her students, enjoying the opportunity to do something other than study.

"I said QUIET!" Maggie hissed at him with fierce eyes, instantly transforming the smiling boy and the others into a meek, alarmed mass.

*"Miss?"*

They were suddenly afraid and watched their teacher intently as she typed something on her computer.

Maggie sent a message to the office asking, "Is this real? Should we start looking in our rooms for items for defense?"

The response—"Real, intruder in the school, emergency personnel notified"—got her adrenaline flowing.

"Listen up, guys," she whispered to her attentive group, I need you to be really quiet, okay? There's someone in the building who shouldn't be here and the police are on their way. He may not be dangerous, but we don't want anyone to know we're in here in case he is, so let's just all stay quiet and stay calm."

Maggie was supposed to slide a green "All Accounted For" card under the door to notify the authorities she had everyone she was supposed to have in her classroom, but chose not to. It would be a sign to an intruder there were people in the room, and this was no drill. She sent an email to the office notifying them of her status.

"Miss?" one of her frightened girls whispered, holding back tears. Maggie looked at her with an expression that said, "Go on." "Miss, will you protect us if someone comes in?"

Maggie whispered back to the group, "Of course I will."

"What will you do?" came another hushed question, and as Maggie looked around at each face in her huddled mob she realized—for the first time since setting foot in the school—her tough-acting students were just frightened young children who needed protection—and rescue from negative influences beyond their control.

She looked around the room.

"Here's what *we'll do*," she said. If everyone had a task, it would give them some sense of control over the situation. No one wanted to be a sitting duck. She had everyone's attention.

"Here, pass these around quickly." Maggie reached into the corner shelves to grab the 4"x5" hardcover abridged student dictionaries. "I know you hate these, but think of them as weapons now, okay? If you hear me yell, 'FIRE!' I want you to throw these books as hard as you can toward the door. Anyone coming into this room without an invitation is going to be surprised because I'm going to grab a desk and charge at them. We're going to attack first."

# *Laurel McHargue*

The students glanced at one another nervously.

"Now, we're going to do something we haven't practiced before, okay?"

Her students nodded, intently awaiting her next words.

Before she could speak again, loud voices and a bang from the end of the hallway startled them all. Maggie recognized the sound of a handgun firing. Within moments, police sirens filled the air.

"I'm scared, Miss!" several students burst, unable to manage whispers.

Maggie moved into double-time and her kids watched as she ran around the classroom laying desks on their sides with the tops facing the door. A couple of students, understanding her intent, left the group to help.

"Everyone—quickly—bring your book and get down behind a desk." Her students did as she ordered. Being at the end of the hallway, she knew she had some time. She called one of her larger boys over to her own metal desk.

"Help me tip this, okay?" she asked, quickly clearing the desktop of items. The two turned it on its side. Maggie called the six students closest to the door to hide in the back behind her desk and moved to the desk closest to the door.

It had never made sense to her that children should be gathered in one easy shot-group, unarmed, in the open, and afraid. At least the student desks had a thin layer of metal underneath which could possibly deflect a bullet.

More silence followed the disturbance and Maggie's students remained motionless—gripping their improvised weapons—behind their desks. She could hear suppressed whimpers from behind several desks. She was startled by her own fear. This was no war zone, yet she had just armed everyone in her care with tools for self-defense. Every sense was heightened and the sound of her own heartbeat was too loud.

Time seemed to stop while they waited.

"You're doing great, everyone, and you do *not* have to throw your books if you don't want to. If you feel safer staying behind the desk, it's okay to stay there." Maggie encouraged her hidden warriors in the most upbeat whisper she could force. "You're going to be fine."

More silence.

# *"Miss?"*

The stillness was shattered endless moments later by the shaky voice of an office secretary over the intercom.

"The lockdown is over. Please remain where you are until your door is opened by the administration."

Maggie stood and looked around her room. Frightened eyes peeked over desktops and everyone could hear doors being opened from down the hallway. Soon they heard the sound of a key in their classroom door, and Gladys's voice.

"All clear, but remain in your room please," she announced as she opened the door and caught Maggie's eye.

Maggie could tell the woman had been frightened. Gladys was about to continue on her mission, but was stopped by the unusual scene before her: a room in disarray and students still peeking out from their positions on the floor behind each desk. Maggie thought she noticed the slightest hint of a smile on the woman's face before she nodded at her, almost imperceptibly, and left.

"All right, everyone, you can get up now. You did great!" Maggie announced cheerfully, belying the panic still threatening to shake her voice.

Instantly, several students ran to her, sobbing, for comfort. She hugged them all, telling them it was all over and everything was fine.

"But what happened?" The questions started. "Is everyone all right?"

"Let's get this room back in order, okay? And I'll email the office," Maggie instructed her students. "And when you get back to your desks, go ahead and unload those weapons and see if you can find five words you don't know!"

She had to keep her kids busy until she heard from the office; the bell had rung halfway through the lockdown and none of the teachers knew what to do with their students yet.

"Teachers, please keep your 6$^{th}$ hour class in you rooms until the dismissal bell today." It was the principal again, sounding much more in control. "I will send you a memo shortly about today's, ah, incident. Thank you all—students, staff and teachers—for your outstanding behavior this afternoon."

"Okay, everyone, until I find out what happened today, let's see if we can try to focus on our process essays." But Maggie's students were in no mood for school work.

"Aww, Miss, can't we just talk?" The request elicited unanimous vocal support. Maggie would get nowhere with her lesson, especially since her own adrenaline levels were still elevated. Although the lockdown had lasted only 40 minutes, it had seemed like hours. Everyone in the room was visibly shaken.

"Well, I suppose I could tell you a story about how I had to make an escape out of a second floor window when I was in college," she offered, and everyone was anxious to hear the tale. Just as she was setting the stage for the story, however, Gladys appeared at the door again.

"Miss McCauley, the principal would like to see you in his office for a few minutes. I'll stay with your class."

Maggie's heart went into overdrive again and her only thought was that she was in big trouble for her handling of the lockdown. But the assistant principal appeared calm, so Maggie instructed her students to start brainstorming ideas for a "How To" paper and left the room.

She entered David's office and was startled to see Grant sitting on the office sofa, unnerved and pale as death.

"Oh my God! What happened!" Maggie blurted, hurrying to his side.

"I'm okay," he said, "just a bit shaken up, you might say."

"It was Razz," said David. He came in through the back door of the gym while Grant was having the kids do shuttle runs. That's how we found out about it—a group of kids ran around to the front of the building and told us what they saw. He had a handgun."

"Are you okay? Are you shot?" Maggie scanned Grant for signs of blood.

"No, no," said Grant, still shaking. "Did you know our new guard has a concealed carry permit? I didn't, but I sure as hell am glad he does. Razz came in waving his gun at the kids, telling them to get lost, then he staggered toward me, calling me every name in the book."

"Oh my God, was anyone else hurt?" Maggie asked, trying to control her panic.

"Just Razz," said David, "but he'll live. The kids ran into Gary on their way to the office and he beat feet around back. Razz didn't see him come through the door."

"I just froze," Grant confessed. "He was yelling at me and saying some really nasty things."

## *"Miss?"*

Maggie could feel the heat rising in her veins; anger replaced fear.

"Then Gary told him to freeze and drop his weapon. He was so startled he almost fell over when he spun around and when he raised his gun, Gary took a shot and hit him in the shoulder. That dropped him."

Maggie squeezed Grant's hand trying to soothe the tremors.

"Oh, great," said David, looking out the window. "They're here already."

Two local news vans pulled up to the front of the school.

"How do they find out so fast?" he said, more to himself than to them. "They're going to want to talk to everyone—me, both of you, the kids—so unless you want to make national news, let me handle them, okay?" The two nodded.

"So what happened to Razz?" Maggie asked, wanting to know the full story, "And what do we tell the kids?"

"Razz was taken to the hospital with a police escort. Wow. I feel horrible I said you wouldn't have to worry about him anymore. I'm truly sorry, and I know that doesn't mean much right now. As for the kids, tell them the truth. I'd better go out now. This place will be swarming with press and parents soon. Let your kids know if their parents want to pick them up early, they can sign them out at the front desk. We'll make an announcement soon. And yes, you can let them use their cell phones."

~~~~~~

That evening Maggie and Grant watched the news with Harry over delivery pizza and beer.

"You okay, sport?" Harry asked Grant, handing him another beer and noticing the young man's hands were still shaking.

"Honestly, Harry, I've never been so scared in my entire life. And I just stood there! That son-of-a-bitch could've killed me—*would* have killed me if Gary hadn't been there."

Maggie rubbed her hand across his back as he spoke and Bones whined at the intensity in the atmosphere.

"It's okay, Boy," Harry said, ruffling the dog's head, settling him down.

"He probably wouldn't have hit you as unstable as he was," suggested Maggie, but they all knew her attempt at diffusing Grant's fear was lame.

"So, will the two of you be making an appearance on any of these news channels?"

"Not if we can help it," said Maggie, but as the words were out, they heard her name on the television.

" . . . and then our teacher, Miss McCauley, gave us books to use as weapons, and we all spread out and hid behind our desks . . . "

Maggie's jaw dropped as several students recounted the defensive positions they'd taken in the classroom and how their teacher was going to lead the charge against anyone who tried to get into their classroom. They were excited and proud.

Grant stared at Maggie. Harry smiled.

"Oh, shit," said Maggie.

"How come you didn't tell me anything about that?" Grant sounded hurt.

"Maybe because what *you* went through trumps anything I did?" She tried to play off the actions she took to keep her students safe. "I wasn't in any danger. You almost lost your life!" The reality of the situation came crashing down on her.

Her cell phone rang and it wasn't a number she recognized. She let it go to voice mail, but it rang again. And again. Harry turned off the television.

"Looks like you might have to make an appearance after all," Harry said. "And hey, perhaps all this publicity will be what the school needs to stay open?"

"Or not," Maggie said, regaining control of her emotions. "It might just be the last straw."

"Wish I could think of something to lighten your spirits, kids," said Harry when the two were ready to leave.

"Tomorrow's going to be a long day." Maggie hugged Harry goodnight. "But we'll be okay. Don't worry. See you in the morning, my friend."

Grant walked Maggie and Bones back home and, uncharacteristically, turned to leave.

## *"Miss?"*

"You could spend the night if you want." Maggie was worried about Grant.

"Thanks, Maggie. You know I'd love to, but not tonight," he said. "I've got some thinking to do. Will you be okay?"

"Yeah, sure I will. Hey—I'm worried about you."

"Don't be, okay? I'll be fine. See you tomorrow," he said, and hugged her before leaving.

Maggie listened to six voice mail messages when she got home, five from reporters, one from David. She called her boss.

"I hate to ask you to do this," said David, "but I've got tons of requests to talk to the combat teacher. Any chance you'd give a quick interview tomorrow morning before classes start?"

"Do you think I should?" Maggie asked, hoping against hope he'd say no.

"I think it would be a positive thing for the school, but I don't want you to feel like you have to. I've had parents calling me all evening telling me how much they appreciate how you handled the incident, and no other teacher thought to do what you did. So yeah, I think you should."

"I'll be there," said Maggie, "but can we leave Grant out of this? He's having a really hard time with all this."

"Absolutely. He just called in to take some time off. I can only imagine how shaken he is right now. Get a good night's sleep, Maggie, and I'll see you in the morning."

But a good night's sleep was impossible. What questions would they ask her? How long would it be before things would return to normal at the school? Why was what she had done so newsworthy? And what was up with Grant?

Maggie tossed and turned all night, and Bones finally jumped from the restless bed to nestle down in his sparsely used dog pillow for his own doggie-dreams. At least one of them was able to leave their day's events behind.

# ~ 20 ~

MENTALLY EXHAUSTED the next morning, Maggie jumped out of bed with the false sense of energy that comes after a sleepless night. She was thankful she and Grant had been able to sneak undetected through the mob of reporters the previous afternoon.

The confusion of parents and students gave the press plenty to focus on and there were enough student eye-witnesses to Razz's gun-wielding to fill hours of air time. She was next in line for the media's scrutiny.

She got to school an hour earlier than necessary hoping to collect her thoughts before her television appearance, but they were already on scene interviewing Gary. He was the true hero of the day, and David was standing by his side.

As soon as they saw Maggie approach, however, all cameras were on her and the flood of questions began. Maggie blocked them all out until she joined her boss by the front door.

"Miss McCauley, is it true you were involved in a love triangle with the perpetrator and the victim?"

"Is it true that he was taking revenge against your boyfriend?"

"Can you tell us more about the military training you did with your students during your lockdown?"

"What do you think about arming teachers in light of the ongoing mass shootings in schools?"

"Weren't you putting your students in danger by expecting them to go on the offensive against an armed assailant?"

## *"Miss?"*

Maggie was overwhelmed by the barrage. She looked to David for reassurance.

"Just say whatever you believe is appropriate," David whispered to her. "I'll back you up." Maggie faced the crowd.

"The actions I took in my classroom were intended to maximize the safety of my students. I chose to disperse them throughout the class behind some degree of cover in the event an armed assailant would gain entry into the class, and to arm them with something they could throw—but only if they wanted to—to startle an intruder. The man who violated the law yesterday is emotionally unstable and I will not pretend to guess what his motives were. My personal relationships have never interfered with my work. And yes, I do believe those of us who are responsible for the safety of your children should be armed with something other than dictionaries and desks."

"That's all we have time for," said David, motioning for Gary and Maggie to retreat into the school. "We appreciate your concerns, and now if you'd please respect our need to get back to the business of education."

Despite the continued questioning, David simply smiled, nodded to the cameras and followed his teachers inside. The three gathered in David's office and this time it was Maggie who was shaking.

"Love triangle? Are you fucking kidding me?" she blurted out as soon as David closed his door. "And military training? Holy shit, Dave, am I going to need a lawyer?"

"No, Maggie, you didn't do anything wrong and please accept my apology for putting you up to that. I had no idea they'd spoken with Razz before coming here and believe me, I was as surprised as you were about the questions they asked. You handled it well, though, so let me take it from here."

"I was about to ask the lawyer question too, Maggie," Gary added. "Most of you didn't know about my concealed carry, but the district knows."

"Gary, I have no way of thanking you for what you did yesterday," Maggie said to the man she knew so little about. "If you hadn't been there—or reacted so quickly—well, I don't think we would've been open for classes today."

"We're going to have an assembly first hour today to let everyone know what's happened and to dispel any rumors," David told the two. "Maggie, I'm assuming everyone knows by now that you and Grant have been spending time together?"

"Yes," said Maggie. "The kids tease us every once in a while, but for the most part, it's not a big deal."

"Good," said David. "There will be no discussion of love triangles or revenge or any of that. I'll let them know Razz is—as you put it this morning—emotionally unstable and his actions were irrational. I spoke with Grant this morning and he said it was okay for me to say he felt like Razz hadn't been friendly with him ever since he's been here, and again, mention the fact that there was never any rational cause. They don't need to know any other details."

"Will we have to speak at the assembly?" Gary asked.

"No. I'd like to keep this short and sweet. I'll need to acknowledge your part in the takedown, though, Gary, and the kids will be very interested in your weapon. I know you know how to handle that. And if I haven't said it enough yet, I think you deserve a medal. The mayor left a message last night requesting a meeting with you. I've forwarded his contact info to your email so you can get back with him when you're ready. I'd like to say you should take the day off, but if it's okay with you, I think having you around will make everyone feel safer, and we're really going to need that for the next several days."

"No problem, sir," said Gary. "I wouldn't want to be anywhere else."

Maggie smiled at the newbie formality.

"And Maggie," David turned his attention to his other media celebrity, "the superintendent would like to talk with you about being a member of the district's ERT. For now, though, let's do our best to get back on track in our classes."

Although Maggie felt honored to be asked to be on the Emergency Response Team, all she could think about was how she'd have more unpaid demands on her time. Still, she was more qualified than most to be on the team and would accept the invitation.

"Teachers, please guide incoming students directly to the auditorium for a first hour assembly," came the directive over the intercom. *Good,* Maggie thought, *let's get this over with.* Normally, students would go to their first hour class for attendance before being herded to the auditorium. David's decision to bring them in right away would minimize wasted time.

The media remained outside the school the entire day and as students entered, many with parental escort, they were abuzz with excitement. Many of them had been interviewed, and the thought of being on television was far more exciting than anything they'd previously experienced. It was certainly more exciting than writing a process paper.

"Ladies and gentlemen," David began his speech when the students were all seated and surprisingly quiet, "our school has just experienced an act of violence, but I am happy to say that because of the smart actions taken by our staff—and by you students too—we're all okay. Go ahead and give yourselves a rowdy round of applause for a job well done!" The principal knew his audience and within moments, both students and staff members were cheering loudly and high-fiving one another.

David waited for several minutes for everyone to settle down before he continued with what he called the details of the event. He made it clear the act was perpetrated by someone who didn't have a healthy mind and there was no sensible reason for it. He acknowledged many people had enjoyed a great relationship with Razz in the past and even though he'd been injured, he'd be given the help he needed to get healthy again.

He discussed the district's decision earlier in the year to bring in security personnel who knew how to use handguns in all the schools and mentioned how fortunate North was to get the first trained guard. He thanked Gary, initiating another round of cheering and applause, and instructed everyone to be respectful of his position.

Maggie made a mental note to talk about situational irony with her students before the state test. The takedown of a dismissed security guard by his replacement would be much more relevant to the kids than any unanticipated scene from Shakespeare, and perhaps they just might be able to make that connection.

"Now, I know you all heard about the kids at the high school who asked to be tased by the Sheriff's department during the career fair last year, but let me assure you, Gary will *not* be letting you near his firearm, so don't even ask!"

There was laughter in the audience as students remembered the scandal and the dismissal of several imprudent law enforcement officers the prior year.

David closed his talk by encouraging everyone to put the event behind them and to focus on the future. He recognized there would be lots of excitement for the next several days with the reporters around and asked them all to do their best to represent their school in a positive light.

"And if any of you feel you'd like to talk with someone about what you experienced yesterday, please let one of your teachers know. We'll have specialists here for anyone who'd like to talk. Let's get back to work, Eagles! Let's show everyone out there how strong we are!"

The auditorium emptied with the sound of applause still ringing in the air, and the energy from the assembly remained palpable throughout the day.

~~~~~

As soon as Maggie's first hour class got seated, hands went up. They had all heard the details of the irregular lockdown scenario from their 6th hour friends and wanted to talk about Army training.

"Will you teach us self-defense, Miss?"

"I sure will!" said Maggie, surprising them all. "Now pick up those dictionaries and let's start learning some new words, because intelligence is going to be your best defense ever against being victimized in the future!"

"Aww, Miss, that's not what we mean!" her students objected.

"Well, okay, but just one quick self-defense lesson and then back to working on your brains, okay?" Maggie decided she should capitalize on their enthusiasm. "Who wants to volunteer?"

With everyone doing the "Oh! Pick ME!" dance, Maggie selected the largest boy in the class to join her up front.

"I'm going to show you all how I was taught to escape from a strangle-hold," she said, and everyone, including the large boy, laughed nervously.

"Go ahead and grab me by the neck," she told the boy, but he was reluctant. "It's okay!" she continued, "You don't have to squeeze really hard, but just pretend. I won't hurt you."

"Do it! Do it!" his classmates called out, encouraging the nervous boy.

When he finally put his hands on his teacher's neck, Maggie dropped down and away from him, quickly swinging her right arm over and breaking his hold as she turned to her left and ran away.

"Whoa!" her students responded. They were on their feet, and the volunteer stood looking at his hands and smiling.

"I can't guarantee that move will work every time, but if you act quickly and aggressively, you might startle your attacker and get away. Have any of you been told about how to inflict damage on an attacker if he still has you trapped?" she asked.

"I know," said one of her girls. "My mom told me to kick him in the balls."

Her statement made everyone laugh and Maggie waited until they had settled down.

"Yes, that's one of the places you should attack if you can, but don't forget to go for the eyes, nose, throat, and even stomp down on their feet if you can. But let me caution you. Don't do anything that could make your situation worse, especially if they have any kind of weapon. I would highly encourage you all to see about taking a self-defense class at the YMCA, and maybe ask your families to take it with you."

"Now back to our lesson," she said, ignoring the moans and waiting until everyone was seated.

"How many of you remember the talk we had last semester about how you feel when you don't understand what people are talking about?" Heads nodded all around. "And who can tell me what it means to be a victim?"

"It means someone does something bad to you."

"That's right, Rico. And does anyone want to be a victim?" Maggie looked around the room at all the shaking heads. "Then could someone please tell me why anyone would choose to be a victim?"

"Whadaya mean, Miss?" asked Ebony.

"What I mean is, if you keep making the choice not to learn things, then the people who choose to make themselves smarter will end up being the ones who'll make all the decisions in the world. They'll be the ones who get hired for all the good jobs, and they'll be the ones who'll make decisions that could affect your life."

"But how does that make us victims?" asked Jack.

"Good question," said Maggie, trying to think of an example they could understand. "Have you all heard about The Dream Act?" Many of her students were undocumented. She explained it simply to those who weren't sure what it was.

"Well, the people who'll decide whether or not it happens are people who are educated, and if people coming into our country don't learn how to speak English well, then the people making the laws won't see any need to help them become citizens." She was greatly simplifying her explanation, but wanted them all to understand her point. When she talked like that it made them angry, but it also kept their attention.

"That's just racist, Miss!" said Juan.

"Perhaps it is, Juan, but let me give you this scenario. You and Trevor are applying for the same job. You both have the exact same grades, you're both excited about the job, you both have the same qualifications the boss is looking for, but Trevor speaks English really well, and you don't because you've grown up in a home where you only speak Spanish, and you've made no effort to learn the rules of English. Who do you think will get the job?" Maggie could see students around the room squirming and wondered if she had been too "real" with her example.

"But that's not fair, Miss!" Juan continued.

"Then it's time someone told you—if they haven't already—that nothing in life is fair and the best thing you can do for yourself is to do whatever it takes to make sure you have a fair chance at being as successful as you want to be later on. The hard truth is that if someone has a difficult time understanding you, then it doesn't matter how smart you are or how great your ideas are, they're going to pick someone with better communication skills. I told you at the beginning of the year—and I wasn't kidding—being able to communicate effectively is the most important thing you can learn in school, and that's why dictionaries will always be excellent weapons against ignorance—and, possibly, intruders!" Her humor broke the tension.

"Oh, Miss! Could I throw my dictionary at the door and see if it would work?" asked Trevor, and Maggie regretted her last statement.

"Yah, Miss, can we?"

With the flurry of requests, she had to make a smart decision. Trevor had been performing surprisingly well since restarting his medication and Maggie knew what an effort it had been for him to rein in his old habits. There were also several small dictionaries destined for the trashcan at the end of the semester.

"Here's what we'll do. Trevor, Juan, and Linda, come stand over here." She motioned them to the front of the room. Linda looked surprised, but smiled and joined the group. Maggie handed them each a tattered dictionary. "Everyone else move to the sides of the room." They complied in an instant.

"I don't want you to throw these at the door, because if you miss, you might break the window, but when I say 'FIRE,' go ahead and throw these at the brick wall behind my desk with all your might, okay?"

Nervous laughter erupted around the room and Maggie wondered if she was making the right decision. It was too late to turn back.

"FIRE!" she yelled, and the three books smacked the wall with a force that left no doubt about the effectiveness of their impact. Two of the books split apart and everyone laughed. Maggie got everyone seated again, denying more requests to try the experiment.

"This is the only class I'll let do that today," Maggie told them, "so you can let everyone know if you had to throw a book at someone across a room, whether you're a boy or a girl," everyone laughed and looked at Linda, "you could certainly do some damage."

"But I still don't get what learning has to do with being victims or not," said Jack. "Mr. Powell is smart, and he was still a victim yesterday."

"Hey, where is he? Is he okay, Miss?"

Maggie had hoped no one would catch the flaw in her argument.

"Yes, he's fine. The principal decided it would be a good idea for him to take some time off, but he's fine, and thanks for asking. I'll let him know about your concern. But back to your question, Jack, there are different threats we need to arm ourselves against. The threat Mr. Powell faced yesterday was a physical one and since he didn't have a weapon, he was at a huge disadvantage. Still, I'll bet if Gary hadn't shown up when he did, Mr. Powell might have been able to use his excellent communication skills to talk Razz out of doing something stupid."

Maggie was stretching her point, but wanted to remain focused on it.

"The threat I was talking about has to do with intelligence versus ignorance, and that's one *you do* have control over. You can either say, 'I'm not gonna do nothin' cuz everyone's just racist,' or you can decide to work hard—and it will take hard work—to improve your vocabulary and your knowledge of other topics so you can present yourselves with confidence and start changing people's ideas about you. And yes, Juan, there are still a lot of racist people in the world and you're going to have to work harder than your white classmates to convince people you can do a job as well as they can, just like I had to work extra hard as a woman in the Army to convince people I deserved to be there as well as my male peers."

"That ain't fair," mumbled Ebony.

"As I said before, there's nothing fair about it, but the reality is that America is still very much a white man's world. But have any of you heard President Obama speak?" Maggie asked, and several students nodded. "And what can you tell about his intelligence when you listen to him?"

"He sounds real smart," said Rico.

"Do you think he could have become president over an all-white guy if he didn't sound like he was smart? I'm pretty sure he had to work even harder to get where he is today than I had to work to prove I could do my Army job well."

There was a moment of silence. Maggie glanced at the clock.

"Well, you've managed to avoid working on your process papers today," she saw flashes of smiles around the room, "but tomorrow I want you to come in with your topic for a "How To" paper. Choose one of the topics from this list." She handed out a sheet full of ideas just as the bell rang.

Maggie spent the rest of the day discussing the same issues with the rest of her classes. Even her rowdiest classes were attentive and chatter in the hallways between classes was all about the shooting and the news.

~~~~~

"So, when will you be giving us our mandatory faculty self-defense training?" Kirby teased Maggie at their team meeting.

"Not you too!" Maggie said in mock exasperation. She told the group about her self-defense lesson and dictionary drill as a heads-up and hoped she wouldn't be reprimanded for it.

"Are you kidding?" said Matthew. "If I didn't like you so much I'd be jealous of all the attention you're getting. But hey, how's Grant doing, really?"

"Not so great," Maggie said. "I'm going to call him at lunch and convince him to come back to school. He didn't even tell me he was taking a few days off."

"He'll pull through," said Kirby. "I think I'd need time off after being on the wrong end of a gun too. But back to the real world now, we have seven more weeks before the test and I'm supposed to tell you all to make sure you're using the past test released items in your classes every day."

"Yeah, yeah, we are," moaned Amber. "And by the time they get the actual test, they'll be so tired of seeing the same shit they'll just bubble in pretty patterns to be done with it."

"Let's hope not," said Kirby, "although at this point I honestly don't know it'll make any difference."

"What do you mean?" asked Maggie.

"Well, let's just say what I've been hearing at the district level isn't sounding too good for us. It's like they've already made a decision about the school but they're not saying it out loud."

"Great," said Matthew. "So much for tenure."

"But hey, don't pay any attention to me. I could be wrong—I have been once before," Kirby said in her usual straight-man tone, "and they're not going to say anything until after the God-Almighty test."

"I still can't believe Razz got in with a gun yesterday," said Amber. They all nodded silently. "Do you really think teachers should be armed, Maggie?"

"Well, I don't think we should be carrying handguns, but I do think we should at least have something like direct-shot mace canisters. I think it's a good idea to have well-trained, armed security guards or Resource Officers in schools, though, like Gary."

They all agreed.

"Let's just hope nothing like this ever happens here again," said Matthew.

"A wise man once told me hope is not a method," said Maggie. "If Gary hadn't been here yesterday, we'd all be hoping someone would see a need to have armed guards in all our schools today."

"Good point," Matthew agreed. "So, are we still hoping they'll keep North open next year?"

"I don't even know anymore," said Kirby. "Let's just keep being our awesome selves, though, in case we need to find new jobs soon."

~~~~~

"You've got to come back to school, Grant," Maggie said. She was surprised he answered his phone.

"I know, I know, it's just that I don't know what to tell the kids. They must think I'm a chicken," he confessed.

"Are you kidding me?" Maggie said. "You're as much of a hero as Gary is right now! All they could talk about today was how you held your ground with a gun pointing at you!"

"But I was scared shitless! I couldn't have moved if I wanted to."

"Fine, but they don't know that. All those kids saw before running out the door was you standing there, and by the end of the day they were all convinced you would've talked the gun out of his hand if Gary hadn't shown up." Maggie didn't mention her part in the talk-down story.

"Seriously?" he asked.

"Seriously, and if you don't get back on that horse, well, you know what I'm trying to say. They need you back here. They trust you. They don't even know the sub they found for you and right now they need things to get back to normal as much as you do."

"I guess I never thought of that," he said. "I'll let Dave know I'll be back tomorrow."

"Good!" said Maggie.

"You think you might blow off classes tonight?" he asked. "I sure could use some company."

"You know I can't. Let's catch up this weekend, though. Everyone will be glad you're back tomorrow, so be ready for a lot of attention. The press will be gone too, so you missed out on that whole thing."

"Yeah," he said. "I watched the news all day today and I couldn't believe the questions they were asking you. God, Maggie, I'm so sorry you had to face them alone."

"I wasn't alone," she said, although she understood his intention.

~~~~~

Maggie drove straight to the library after school to prep for her evening class. Sitting at a quiet table with her book opened in front of her, she zoned out for a moment, feeling as if she had shouldered the brunt of the past days' events and realizing she needed a shoulder to lean on as much as Grant.

She closed her book, emailed her instructor she hoped he would understand her absence and drove home. The emotional exhaustion had finally caught up with her.

Harry was pleasantly surprised when she showed up with Chinese food for two and by the end of dinner, she knew what she had to do. She'd wait until the weekend, though. There was only so much more she could add to her list of caring for others for the next couple of days. It was time to take care of herself.

~ **21** ~

---

G RANT RETURNED TO SCHOOL the next day to become the instant
new hero, and at the end of the week, Maggie was able to provide
another relevant example for demonstrating the word of the day: Fickle
Friday. Despite the horrendous event just days prior, life at North got back
to normal quickly, the media moved on to a story about a child abduction
and squabbles between students once again took center stage.

The weekend, however, was a different story and left Maggie
completely wrung out. Grant had pleaded with her again to hang in there
with him, but Maggie was certain she needed to set him free.

She needed more, and she needed to stop encouraging hopefulness for
their future together. Grant deserved the truth. Her time with him had made
her realize that—although she had always been able to take care of herself—
she nevertheless wanted to be with a man who could make her feel safe,
who could challenge her in ways that would make her better, and who was
decisive and clever and at least as confident as she was under stressful
circumstances. She wanted a man she could respect unwaveringly. She
wanted a man like Sam.

It was February and although Maggie had stacks of testing materials
to wade through with her students, she wasn't willing to give up the poetry
unit she had developed. Because there would be poetry questions on the test,
she justified moving forward with her plans to have students create their

own books of different types of poems. She'd find a way to work in some test questions.

But first she'd need to report one of her students to the counselor, Anne. It was a report that would be shared with the principal. While the majority of Maggie's students had done a fair job of constructing their "How To" essays having selected fun, easy subjects such as "How to make a cheese sandwich" from a list of acceptable topics Maggie had assigned them, Naldo had written his paper on "How to kill." It was blunt:

*"First go down town and knock someone out then take them to your house and tie them up and slice them open and eat there organs and go outside and bury them and go inside and whatch TV."*

Perhaps if he had added how he felt *melancholy* after completing his task, Maggie wouldn't have felt so horrified after reading it. He hadn't, though.

Maggie figured she'd probably be told Naldo was just looking for a reaction or some attention. She hoped that was all it was, but she also wanted to ensure the reaction and the attention would be appropriate and sufficient.

Maggie met with Naldo and Anne in Gladys's office during lunch.

"Naldo, did you write this paper to get a rise out of your teacher?" the counselor asked.

"No," he responded, simply.

"Do you know who Jeffrey Dahmer is?" she continued.

"No," he repeated, his expression blank.

"Do you know why we might be concerned about the topic you chose to write about?"

"No."

"Sounds like he's just looking for attention," said Gladys after releasing the boy back to lunch.

Anne called Naldo's mother. "She's not at all concerned," she reported after hanging up. "She said it was just because of the kids he's hanging out with. She said it was a joke."

"I hope he knows the 'F' he's earned on the paper is no joke," said Maggie, who was more concerned than his mother by the fact that the boy saw nothing wrong with what he'd written, or that he'd selected a topic not on the assignment sheet. She wondered if she should have given him extra credit for being creative and thinking outside the box.

"I'm suspending him for a day," said Gladys. "Maybe that'll give him some time to think about what he's done."

"But isn't that kind of like rewarding him by giving him a day off? If he doesn't know what he's done wrong, a day at home won't help him, and then he'll be even further behind in his requirements." Maggie was stunned.

"Well, what would you suggest then, Miss McCauley?" The assistant principal's tone was patronizing.

"Isn't there any way we could have him do some community service, like maybe have him spend the day helping some of the elementary kids with reading or something? Or better yet, find him a desk in the library and have him redo his work?" She never understood the rationale behind giving kids time off for bad behavior and wanted to ask if there might be a book with "thousands of ideas" for consequences that would fit the crimes.

"It would require someone to monitor him and you know how short we are on resources," Gladys said, tidying up some papers on her desk and looking at her dismissively.

Maggie headed back to her classroom feeling dejected. But she wasn't the only one feeling that way. Almost as if Maggie's discussion with Grant had caused repercussions throughout the school, or maybe because Valentine's Day was right around the corner, dating tiffs cropped up daily between students and the melodrama of seventh grade break-ups infused the atmosphere.

The biggest news was the break-up of Leanna and Juan, who'd dated for over a year. Maggie had always wondered why the pretty, smart girls always hooked up with academically challenged bad-boys in the school. She'd seen it play out since the beginning of the year. She followed Leanna—who was crying—into the hallway, and they were joined by Leanna's friend.

"My momma told me no boy under the age of 15 is worth crying over," Leanna's best friend told her, and Maggie was able to laugh with the two girls.

She decided to capitalize on the emotional heaviness they all were feeling by having her students write a simile about love. The kids would need to be able to identify this figurative language term on the impending test.

"So here's what we're going to do today," Maggie told her classes. She wrote in big letters on the front board, "LOVE IS . . . ," and then asked them to finish with a simile.

"Go ahead and write down as many things as you can imagine love to be like, and then if you're feeling extra-creative, try to use a semi-colon after it and add an independent clause to explain what you mean. For example, you might write 'Love is like an English class; it can be really frustrating.' Or for those who want to get an 'A' this semester, '. . . it can be really fulfilling'!" Everyone laughed, and Maggie looked forward to reading their responses.

"What do you mean by an independent clause, Miss?"

"What does it mean if *you* are independent?" Maggie asked the class.

"It means you're on your own and you don't need anyone's help," came the usual response.

"Good! So an independent clause is basically just a group of words that can be on their own, like a complete sentence. On either side of the semi-colon you need independent clauses—ones that could be sentences all by themselves—and the semi-colon just means the ideas on either side of it relate to one another somehow. You could put a period after the first statement and then start the next statement with a capital letter, but when you put them together with a semi-colon it lets the reader know the ideas work together and it makes for a more interesting sentence."

The answer seemed to satisfy her students and perhaps they'd remember the mini-lesson when writing their essays for the state test.

Maggie was startled by the depth of feeling this simple exercise brought out in her students and before each class ended, she had time to share the responses anonymously.

"Wow, you guys, these are truly beautiful!" she gushed before reading them aloud. "Check these out! Love is:

- *Like the wind; it comes and goes.* How true, right?
- *Like glass; be careful, it can break.* Hmmmm, nice. Try the word 'shatter' and see if that makes it sound more powerful.
- *Like going through pain with a smile on your face.* Oh! This one makes me sad.

- *Like school; you learn so many things.* Aha! Here's my 'A' student!
- *Like crossing the highway and getting hit by a semi.* Yikes!
- *Like getting your neck twisted off your head.* Eek! Who are you people dating?"

The students loved hearing their work validated. They even tolerated their teacher's goofy editorializing.

"So, can anyone here tell me the difference between love and lust?" Maggie asked, witnessing far more of the latter in the hallways every day.

They couldn't, so she turned English class into a cross-curricular science lesson about the chemistry between two people and the biological processes that occur—often instantly—to make people think they're in love when they're really just trying to keep the human species alive.

She hummed a horrible rendition of Bloodhound Gang's "Bad Touch" and her students all chimed in on the line about doing it like they do "on the Discovery Channel."

"That, my dears, is lust, pure and simple, and it's the first thing most of you feel when you see someone you think is hot."

They snickered.

Maggie was straying from her prescribed testing curriculum, but she knew most of her students were already sexually active and believed a few real-life lessons would be more beneficial to her horny hordes than another irrelevant test worksheet.

"Miss, can we ask you a question?" A shy request came from the back of the room.

"Certainly. What's up?" Maggie wondered what can of worms she had just opened.

"Well, is it true you can't get pregnant the first time you, you know, do it?"

*SHIT! Shit-shit-shit!* Maggie thought, panicking briefly while deciding how to handle this question. Many of her students were already sexually active, but most were still naïve about consequences. More than one middle school girl was currently pregnant, and it was pretty clear her students weren't getting accurate information from their parents or friends. This was a question she couldn't avoid.

"I'm not sure where you're getting your information, guys and gals, but what you just asked me is absolutely false. You certainly can get pregnant the first time—and *any* time you have intercourse." Maggie was concerned by the nervous expressions she noted on several faces around the class.

"And by the way, ladies, if a guy ever says you need to 'do it' or go 'all the way' to prove your love for him, then he really doesn't love you, he's just playing you."

More worried glances passed around the room and Maggie was more than ready for this day to end.

"Thanks, Miss," Bernicia said to Maggie on her way out the door, and then threw her an even bigger surprise by wrapping her arms around her in a powerful bear hug. The girl had made gains in controlling her outbursts lately and although she'd never opened up completely, it was clear she no longer viewed her teacher as the enemy.

"Any time, Bernicia." Perhaps what she was doing each day at the school just might be more important than any other job she could have taken.

"Love is like going through pain with a smile on your face" had been Bernicia's simile.

~~~~~

Sadly, others in the school weren't feeling as hopeful as Maggie about their impact on students and by the end of the month, even Matthew— an eighth year teacher—was routinely losing his composure. He confessed at one of their team meetings, which Grant had decided not to attend anymore, that he was filled with frustration and self-doubt. The team decided not to snitch on Grant. They realized how hurt he'd been by Maggie's decision. Also, their meetings had little—if any—impact on physical education classes.

"You're not alone, buddy," said Kirby, patting Matthew on the back. "Janet just told me there's no way she's coming back next year."

Janet, a 6th grade teacher with 15 years of teaching experience, was one of the best. Even she couldn't handle the constant change of new programs designed to get their school back on track.

Maggie wondered if the problem was that North wasn't a typical middle school, but she had nothing to compare it to.

"Our population is just so ridiculously needy," said Amber. "A lot of them don't even have their basic life necessities met. It's no wonder they have no attention span."

"Yeah, and my peanut butter budget is getting low," said Kirby. She had confessed to Maggie earlier in the year how she kept a supply of bread, peanut butter and jelly in the back of her classroom. Her students knew if they were hungry, they could help themselves. She used her own meager funds to provide this gift knowing if a kid's stomach was growling, he likely would be neither interested in nor capable of focusing on something as irrelevant as the dynamics of a water cycle.

"It sure doesn't help that their parents expect us to fix them, either," said Maggie. "Remember Mateo?"

"Who could forget that upstanding young citizen," said Matthew. They were all noticing Mr. Mild-Mannered's change of attitude toward his work lately and were sad to see him succumbing to the sense of defeatism infiltrating the school.

~~~~~

*Love is not a sin nor is it a tragedy. Love is more than just caring about someone, it is about having faith in them, respecting them and always being there for them. No matter what happens, your love, faith, and respect for them will always matter.*

When Maggie collected her students' completed poetry books, she was delighted once again to see many of her students were capable of communicating far more maturely than they were willing to express publicly. Knowing their teacher would share their poems only if she had their permission, they were open and honest in ways surprising even to themselves.

## "Miss?"

*I fear*
*Police because they take you away*
*Evil because it's scary*
*Myself because I get mad sometimes*
*I hope*
*To go to college so I can get a better education,*
*To graduate and get a better job,*
*To be a professional soccer player because you get paid a lot*
*I wonder*
*If I'm going to live long*
*If I will have a good family so we can live long*

The simple cookie-cutter format poems allowed students the liberty to be both honest and concise and gave Maggie a glimpse of their world she would not otherwise have seen. Many of her male students had plans to make it big in the professional soccer world, but few understood that even in pro sports, education is part of the package. Although she was encouraged to see these young men looking to healthy role models for inspiration, she failed to see the kind of work ethic necessary to make their dreams come true.

The most intensely personal poems from all her classes came from Bernicia. Most of them made her sad, but not nearly as sad as her poem entitled *Pain:*

> *Stuck in a blackened world of silencing abuse to the mind, depressing taste of my bitter disease of hurt, thoughts of suicide and tear jerking misery, life looks dark and cloudy as though these feelings are everlasting.*

This was a 13-year-old girl. Maggie was supposed to prepare her to be successful in life after school, but the painful reality for this child would likely be a life filled with sorrow and loss. Maggie would have to talk with Bernicia about seeing the counselor since there was mention of suicide in her poem, but doubted the girl would open up to someone she had no reason to trust.

Many of Maggie's students still claimed they didn't like poetry when the unit was completed, but she witnessed the unmistakable expressions of delight and pride in those who were most obstinate when she read their poetry aloud to the class. Even Bernicia allowed Maggie to post a couple of her poems on the display board in the classroom.

Perhaps the best lesson Maggie learned from squeezing her poetry unit in around the boxes of pre-test material was her students were more resilient than she had thought. In the midst of impending state test stress, puberty, and the looming threat of having their school closed, they were able to channel their frustrations into poetic expression.

Despite having little or no encouragement or academic support from their homes and having experienced much more life than children their age should experience, they nevertheless came to school every day and tolerated a system that oftentimes made no sense to them.

*Where was the poetic justice?* Maggie wondered with just three weeks remaining to bridge the gap between what English skills her students had mastered and what they should have mastered. The gap remained gargantuan.

## ~ 22 ~

M ARCH 4<sup>TH</sup>.

*If only we could,* thought Maggie after writing the date on the board. With fifteen class days remaining before a full week of state testing, she had the panicky feeling she had taught her kids nothing. Nothing that would translate to stellar performances on the test, anyway. About the only thing she could concentrate on was having her students memorize terms she knew would be on the test. Yes, they were terms they'd been using all year, but that gave her no confidence they had internalized their meaning or how to apply them.

"Who can tell me what a bibliography is?" She asked what she thought would be an easy question.

"It's a story about a person," someone suggested, and several heads nodded in agreement.

*Oh boy*, she thought, her fear validated.

"Does anyone have a different answer?" She hoped someone would be bold enough to disagree.

"I think it's like a list of books or something," said Ebony, who had been trying her hardest since the beginning of the semester to reverse a lifetime of poor performance.

"Yes! Excellent! So then what's the other word for a story about a person? Think back to when we read *The Diary of Anne Frank.*" She was stretching here, but hoped there'd be some flicker of remembrance.

"A biography!" someone shouted out.

"Yes! Good! I can see how these two might be confusing, so let's take a look at the words." Maggie wrote the words side by side on the board.

"What other words start with 'bio'?" she asked.

"Biology," said several students.

"Good, and what is biology all about?"

"Things that are alive?" someone offered tentatively.

"Yes! And so if you know 'bio' is about something that is or was living, then you can make a connection to a person who is or was alive. Now let's take a look at the word 'bibliography.' Juan, what's the word for library in Spanish?"

Maggie wanted her second language learners to be confident about making educated guesses based on the similarities between the two languages.

"It's biblioteca, Miss," he said, smiling a little.

"And what's in a biblioteca? Not that any of you would ever go to one," Maggie teased them good-heartedly.

"Books," came the unanimous response.

"Good! So you can make the connection between a library and a list of books, which is what a bibliography is, or even think of the word 'Bible' if it helps you remember it's about books. You'll need to remember the difference between these words because you'll get questions on the test about where you might find a list of references someone might use for a research paper, and you *don't* want to choose biography as the answer."

*Perhaps they'll all get at least one answer right*, she hoped, trying not to let the reality of their limited knowledge drag her into depression.

"So if a biography is a story about a person, then who can tell me what an autobiography is?" She wrote the word on the board.

Rico raised his hand. Like Ebony, he was also making a concerted effort to stay on the right path.

"Yes Rico? And thanks for raising your hand." Maggie did her best to reward behavior she wished to encourage in her classroom.

"It's a story about a car?" he responded, and Maggie burst into laughter, believing her student had just made a clever pun. The instant look of confusion on Rico's face, however, told her his response had been serious, and she was keenly aware of needing to act quickly to ensure she didn't just lose the tenuous trust of a young man who was always one step from the edge of making self-destructive decisions.

"That's excellent, Rico!" Maggie said with exuberance. She couldn't take back her laughter, so to save face, she'd explain to the class what Rico had just done, however inadvertently he had done it.

"What Rico just did was make a pun on the word autobiography. You all remember a pun is a play on words," she said, giving them credit for knowing the term, "and another word for car is automobile, so he just made a joke that if a biography is a story about a person, then an autobiography is a story about an automobile! I love it!"

Maggie prayed her explanation would work. As students laughed when they understood the pun, Rico's expression of confusion changed to one of gratitude. He looked up at Maggie and smiled.

*Phew!* Maggie thought, and moved on with a review of literary terms from the back of their text books.

~~~~~

"We're doomed," Maggie told Harry that evening before sharing the embarrassing situation surrounding Rico's response and bemoaning the lack of information retention among the majority of her students.

"I believe you're hyperbolizing," Harry responded. "And I'll bet you didn't think I'd remember the meaning of that word after all these years."

"Are you kidding me? With all the crossword puzzles you've destroyed since I've known you? If only you could sit in for one of my kids on test day."

"So tell me, how's Grant doing with his recent upheavals? I don't mean to pry, but I've been concerned about the young fellow."

Even though Harry hadn't meant to come off sounding accusatory, Maggie felt guilty. She had contributed significantly to Grant's recent slump and wasn't sure what to do about it.

"I think he's still struggling with everything," she said. "He was his old self when the kids were all talking about how he didn't run away when he had a gun in his face, but you know how kids are—they're not going to keep him in the news for long."

"And you? You can't keep blaming yourself that it didn't work out with him, you know," Harry said, and Maggie was grateful for his depth of observation.

"I can't help it," she confessed. "He didn't deserve to be hurt, and it's not his fault he doesn't have what I'm looking for. But am I wrong for feeling like I need a man who has a history more like my own?"

"What do you mean by 'history'?" he asked.

"I guess I mean my military background. I don't want to feel like I've got to explain why I'm tired all the time because of the nightmares I keep having."

Maggie intellectually understood it would take time to get over the repetitive nightmares, but felt Grant would never fully understand.

"At least Bones doesn't ask what's wrong all the time," she said, and hearing his name, the dog lifted his head from her lap and licked her chin.

"I see what you mean," said Harry. "It took a long time for me to feel like a civilian after I finished my time and even now, I don't completely. And you're right. Unless you've lived through what we've lived through, you just can't understand the whole experience. My beautiful Pat was a great comfort to me when I returned from Germany, but I know she always wanted me to share more than I was willing to tell. It made me feel bad. But let's not dwell on the past—did you hear about the kidnapping today?"

"Oh no! Who? Where?" Concern spread over Maggie's face.

"Don't worry," he said, "it's over now. He woke up!"

"Oh! You! You had me going there! Talk about word play—you're the master!" Maggie was happy to end their evening with laughter.

~~~~~

At the end of the week, Kyle never showed up for his last hour class. Maggie had seen him by the gym kissing a girl before lunch when he should have been in another class, so he wasn't absent. She was growing increasingly concerned about the boy's behavior. She'd already written him up several times, but his offenses were low on the administrative radar compared to others. When she opened her door halfway through class to check on some commotion in the hallway, she saw him hanging around the lockers with two 8th grade girls.

## *"Miss?"*

"Kyle, are you coming to class today?" Maggie asked.

"Yeah, I was just working with Miss D.," he said, making his way over to her. Miss D. was a custodian.

"Then go get a note from her, please, and get back here quickly," Maggie requested.

Maggie was surprised when Miss. D. brought Kyle back to class and said he had helped her move some chairs, but in the full story, she had released him when the bell rang. Maggie thanked the woman and let Kyle know she'd be writing him up once again for skipping class. He shot her an "I don't care" look and slumped in his seat.

Shortly before the bell rang, Maggie put a note on Kyle's desk which read, "You will stay after school today to complete your assignment—I will call your home." He crumpled it up and pushed it off his desk.

When the bell rang, Kyle shoved past her at the door yelling, "Too bad, so sad!" over his shoulder. Maggie drove home feeling defeated by a system failing teachers as much as it was failing students.

~~~~~~

Gladys called a special team meeting early the next week.

"Maggie, how often have you re-visited the behavior plans you have with your students?"

It took a lot of bad behavior from a student to get Maggie to write up a disciplinary referral form. She was always willing to give a kid a break and she hated giving up control of a student for others to deal with, but there were some—like Kyle—who'd simply worn her down too far. Those were the ones she needed administrative help with, and it seemed "the office" didn't want to deal with them either.

Gladys pulled out the *One Thousand Ideas* book and set it on the table.

Maggie wanted to say, *"How often have I re-visited those futile plans? How about never. Haven't done it. Don't have the hours in the day. Perhaps if you'd stop suspending kids and help us find a way to keep them in school, I might be able to do something with them."* But it was clear Gladys believed the problem was with her teachers.

"It's been a while." Her response was flat. She suppressed her urge to choke out the condescending woman. It would be so easy. So quick.

"I know you have a lot of homework, Maggie, but I really think you need to be making some calls home tonight. That goes for the rest of you too. You won't be able to move forward with your teaching until you get your classroom management under control."

The team looked around at one another, disbelief and anger palpable in the air.

"How many of these techniques have you tried?" Gladys asked no one in particular, expressionless.

The year was almost over, the school's status was up in the air and yet she still treated her overworked employees as if they were the enemy. She just didn't get it.

When no one responded, Gladys strongly suggested they all consider starting their next day with a Town Hall meeting during which they would capture on butcher paper all the things their students felt weren't working for them in the classroom. She wanted them to report their findings back to her by the next day.

"I'll leave the book with you, Kirby, and you can share the Town Hall format information with your team." She left the room.

"I don't know how much longer I can do this," said Maggie. "She's hated me since day one and everything I do is wrong. Sure, I'll get right on those phone calls, Your Highness, because I know how effective they'll be." She was ready to explode.

"Hey, we're on this elevator together, kiddo," said Kirby, making a reference to another one of the 'Let's Fly' poster techniques. "And you should know by now you're not her only target."

"Since when did the world decide that 12-year-olds should be making decisions about how we should be teaching?" asked Matthew.

"Since testing companies convinced Big Brother they all had the solution for academic success," said Amber. "You should know something about deep pockets, Mr. Social Studies."

"We have nine days left until testing and we're going to dedicate one of them singing 'Kumbaya' with our students. Why should any of us even try anymore?" asked Maggie.

"Because despite what Gladys says, we know we're great teachers and our students can still learn a few things, and you're the one who told us we should find something good in every day," said Kirby. "Listen, we all know we're working our butts off, so let's not let her shit get us down, okay?"

They encouraged one another and each patted Maggie on the shoulder as they left the room, telling her to hang in there; she had almost survived her first year of teaching.

~~~~~

Much to Maggie's dismay, Gladys showed up for her last hour Town Hall meeting the next day. She asked Maggie for permission to present the rules of the meeting to the class. Maggie was happy to hand her the reins.

At one point, the woman stopped and said, "Now, when I'm talking I expect that I am the only one talking, and that means the rest of you are quiet."

*Wow*, Maggie's sarcastic inner voice whispered. *Why did I never think of saying that before.* If only Gladys knew what the students thought of her. They weren't stupid when it came to knowing what they could get away with, and from the start of school they knew this administrator didn't like confrontation. They could do what they wanted to do when she was around and only maybe would she have someone else take corrective action. They were always willing to guess she'd do nothing.

While Maggie wrote her students' suggestions on the butcher paper, she was aware of Gladys making her way around the classroom to each disruptive student, whispering in their ear—a suggestion she had made to Maggie earlier, because you would never want to reprimand a student publicly—before moving to the next indifferent klatch of chatterboxes.

Student suggestions came as no surprise.

"More music!"

"More games!"

"More candy!"

"No homework!"

The last response surprised her. During the first week of school she was told she shouldn't bother giving homework because she'd never get anything back. She had grudgingly fallen in with her peers' suggestion and stopped assigning it. She hated the message of lowered expectations, but couldn't fight every battle single-handedly.

"No more standing us in line in the hallway. That just makes us more mad at you."

No, they didn't want any discipline and didn't want to do anything unless it was fun.

"You always pick on the same two students when everyone else is acting the same way," said Kyle. Maggie couldn't believe his audacity.

"Please raise your hand if you feel like I've ever singled you out," Maggie announced. More than half the kids raised their hands. She looked at Kyle with one eyebrow raised and could tell she'd proven her point.

He slouched in his chair.

More nonsense ensued despite her best efforts to elicit her students' help. With ten minutes remaining until the end of class, Gladys departed and the students took it as a signal the day was over. They commenced chatting among themselves about the "stupid Town Hall crap" and all but ignored Maggie, who was still standing at the front of the class.

She looked around her classroom and saw so much apathy on their faces that it broke her heart; an ache from deep within her chest threatened to stop her breath. She simply stood there, feeling useless, and when the bell rang, she left the school faster than she ever had before.

~~~~~

"Get a grip, woman!" she shouted at herself in the rearview mirror as she drove home, her hands clenching the steering wheel and anger welling up inside. "It's just a job!"

~~~~~

Maggie returned the next day to several "I'm sorry" notes on her desk. Rumor had it she'd stormed out of the building and quit. Evidently some of her students had seen the look on her face when she flew out of the building. One note, however, stood out from the rest, and it was from Kyle.

*"Miss?"*

*"I'm sorry for the things I've done in your class that have gotten me in trouble. I know I've done bad things, but it was just to get my mind off the real bad things in my life. If you can give me one more time, I promise I can really turn myself around."*

Humbled by the evidence showing she wielded far more influence on her students than she believed she deserved to have, Maggie accepted the notes and the hugs and promised her students once more she'd never abandon them.

Screw Gladys and her condescending attitude. Screw "Let's Fly" and all the other crap that interfered with doing what she had been trained to do. Screw the growing rumors of their school closing at the end of the year. Maggie was going to teach her heart out until the fat lady sang.

## ~ 23 ~

SEVEN MORE DAYS.
Magnanimous Monday, tenacious Tuesday, wistful Wednesday, and today was thrifty Thursday. Maggie had tried since the beginning of the year to expand her students' vocabulary, but with each new word she taught, she discovered there were multitudes that eluded them.

"Miss, what's this mean?" asked Shareena, who had been good as gold the past month and was always ready to be her teacher's enforcer.

The girl had even reined in her penchant for pinching. She pointed to a word in one of the answers to a question about how DDT could make people sick. The answers followed a reading about pesticides and how one woman stopped the rampant spraying of fields in the early 1960s.

"Steak? Who knows what a steak is?" Maggie asked the class, trying to hide her surprise. The kids looked around at one another waiting for someone to answer.

"Isn't it some kind of meat?" Jeanie's voice was barely audible.

*Holy mackerel*, Maggie thought. *Here I am teaching them SAT words and they don't even know what a steak is.*

"Yes, it's a slice of beef that comes from a cow," Maggie told the class matter-of-factly. "Does anyone have any other questions about words on the worksheet?"

"Yeah, I don't get question number three," said Naldo, and several students said they didn't understand it either.

"Okay, let's read it: 'What life experiences did the author draw from when she wrote her book?' What is it you don't understand?" Maggie asked, trying to be helpful.

"I don't get the part about drawing—it doesn't say anything about her drawing," said Naldo, and Maggie recognized what the issue was.

"Right! I can see how that would be confusing. This is one of those bizarre English language things where one word can have several meanings. What if I said to you, 'would you please draw a name from this hat?' What would I mean?"

"It would mean pull it out," said Jeanie, more boldly this time.

"Good! So now what do you think the question is asking, Naldo?" Maggie hoped he and the others could make the connection.

"What life experiences did the author pull out, ah . . .," Naldo struggled with his response while Maggie struggled to be patient. "Use? Does it mean use?" he asked tentatively.

"Yes! Good! So it's basically asking you to look through the reading and find things from her life she could use to write a book about the horrible things DDT was doing to plants, animals, and even people."

Maggie thought she could hear the fat lady clearing her throat.

~~~~~

That evening Maggie went to a girls' basketball game. Despite the workload from her routine class prep and her certification classes, she did her best to attend as many after-school events as she could. Her students always smiled when they spotted her. There were few parents at most games and it was embarrassing when visiting teams had a larger cheering section than the home team. Maggie sat down by a familiar face.

"So, will our school be closing?" asked one of the player's moms—one of the few who did show up occasionally.

"I wish I could tell you one way or the other," Maggie said. "We haven't been told yet, but I know the teachers and the principal are working non-stop to convince the state to keep North open."

"What we need is more Hispanic teachers for our kids," said the mother, seemingly unaware of the impact her statement might have on Maggie.

Maggie struggled to hold her tongue; she could feel the heat rising in her face. What could she say? What she wanted to say was, *"So where are these Hispanic teachers?"* She wanted to tell the woman it took a tremendous degree of dedication, patience and higher level education to become a teacher and she was seeing no emphasis at all from parents of her students on the value of schooling.

The truth was, there were no Hispanic teachers at North despite the large Hispanic population. The woman's comment made her feel defensive.

But she bit her lip and nodded her silent agreement.

The visiting team won 39-2.

~~~~~

"Miss, Miss, Come quick!" the distraught student beckoned Maggie between classes early Fortunate Friday morning.

She dashed to the end of the hallway to see Linda sprawled face-down on the floor, crying hysterically, with Ebony standing over her and looking smug. It was a good thing Maggie hadn't seen it happen, or both girls would have been sprawled on the floor and Maggie would have been kissing her classroom goodbye.

According to observers, Linda had said something snitty and Ebony had slapped her in the face, hard, and down she went. There had apparently been some coaxing from one of the 8th grade boys. Maggie called for security and helped Linda to her feet when they arrived. Though not seriously injured, she was humiliated. The two combatants and the 8th grader were escorted to the office and everyone returned to class.

Spring fever started early in Colorado.

~~~~~

Friday afternoon while Maggie was helping a student with a Test-Ready paragraph practice, Bernicia smacked Juan in the chest for no apparent reason, knocking his breath out. By the time Maggie got to the boy, he was hyperventilating.

"Get off of him!" Maggie screamed at Bernicia, who was pinching his cheeks so hard it left marks.

## *"Miss?"*

"What is wrong with you?" she asked the girl, instantly regretting her words. After the progress she'd made with Bernicia during the poetry unit, the troubled girl had made gains in her school work. Maggie's thoughtless comment could negate it all. There was plenty "wrong" with her student and everyone knew it.

Gary, who had been walking by the room when he heard Maggie raise her voice, entered the room.

"Miss McCauley, do you need assistance?" His voice, like his demeanor, was calm. Since the shooting, anytime he walked into a classroom, students hushed. They idolized him.

"Actually, would you mind talking with the kids for a few minutes while I escort Bernicia to the office?" Maggie asked.

Juan had regained his breath and claimed he was fine, and Maggie wanted to be in on this disciplinary decision.

David met with Maggie and Bernicia and while Maggie was explaining the incident, David retrieved Bernicia's file from a cabinet.

"I don't understand why you're always picking on me," Bernicia said to Maggie, working up a hearty crop of crocodile tears and assuming an air of innocence. "Yours is the only class I get in trouble in," she pouted, wiping her eyes.

"Your file tells a different story," said the principal, staring her down. "Let's take a look at your history of discipline, shall we, Bernicia?"

"My name is 'Bernicia'," the girl spouted back at him indignantly, her little-girl-innocence gone.

David hadn't yet mastered the Hispanic pronunciation—with an 's' sound instead of an 'sh' sound, and the girl was offended by the Anglicized *Berneesha.*

Maggie was appalled by her arrogance. David just ignored it.

"Looks like this isn't the first time you've physically attacked another student," David said, flipping through a file an inch deep. Maggie wondered what good any of the paperwork did if it just ended up being added to the heap.

"But—"

"No!" David shot back. "If I see you in this office one more time this year, young lady, or if I hear you've touched anyone again in an

~ 195 ~

inappropriate way, I'll bring in a law enforcement officer. Do you understand what I'm telling you?"

Maggie's heart skipped a beat.

Bernicia nodded, the wind knocked out of her sail this time.

"You'll spend the rest of the day downstairs in detention. I'll let them know you're on your way."

And with that, Bernicia departed. Maggie thanked David, who looked as if someone had been using him as a punching bag.

"For what it's worth, Dave," Maggie said, "I think you're doing an amazing job here."

He nodded, attempting a smile, and Maggie returned to class.

~~~~~

One more class and Maggie could go home for the weekend. Sure, she had about six hours of homework to complete, but at least she could do it in peace. The weeks had become increasingly more exhausting and this one had been a doozie.

With only ten minutes remaining until the dismissal bell, Maggie noticed a distinct rise in volume near the door before the eruption.

"Fuck you!" Leanna yelled at Kyle. Her romantic break-up was starting to affect her typically stellar behavior.

"No, Fuck you!" he responded, and Maggie was between the two in an instant, an unexpected sense of déjà vu making the hair prickle on the back of her neck.

"Are you kidding me?" Maggie shouted, positioning herself between the two, who continued with their verbal barrage despite her presence.

"Give me a break, people! Give me one stinkin', hairy break, would you please?" Maggie looked from one to the other, exasperated, and then the giggling started.

"A stinkin' hairy break, Miss? What's that?" someone asked, and before she knew it, she was laughing too. Everyone in the room—everyone except Kyle—laughed until the bell rang.

~~~~~

# *"Miss?"*

Before she could go home, an urgent message appeared in her in-box. She was asked to answer some questions emailed to her from a young girl who was considering being a teacher. She had visited one of Maggie's classes earlier in the year, and had follow-up questions for her report:

*1. Could you tell me how you formulate your grading criteria, particularly in light of the fact you have such a range in student ability?*

*2. Do you feel your administration supports the goals and aims of your department? It seemed many of the students were not at grade level. Is it because they are on an Individual Learning Plan? I just didn't get the sense that the admin supports your efforts in terms of discipline and consequences for the students.*

*3. I don't have the experience to say what can be done to help this student population, but what is in place doesn't seem to be working. I was hoping to get your insights since you are in the trenches and I really was very impressed with your ability to remain calm and keep the focus on the objectives for the class. I loved your teaching style and think you bring a great arsenal to the classroom. I am inspired by you, but discouraged by the situation at your school.*

*We are sharing observation experiences and nothing even comes close to this in the other schools observed. Most noted a disruptive student or two, but none compares with the battle you face daily. Nothing was even close. I was also curious if when you applied for the job you were told how challenging this student base was? You have been so generous with your time. Hang in there.*

Perhaps it was because Ebony was suspended and Linda's mom called the office to say she was going to pull her out of school—an idle threat; perhaps it was the fear she might have had to provide CPR for one of her students that day; perhaps it was the constant battle of Kyle against the world, or perhaps it was simply that in one more week, the testing would commence and then there would be a blissful spring break. Whatever it was, Maggie burst out laughing after reading the young girl's questions, appreciating the many references to her school being like a battlefield, and laughed until the tears ran down her cheeks. When she stopped crying, she shut down her computer and left the building.

Fortunate Friday? No. Maggie knew that, without a doubt, it was an F-You Friday.

*"Miss?"*

# ~ **24** ~

---

$\mathbf{F}$IVE MORE DAYS.

The atmosphere in the school was surprisingly sedate for a Monday morning and Maggie figured it had something to do with all the kids who were suspended for their actions from the previous week. She'd heard from other teachers about how their last week had been unusually demanding too, and hers weren't the only students out of school for a couple days. It made her feel a little better knowing she wasn't alone in her constant battle to maintain some degree of propriety in her classroom, though the overall message for the future outlook of the school was bleak.

Maggie hated the suspension policy, but she wasn't about to complain today. She wondered if she should volunteer to lead a boot-camp prep school for students during the summers. Most of what they learned in their previous grade was forgotten during the ten weeks of vacation, and precious time was lost each new school year with re-teaching skills the kids should already have mastered.

Plus, they could all benefit from a vigorous exercise program. Maggie was appalled by the rampant obesity throughout the student population. Grant's physical education classes kept the kids moving, but it was too little, too late.

During the morning's "Let's Fly" session—which Maggie couldn't believe was still requiring this late in the year—Rico asked if he could present one of the metaphors. His teammates volunteered to help him with the overheads. The metaphor was about tearing off the negative labels we put on ourselves.

"I ain't got no negative labels," Dashay announced proudly. Maggie cringed.

"Bossy!" Rico shot back at her.

Dashay jumped to her feet and marched over to him in a threatening manner. The two had been on good terms all year and Maggie hoped Rico was simply poking fun at her, but she wasn't sure.

"Hey! How about the Defense Mechanisms metaphor we learned about last week?" Maggie shouted at them.

Dashay looked at Rico with her hands on her hips, he smiled at her, and she laughed.

The rest of the kids in the group all enjoyed the interaction, and the reality of how quickly people respond in a defensive manner when they're caught off guard hit home.

"Mom—I mean Miss," said Rico, "what's in the cans?"

Maggie hid her amusement. It wasn't the first time a student had accidentally called her "Mom" and it was as embarrassing for her as it must have been for her students. She pretended not to hear the mistake, but Dashay didn't miss the opportunity to rub it in.

"Hey, if you two don't stop it right now, it's to bed with no dessert tonight," teased Maggie, shaking her finger at the two and putting on her best "Mom" face. She had to admit that even though the program was contrived, she did enjoy her small group of students, and the discussions were generally productive.

"So, after you finish attaching your labels to your cans, go ahead and open them!" Maggie announced to the group, passing out a few can openers. The preparation for this session included opening empty soup cans from the bottom and filling them with treats, then gluing the bottoms back on so they appeared intact. After finishing the exercise, the kids would be rewarded with sugary treats, just what the population of youngsters who showed up each day working on their second can of "energy drink" needed.

~~~~~

During her lesson on idioms, another language skill Maggie's students were weak on, she started with one she believed they'd heard at one time in their lives.

"What does 'Don't chop off your nose to spite your face' mean?" she asked. She waited. She remembered the difficulty they all had with the literal translation of the word "draw" from a previous exercise. When she got no response, she tried to make the expression more meaningful to the kids.

"Think about it this way. You hate your teacher, so what do you do?" In her mind, Maggie understood that oftentimes, students who don't like their teacher will not do the work, and will ultimately get bad grades.

But that wasn't the connection Naldo made.

"I'd kill you," he said, stone-faced.

*So there he goes again*, Maggie thought.

"How about a less dramatic way of interpreting it?" she asked, trying to make light of his response.

"I'd have you assassinated?" came the next response, working off of Naldo's answer.

"Any other suggestions?" she asked, smiling at Naldo and letting him know she was on to his game, though she still secretly believed he could become the next Dahmer.

"We wouldn't do our work," someone finally said.

"We'd misbehave," said another. They finally got it.

She spent the rest of the class going over different idioms, what they meant, and suggested ways they could insert them in their writing and poetry.

During class, Jeanie had surreptitiously taped a poem about sadness she'd written the previous month to the front board and when Maggie noticed it, she asked the girl if she could read it to the class. She agreed, shyly, and Maggie made a point to read her poem just as it was written to show the kids they could express much without punctuation in poetry. Jeanie was finally proud of something she had done, and was able to accept the praise she got from her teacher and her classmates.

"I'm getting pretty good at headstands too," Jeanie whispered in Maggie's ear after the applause died down.

By Thursday morning Maggie was starting to feel things just might turn around for once. She'd been successful at interjecting her own curriculum around the stacks of mandated pre-pre-pretesting materials and she could practically taste spring break. Although she couldn't leave town because of her certification course requirements, she was practically giddy with the thought of going on long morning runs again with Bones.

She was looking forward to a quiet, easy day. Students would work on revising the written response to a prompt they'd started on Wednesday, and it would take them the full class period to complete. Because she had no real preparation to do before students arrived, she allowed herself an extra half-hour and got to school just fifteen minutes before the first bell.

When she approached the front door, however, her heart sank. The students, whose typical morning routine involved shoving, shouting and laughter, were huddled in small groups and many were crying. Maggie ran into the building and straight to the office. There, she witnessed the same scene.

She looked around the crowded office trying to comprehend what was happening. Kirby, her staunch, wise-cracking mentor, was crying on Matthew's shoulder. Her boss was distraught. Two police officers stood by his desk, professional and unemotional. Teachers from other teams were starting to show up. Amber and Grant were stone-faced in the corner, but when Grant saw Maggie, he went to her and grabbed her to him.

"It's Kyle," he said, his voice breaking. "A friend found him early this morning."

"NO!" Maggie shouted, pushing him away and stepping back. She felt as if she were suffocating. "What? What do you mean 'found him'?"

"Would you like us to handle the briefing, Sir?" one of the officers asked David quietly.

"No, no, John, I've got to do this. Thank you, though. Please stay. We might need some extra help today." David worked on regaining his composure. Most of the others were a wreck.

Maggie stood, unmoving, still trying to understand what she was hearing.

"I'm really going to need your help today, people," David addressed his crowded office. "We'll bring the kids directly to the auditorium. I've got counselors from surrounding districts on their way to be available for anyone who needs them. If you'd now please go to the auditorium and prepare for the kids to arrive, I'll be there shortly."

Kirby grabbed Maggie's hand and walked out with her. Grant, Amber and Matthew followed closely behind. Maggie was unable to speak, as were the others, who were doing their best to reel in their emotions.

The morning bell startled them all and within moments, the stunned mob entered and found seats. David took the stage.

"As I'm sure many of you have already heard," his voice wavered, "we lost an Eagle this morning."

Many students around the auditorium continued crying, just as many sat expressionless, and the sudden reality of the situation hit Maggie like an avalanche.

"I don't imagine there's anyone in here who didn't know Kyle. He made it his mission to make people laugh every day, even when it got him in trouble." David grasped the podium, his head down, and allowed himself a moment before continuing.

Maggie stood, her body numb. Somehow in the somber crowd she saw Leanna, whose despair appeared deeper than most.

David looked up and continued.

"I want you all to know that although we may never understand why this tragedy occurred, Kyle would want you to remember the times he made you laugh, and the times he drove his teachers crazy."

Maggie heard subdued laughter over sobbing around the room and even found herself remembering the scene of the crazy boy who humped her classroom door, months ago, before he turned angry. *But what had happened to make him turn so very angry?*

"We'll have counselors available all day today and school will be closed tomorrow for students in memory of our lost Eagle. Teachers, we will still meet in the morning. The school will stay open today and those who would like to go home may do so if you have a parent who can pick you up. Teachers, please return to your rooms now and we will resume a normal bell schedule shortly."

The teachers drifted out of the auditorium like zombies. Maggie was going to have to be stronger than ever for her grieving students.

Within moments they were surrounding her, hugging her and each other, crying. Every class was the same, somber and reflective. There would be no lesson today. She suggested they might write down how they were feeling, and some did. Somehow, the day came to an end and the school emptied, slowly. There was no running. There was no shoving. There was no laughter.

David asked the 7$^{th}$ grade team to meet in his office once the students had all departed.

Maggie met Grant in the hallway, and when he opened his arms this time, she accepted his embrace.

"What happened?" she asked, finally letting down her guard.

"I don't know. I think we're about to find out," he said, and the two joined the others who were arriving as they had—in a daze.

What they learned from David was that sometime after midnight, Kyle had shot himself. An 8$^{th}$ grade friend who walked to school with him in the morning found him on the kitchen floor. The front door was open. The police had to find his mother—she was in a bar. His father had walked out on the family two weeks ago. That's all anyone knew.

~~~~~

*What had he written in that note?* Maggie struggled to remember. She riffled through the folder labeled "MISC" in her desk drawer.

*". . . it was just to get my mind off the real bad things in my life . . . ."*

Maggie ran back down the hall to show the note to David, to confess her negligence in not sharing the note with the counselor, but he was gone.

And now Kyle was gone too.

~~~~~

Because Maggie knew she wouldn't sleep, she thought about asking Harry if he'd mind keeping Bones overnight, but then changed her mind. She needed the comfort of her unconditionally loving little buddy.

Harry was a true friend. He listened to her litany of perceived failures and then told her why she was wrong on every count. Still, she would agonize over thinking she had failed to see the warning signs leading to the boy's tragic decision.

*"Miss?"*

## ~ 25 ~

"MAGGIE, KYLE WAS in Anne's office at least once a week this semester," David told Maggie, gently placing his hand on her shoulder before the rest of the staff arrived Friday morning. "You didn't withhold anything and we've all been trying to help him, so stop beating yourself up, okay?"

"I still can't believe he's gone." She looked down at the note in her hands. "I thought he was finally going to be okay."

When she looked back into her boss's kind eyes and noted he probably hadn't slept the night before, she couldn't stop herself from embracing him. Though startled by her boldness, he allowed himself a moment of weakness and the two comforted one another in silence.

Kirby was the next to arrive and she also looked like hell. Within moments the rest of the staff stumbled into the conference room and the atmosphere had never been more somber.

"I honestly don't believe any of us were prepared for this," David said. Everyone nodded. "And now I hate to mention this, but in addition to our testing next week, we've also got a school board meeting scheduled for the Wednesday we return from spring break. There will be representatives from the state there and we're looking for people—parents, staff and students—to speak about our school."

"Do you honestly think what anyone says now will make a difference?" asked Matthew. "I've been hearing from my friends in other schools that they've already made the decision to shut us down."

All eyes were on their boss.

Laurel McHargue

"To be truthful with you, no one has had to courage to say that to me yet, but I'd be lying if I told you I didn't think you should be updating your résumés. I've already made inquiries in some schools in the area and I think you should too."

A groan spread through the group.

"I'll be happy to provide letters of reference if it comes to that. But let's stay focused. I know I'm asking a lot from you, but we've got to keep up a good front here and not let the kids know anyone is giving up just yet."

Maggie believed too many people had given up on the future of her students a long time ago.

"Does anyone know if there will be a service for Kyle?" asked Amber.

"The family asked that their privacy be honored. I believe his father will be back in town today and they're planning a small family gathering. That's all," said Anne, who had been talking with the boy's mother. "If any of you would like to come in and talk with me today, I'll stick around. This has been hard on everyone, so you don't have to pretend you're not affected."

"Keep a close eye on the kids too," said David. "I don't even want to consider the possibility of a copycat."

"Yes," affirmed Anne. "Please let them know my door is open. I'll be happy to come in and talk with groups as well."

On the way back to her empty classroom, Maggie heard her name called.

"Maggie, would you have a moment to talk this morning?"

Elizabeth Cole hadn't given Maggie the time of day all year and Maggie had been successful in avoiding the unpleasant woman since her run-in the first week of school. She had no idea what the woman could possibly want to talk about, but she had nothing to do in her classroom and was too tired to try to improvise a reason for saying no.

"Sure, would you like to come to my room?" Maggie asked, and Elizabeth walked with her to the classroom she had never yet stepped foot in.

When the two arrived, Maggie pulled up another chair to the one by her desk. Elizabeth looked around the brightly decorated classroom and Maggie thought the expression on her face flashed a hint of approval.

"I've come to apologize," she said abruptly.

"I don't understand," said Maggie, confused.

"I was rude to you, and you didn't deserve it," she said, simply. "I've had close to a year now of hearing about how 'awesome' you are from our students and I've seen how you interact with them. I've heard about how you go to the games and stay after school and open your room for students at lunch."

Maggie had caved to requests from her students to eat lunch in her classroom right after the incident with Razz, and each day the group had grown.

"I thought I owed you an explanation," Elizabeth continued, "and I haven't shared this with anyone at the school before. I lost my husband in Vietnam."

"Oh! I am so sorry," said Maggie, feeling inexplicably guilty again, but not wanting to hear more. There was enough sadness in her heart already.

Elizabeth shook her head as if casting off a bad dream.

"I was young and he was the love of my life. He was supposed to come right home and start a family with me. I never remarried, never had children, and since then, I've just been so darned angry at the military and at everyone who comes home to carry on with their happy little lives." She spat out the last few words.

"It's not your fault that you came home," she continued, "and I had no right to be angry at you." Elizabeth picked at her fingernails, nervously awaiting Maggie's response.

"Elizabeth, thank you. I lost my fiancé too. His name was Sam. We were only together for a couple years, but I knew he was the man I would spend the rest of my life with." Tears blurred Maggie's vision. The culmination of emotional challenges since her military service had ended overwhelmed her.

"And I *do* feel like it's my fault I came back," she continued. "The mission he went on that day should have been mine. Our battalion commander asked for a last-minute situation briefing and I was the best at setting up presentations. Sam and a group of his soldiers volunteered to go instead. There was an ambush. None of them returned."

Nearly two years after his death, Maggie still found it impossible to stop thinking about Sam. He haunted her subconscious and made love to her in her dreams.

"I didn't know," said Elizabeth. "I'm so sorry, Maggie. So very sorry."

~~~~~

"I know you guys are going to crush this!" Maggie proclaimed to the group of students who would be in her room for testing all week.

She was pleased she had her "Let's Fly" group in addition to others from different classes. David had changed the testing schedule to start right away on Monday so they could finish on Thursday and take off the Friday before spring break. It had originally been scheduled to start Tuesday, but no one wanted to spend a full day of being preoccupied with talk of the suicide and worry over inadequate test preparation.

"You're going to do well not because I'm asking you to, not because of how it will look for the school, but for yourselves. You're going to destroy the perception of inferiority you know other people have of our school. You're going to do well because you believe in yourselves and I believe in you too."

She looked at each of the twenty-five students' faces and saw a mixture of sadness, resignation, gratitude, and hopefulness. There was nothing more she could say or do.

"Miss, what happens to our scores if they close our school?" asked Ebony.

Everyone knew the results of the test wouldn't be available until August, shortly before the start of next school year. The timing of the whole testing cycle was ridiculous.

"I believe your scores would then be sent to the school you'd go to next and I think they could use them to make decisions on where to place you in your next classes. But don't worry about that right now, just do the very best you can, okay?"

Maggie passed out the first round of tests one by one, smiling at each student in turn. She read the canned instructions verbatim and then stood back—amazed—and watched as each of them worked harder than she had seen them work before. She could not have been more proud of them.

~~~~~

Spring break passed quickly. Maggie caught up on her certification program requirements and even knocked out a few due the following week. She allowed herself to sleep in until Bones was ready to go out, and in the evenings, she enjoyed leisurely visits with Harry.

"Have you always been a great cook, Harry?" Maggie asked one evening over a roasted chicken and vegetable dish.

"I had to learn pretty quickly when Pat died, otherwise I'd have perished," he said. "That reminds me of a time little Johnny and his family were having Sunday dinner at his Grandma's house."

Maggie was always impressed her friend could pull up something for every situation. She smiled, waiting for him to continue.

"Everyone was seated around the table as the food was being served, and when little Johnny received his plate, he started eating right away. 'Johnny! Please wait until we say our prayer,' his mother said. 'But I don't need to,' the boy replied. 'Of course you do,' his mother insisted, 'we always say a prayer before eating at our house.' 'That's why I don't need to say a prayer,' little Johnny explained. 'This is Grandma's house and she knows how to cook!'"

It felt good to laugh again. Distancing herself from the school, the recent tragedy, the politics, and the daily drama of student life was helpful. By the end of the break, she felt refreshed and ready to take on whatever life would toss her way the last weeks of her first year of teaching.

# ~ 26 ~

THE FIRST DAY BACK from spring break might as well have been the first day of school. Students had moved on with their lives and were rowdier than ever, the stress of testing was over, teachers could finally focus on lessons they believed were important, and summer vacation was right around the corner.

If only they knew what the decision would be concerning the fate of the building and its inhabitants the following semester.

"Miss, if they close our school, I'm droppin' out," Bernicia announced as soon as class started.

Her statement triggered a smattering of agreement from several others.

"Why, Bernicia?" Maggie asked, concerned. She had sensed an atmosphere of rebellion in the hallways between classes and knew everyone was focused on what would happen at the school board meeting later that week.

"Just look at me," she said. "I'm fat, I'm loud, and no one will like me."

Her statement paid off as the majority of her peers declared how much they loved her and told her how beautiful she was, but Maggie could hear a note of desperation in the brazen girl's voice.

"Bernicia," Maggie addressed her with assurance, "you will *own* whatever school you end up in!" Maggie added the head-joggle while she spoke and even Bernicia burst out laughing at her teacher.

"It's true, Miss," said Juan. "Everyone's talking crap about us at the other schools. They don't want us there."

There were several other middle schools within an easy bus ride, and she'd heard rumors that, if the school closed, students would be dispersed in a way most expedient to accommodate the new bus routes. The fact that they were already discussing alternative bus routes was telling.

"Let me just give you my philosophy on life," she said. "You know I've spent some time in the Army, right?"

They nodded.

"And do you know that when you're in the Army you have to move around a lot?"

"What's a lot? Please be specific!" Leanna said in her best teacher voice, cracking up her friends.

Maggie was glad to see the girl rebounding from the turmoil of the past few weeks. The students all knew in addition to "I dunno," using "a lot" was another of their teacher's pet peeves.

"Let's just say, Miss Wisenheimer, that I moved four times in five years," said Maggie. "That includes a couple of moves for some schooling. Anyway, I believe that change is a good thing."

"Why?" asked Bernicia.

"Because it forces you to meet new people and learn about different places and see things from a different perspective, and when you do, you grow because you will learn new things about yourself too."

"What do you mean by see things from a different perspective?" asked Juan, who was feeling more confident now that Maggie's tone had become animated.

"Hmmmm. Okay, everybody up!" Maggie shouted, and her students got to their feet.

This didn't sound like a "line up in the hallway" command.

"Go ahead and stand on your chairs," she directed.

Half the class stood upon their chairs right away, others moved more slowly, and some, like Bernicia, chose not to.

"You're crazy, Miss," said Juan, and Maggie just nodded.

"Now tell me how the classroom looks from your new perspective!"

"Bigger."

"Brighter."

"More open."

Several students were able to touch the fluorescent light banks in the ceiling, and Maggie had to warn them not to electrocute themselves. Still, Juan pulled his hand back quickly after touching one of the hot light bulbs.

"You can come down now," Maggie announced, and her smiling students slowly resumed their seats.

"That's just one example of how you can see things from a different perspective. Turn over your worksheets and sign your names on the back now, but use the hand you don't normally use."

"I can't do that, Miss!" protested Juan.

"What do you mean you can't?" Maggie feigned incredulity. "Don't you know how to spell your name?"

"Well, yeah, but…"

"Don't you know how to form the letters?" she continued. Her students chuckled.

"Well, yeah, but…"

"Is your left hand broken?" She was playing with him, and students around the classroom were already laughing at their messy first attempt at using their non-dominant hand.

"So check it out," she continued, "you're already learning something new and making new connections in your brains by changing the way you've done something for years! Just imagine how much you might learn if you were in a different school, especially if the school is already doing well!"

All the surrounding middle schools were rated as being far more successful than North—using the same evaluative guidelines—and she couldn't help thinking perhaps it was time her students were given a chance at something better.

~~~~~

Flyers had gone home and phone calls had been made announcing the importance of attending the school board meeting if parents wanted the opportunity to speak on behalf of keeping their school open. The turnout was dismal.

# "Miss?"

Maggie surprised herself by the passion with which she delivered her brief, but heartfelt plea for the board to consider giving North more time.

"I honestly don't believe our students will be able to get the same degree of one-on-one instruction they need at a larger, more crowded school. We've been making real progress this year with our 'Let's Fly' groups and I personally witnessed the effort our kids put into testing this year." But even as she said the words, she could sense they were having no impact.

Her words didn't compare to those from a handful of students who brought the small group of audience members to tears with their expressions of pride in a school most of their families had attended. Her heart ached when they talked about the caring teachers who were always there for them.

"Please give us another chance," one tearful 8th grader implored. "We promise we'll try to do better next year."

Maggie knew, however, that effort didn't always result in success. She'd seen students working diligently on in-class assignments, but because they weren't addressing the requirements, they'd earn poor grades. She'd seen the basketball players pouring with sweat while competing in a tournament, but because they'd fooled around during practices before the game, they'd lose.

Trying to maintain her professional bearing, but feeling on the verge of tears, Maggie remembered the little Johnny joke Harry had told her the night before. Little Johnny was getting bad grades in school, so one day he stepped up to his teacher's desk and announced, "I don't want to scare you Miss McCauley, but daddy says if I don't get better grades, somebody is gonna get a spanking!" Harry had added the "Miss McCauley" part for effect, and the thought of her friend's chuckle after he delivered the punch line was enough to keep her mind off of the pain threatening to break her down in public.

She studied the stoic faces of each school board member and knew they'd already made their decision.

~~~~~

The school district published their decision to close North shortly after the School Board meeting and by the end of April, committees were formed to reorganize the surrounding schools that would take in students from North, as if what they were doing was a mission of mercy. And perhaps it was.

The atmosphere in the school was a mixture of fear and relief; at least everyone finally knew where they stood and could prepare for the changes to come. David had already found a new principal position and stayed busy writing letters of recommendation for all his people.

Maggie was in the computer lab all day so her students could spend some time researching schools they might be transferred to the following semester. Halfway through one of her classes, Kirby approached her, concern spread across her face.

"What now?" Maggie asked.

"I don't know what's going on in your classroom," Kirby whispered, not wanting to draw attention, "but there are police in there. You go down and check it out. I'll stay here with your kids."

Maggie asked her students to continue on their best behavior until she returned and hustled down the hallway.

"Please get whatever you need from your classroom, Maggie," said David, who met her at the door. "I'm sorry to have to use your room, but it was the only empty one right now."

"What's going on? Am I in any trouble?" she asked.

"Not at all," he said. "There's a gang investigation going on and the police have identified some of our students. It doesn't look good."

The relief Maggie felt turned to heartache and anger the instant she looked into her classroom and saw Rico with two other students she didn't know up against the wall, police officers standing in front of them. Rico caught her eye briefly—flashing her an unspoken, grief-filled apology—before one officer turned him toward the board for frisking. She would never see him again.

~~~~~

"Oh, Miss? Could you tell me what is an orgasm?" asked one of her second language learners during lunch the next day.

## *"Miss?"*

The year was coming to an end, yet somehow the teachers kept on teaching and the students kept showing up for classes. The sense of rebellion was gone and the atmosphere of concession was strangely calming.

This wasn't the first time an unexpected question had arisen. Still, a question of this nature required extra thoughtfulness before answering. Maggie always wanted to answer a question of this sort professionally, accurately, and respectfully.

"What assignment are you working on?" Maggie asked, deflecting her astonishment and buying herself time to consider her response. Students often brought worksheets from other classes to finish during lunch and she would help them with their academic language skills.

"Science," she said. "They were talking about it in this film, but I didn't get it."

Maggie wondered what kind of film Kirby was showing with the word orgasm in it, and thought perhaps her quirky friend had finally lost it. She came to the conclusion it had something to do with the reproductive cycle.

"Okay. Well, let's start with the dictionary then. No, not the abridged version. Get the big one from my desk." Maggie decided to let Webster's unabridged do the work.

"So how you spell . . . O, R, G . . .," the girl fumbled through the pages.

"A, S, M," Maggie finished for her, happy to assist with dictionary search techniques. She would turn this into a cross-curricular lesson, and everyone would learn more than they had anticipated.

The problem with Webster, however, was that the definition was too complex, especially for a second language learner.

"Intense or paro . . . what? Paroxysmal, what is that? Excitement, . . . I don't get this, Miss, this is stupid."

Maggie looked at the definition and felt foolish. Even she didn't understand some of the words in the definition. If she hoped to help her students before lunch was over, she'd have to intervene and provide her own explanation. She did her best to keep it relevant to the reproductive cycle she assumed they were discussing in science.

The students listened with rapt attention as Maggie provided the basics of the physical "climax," a word she said they should remember from their discussion on short story elements earlier in the year.

When she finished her explanation, she was surprised there were no follow-on questions, but several students still looked confused. She didn't often pray for the lunch break to be over, but when the bell rang, she was ready to get back to English lessons.

"Kirby, what kind of films are you showing our 7$^{th}$ grade kids?" Maggie asked her friend when she saw her in the hallway.

"Why?" asked Kirby.

"Well, whatever you showed, it really wasn't very effective at getting across the role of orgasms in the reproductive cycle and I didn't even know you were teaching that stuff this year. I had to explain it to your kids at lunch."

"Oh, my God, Maggie, you're such a dork!" Kirby screeched, and then laughed uncontrollably. Kirby's exuberance attracted the attention of Matthew and Amber, who came over to see what all the hoopla was about.

"Did you know I'm teaching our kids about orgasms this year?" Kirby asked the others, trying to sound serious but unable to control her laughter.

"I thought I was supposed to cover that in social studies," said Matthew, not missing a beat.

"What?" asked Maggie, feeling she was the brunt of an inside joke.

"Let's see," continued Kirby. "When bacteria start to get really horny—Oh God! I can't!" she burst into laughter again and Maggie laughed with her.

"But really, what's going on?" Maggie persisted.

"Do you think maybe it was a film about *organisms*, Maggie?" Amber looked at her in disbelief.

Maggie was embarrassed, but couldn't stop laughing. "Well, I suppose that would explain the confusion on their faces after I finished my explanation!"

# ~ 27 ~

"WHICH SCHOOL WILL YOU be going to next year, Miss, 'cause I want my little sister to have you," said Juan. It was the last day of school.

Maggie didn't have the heart to tell him the truth. Although teachers at North had been told they'd have first pick at any available openings in surrounding schools, the competition for those spots would be fierce. And much like the sentiment her students felt about other schools not wanting them, it was rumored teachers from the failing school might not be regarded in the best light.

But Maggie had already made her decision to move from the area. She hadn't even told Harry yet.

"I don't know, Juan," she said, looking at the young boy for the last time and trying not to appear sad. Her response was truthful. Despite the sleepless nights and frustrated tears she'd endured because of her students, they had nevertheless worked their way into her heart.

"Now, don't you go acting all Miss MelanMcCauley on us, Miss," said Bernicia with authority. The girl was proud of the pun she'd made with her teacher's name. "Change is good, right?"

Maggie knew Bernicia was going to be just fine at her next school.

~~~~~

Grant stopped by Maggie's nearly empty classroom to say goodbye. "I wish it could've worked out between us. I hope you find what you're looking for," he said sincerely.

"Thanks, Grant," said Maggie. "This year was harder than I ever expected it would be. You get a job yet?" she asked, changing the subject.

"Yeah. I'll be starting at Central in August. You?"

"Nothing yet. I'm leaving at the end of the week after my finals. I've been looking at some openings further west, so maybe I'll check out one of those little mountain towns. I've always wanted to learn how to ski and I'll bet a smaller school district would be a piece of cake to work in compared to here." She tried to sound lighthearted.

There was an awkward silence before he walked to her and embraced her gently. There were no more words. He released her, tousled her hair, and walked away.

Maggie had said goodbye to Matthew and Amber earlier that day and had thanked David for being the most patient boss she'd ever had. There was talk of Gladys taking an 8th grade English teaching position, and Maggie felt sorry for her students. Most of the staff would stay employed in the district the following year, and Maggie was happy her students would see some familiar faces in their new schools. She carried her last box to her Jeep and found Kirby standing there.

"I'm gonna miss you, killer." Kirby grabbed Maggie roughly in a bear hug.

"When I get settled, you come out and visit me, okay?" Maggie told her eccentric friend. "We'll go to one of those hot springs and you can paint the mountains."

Kirby hadn't yet found another opening in the district for a science teacher and took it as a sign it was time to develop her skills as an artist.

"Only if I can be the guest teacher in your classroom for your orgasm lesson!" said Kirby.

Maggie hugged her tightly again, appreciating the way Kirby could end any uncomfortable situation on a funny note.

~~~~~

# *"Miss?"*

"I knew you'd understand," Maggie told Harry after breaking the news of her move.

"Well, I didn't figure you'd be hanging around here much longer, Captain." Harry cast a surreptitious glance at Bones. "And I've been thinking lately about moving over to Vail with my sister soon. She's got kids and they've got kids and there's always something needing to be fixed. Thought it might keep me out of trouble for a while, now that I won't have you two to worry about." He looked at Bones again, shuffling his feet, and Maggie could see he was struggling to maintain his composure.

"Harry?" Maggie was trying to stay in control too. "Would you keep him?"

As much as it hurt her to realize what a horrible first-time dog owner she'd been, the look in Harry's eyes left no question she was making the right decision. Bones had been a comfort to her in her times of need, but he was also a reminder of a painful past.

"You know he's really your dog, Harry. I could never take him away from you," Maggie said, and Harry hugged her tightly. "And hey, I might not be too far away from your sister's place. You know I'll need to visit my drinking buddy once in a while."

"That would be wonderful, Maggie," Harry said, pulling away. "Just promise me you'll watch your step out there in the mountains. I hear those cowboys can be a crude sort."

"What do you know about cowboys, Colonel?" Maggie teased.

"Well, I heard about this time when there was a doctor, a lawyer and a cowboy finishing their business at a urinal. Now, the doctor, he finished, zipped up and scrubbed from his hands clear up to his elbows. He told the others he was a graduate of Tufts and they taught him to stay clean."

"Go on," said Maggie.

"So then the lawyer finished, zipped up, wet just the tips of his fingers quickly and shook his hands dry. He said he had graduated from Berkeley and they taught him to be environmentally conscious."

Maggie waited for the punchline.

"Our unconventional cowboy friend, when he finished, he just zipped up and walked to the door. When he got there, he looked back and said, 'I graduated from the University of Hard Knocks and they taught us not to piss on our hands!'"

Maggie would miss the sound of her friend's laughter.

"Harry, would it be okay if I called you now and then for a laugh, because I think I'm really going to need one soon." Maggie was still chuckling from his silly joke and trying not to cry.

"I'll be sad if you don't," he said.

~~~~~

The sun was just starting to rise behind her as she drove away from the crowded city. Her rearview mirror had been knocked off while packing her Jeep. She'd have to get it repaired soon, but she was in no hurry.

She had no real plan. She'd spend a night or two in little towns off the beaten path—Leadville, Rifle, Meeker, Montrose—and stop when if felt right. She was confident in her ability to land another teaching job. Her year at North had prepared her for any school that might hire her.

Steve Miller Band's "Fly Like an Eagle" was blasting on the radio and Maggie sang along as loudly as she could to keep the tears at bay.

This was just another change, and change was good.

# ~ ACKNOWLEDGMENTS ~

As this is my first novel, my thanks go out to everyone who believed in and encouraged me. If I fail to mention you by name, it is not by intention.

To Marilyn Hintsa, the very first best friend I ever had. You knew I would be a writer ever since that first day I claimed you as "mine" in kindergarten.

To members of Leadville's "Cloud City Writers" for encouraging me to try fiction. Stephanie Spong Stroh, you first uttered the word "NaNoWriMo" to me and then motivated me to complete what I started; Roger Johnson, your cast of characters inspired me to create my own; Annie Livingston-Garrett, your critiques were spot-on; and Carol Bellhouse, your exhaustive editing, guidance and substantive suggestions made my story far better than it was originally.

To Sherry Randall who opened her "Cookies With Altitude" shop in Leadville for my first writing and poetry groups to meet and consistently validated my effort, and to the Lake County Public Library employees who took us in when we outgrew the cookie shop!

To all the seventh grade students who struggled with me through my first year of teaching and who provided me with countless gray hairs and even more stories to share. You may not know it, but you captured my heart.

To Stefanie Foreman, my first-year teaching mentor and sanity saver. You were my inspiration for "Kirby"!

To Sue Jewell, my follow-on mentor, and to teachers everywhere who continue to show up each day to give their students more than 100% of themselves with the hope that what they give may positively influence the lives of their students.

To Joanne (Cavanaugh) Bowman, Nadine Collier, Kristi Smedley and Heide Collister for your story input and for being forever-friends.

To Charlène Martel, my Canadian critic whose praise is extra-special.

To my nephew Michael Shaughnessy whose insight was brilliant, my aunt Phyllis McCarthy, my cousin Debbie Braga, my brother-in-law Mark McHargue, and my friends Diane Smith, Sarah Smith, Pam Arvidson, Erin Sue Grantham, and Brent Goldstein. Thanks for providing invaluable constructive criticism on my early draft.

To Dahlynn and Ken McKowen, owners of Publishing Syndicate, for adopting me into your family of writers and launching me as a legitimate writer, and to Maggie Lamond Simone for introducing me to them. And to Maggie's brother Mike Lamond for introducing me to his sister! Also to my PS co-creator friends who routinely encourage me through social media (you know who you are).

To David Sargent who formally adopted me as his little sister shortly after my 52$^{nd}$ birthday and edited the earliest version of this novel. I always wanted a big brother, and I'm proud to call you my Bro.

To my ever-more-amazing-each-year husband, Mike, and sons Nick and Jake for the sacrifices you have made for me over the years so I could continue to climb to the peak—of various mountains and of Maslow's Hierarchy of Needs!

To my fabulous four sisters—Christine Stewart, Susan Russo, Charlene McDade and Carol Shaughnessy—and your husbands for always being proud of me and for continuing to live under the delusion that I can do nothing wrong.

Finally, extra-extra-special thanks to Patricia Bernier (my Mum) for holding your breath all those years while I was "finding myself," and to Charles M. Bernier (rest in peace, Daddy-O), my role model for "Harry," who patiently waited for me to find time to write "his" book. It's coming.

# ~ About the Author ~

LAUREL McHARGUE was raised in Braintree, MA, but somehow found her way to the breathtaking elevation of Leadville, CO, where she has taught and currently lives with her husband and Ranger, the German Shepherd. She facilitates the Cloud City Writers group and is available for speaking engagements and workshops. Laurel would love to participate in classroom and book club discussions about her novels and the process of writing.

She also has been known to act.

Visit Laurel in Leadville and/or check out her blog where she writes about her adventures.

www.leadvillelaurel.com

*Leadville Laurel*

## ~ A Personal Note from Laurel ~

I would love to hear from you! I'm serious about the "visit me in Leadville" comment, but until you might make that happen, connect with me here:


**Facebook**: Laurel McHargue (personal) and
Leadville Laurel (author page)
**Twitter**: @LeadvilleLaurel
**LinkedIn**: Laurel (Bernier) McHargue
**Web Page**: www.leadvillelaurel.com
**Email**: laurel.mchargue@gmail.com


Check out my novel *Waterwight: Book I of the Waterwight Series*
on Amazon.com
and let me know what you think!
*Waterwight* ~ ~ ~ There's something in the water!

Looking for a unique journal for yourself or for a gift?
Check out my book *Haikus Can Amuse! 366 Haiku Starters*


And remember, we struggling authors/musicians/artists/actors
love positive feedback.


If you like what we do, please consider writing reviews of our work!
If you don't like what we do, well, if you can't say something nice . . .

My son Jake used this sketch I drew of a student taking a "high stakes test" one momentous year as cover art for my first editions of "Miss?"

The following essay represents my opinions on the current state of public education and ideas for improving the learning environment.

# Flap Your Wings (and maybe stomp your feet a little)!
*Laurel's Editorial*

I have felt overwhelmed countless times in my life. Opening a junk drawer can ruin my day. I'd rather show up for class sick than create a lesson plan for a substitute teacher. The thought of writing a whole book nearly paralyzed me. I couldn't go into a library or bookstore without coming out depressed. What could I write that hadn't already been written? But I had made a promise.

"Someday I'll write a book about this year," I told the first group of 7th graders I ever taught. I didn't know how or when or what type of book it would be, but every student wanted to be in my book, and I still have the roster with their actual names and the names they wanted me to call them whenever I wrote it.

Although I couldn't fit over 100 students into my novel and felt a need to create my own names for the amalgamated students I chose to represent, I fulfilled my promise seven years later and donated over $1,200.00 in proceeds to a graduating student in my community. I also found my real-world model for the troublesome character "Bernicia" and learned something wonderful.

*"Miss?"* is fictionalized for obvious reasons, but the realism of Maggie's first year teaching experience is apparent to all teachers I've spoken with about the story. It certainly helped that I kept a daily journal my first year of teaching.

I discovered quickly they just don't make schools like they used to.

Today's public schools are becoming battlegrounds, figuratively and literally, but they don't need to be that way. Daily, teachers post their frustrations on social media, many who then are written up by their superiors for expressing their feelings. Routinely, citizens become more outraged by the tide of school violence, the recent surge against which we seem to have no power. Companies are developing bullet-proof blankets for students; many suggest arming teachers.

Teacher complaints are well-founded. Much like the companies that will get rich from blanket sales to schools, others are flourishing from quick-fix programs school administrators are eager to employ, and classrooms around the nation are becoming marketplaces.

"But wait! There's more!" . . . and more, and more for teachers to work into their full curricula. They feel besieged. More "professional development" for teachers—on the latest programs—equates to less time doing what they know how to do best: Teach.

"So what's the answer, *Miss*?"

Many of my friends, astounded by the picture I've painted, have asked me this question after reading my novel. There is no single—no easy answer, no quick-fix, and I don't pretend to have the solution.

Struggling schools face a plethora of challenges daily, and three of the most debilitating I've experienced include corrosive work environments, over-testing of students and lack of effective student discipline. Of the three, lack of discipline can be the greatest detractor to success, though potentially it is the easiest problem to remedy.

### *Ideas on polishing potentially "corrosive work environments":*

Are all teachers great at what they do? Of course not. Neither are all administrators, all CEOs, all parents, all community and government leaders, all students. Nevertheless, the current environment in many districts is suffocating and good teachers are reconsidering their profession. Many factors combine to create harsh work environments in schools—a revolving door of initiatives, lack of communication and trust between peers and supervisors, and lack of community support—and I won't even address the issue of low pay in many of our most difficult towns.

Teachers are fed up with having to implement the latest program-du-jour with inadequate training or preparation time, and veteran teachers see through the smoke and mirrors of purportedly "new" programs.

"Just wait five years and you'll see the same things come back," one retiring elementary school teacher recently told me. "They'll just give it a new name." After 45 years of teaching, she should know.

The same is true for instructional standards set for each subject by state departments of education. Weeks have been wasted on reconfiguring curricula to the latest standards that have been tweaked to sound more reasonable, more doable, while the bottom-line expectations remain the same: students must be able to read and write and do 'rithmetic at more advanced levels each year. Rewording requirements so we have four rather than six for Language Arts standards is a wasteful, frivolous exercise.

Teachers know this, and students have never felt the need to fret over the boring banners outlining all they are expected to learn in each classroom.

I recommend leaders in school districts across the nation step back and take a deep breath the next time they're approached by any agency offering a new program, especially from commercial entities, and consider if the potential benefits are worth the time needed to invest in adequately implementing the program. Consider as well that even if a program has demonstrated success in a small town in Maine, it doesn't necessarily mean it will deliver the same results in a rural Texas town.

Let me take my recommendation one step further and suggest school leaders look within their own pool of teachers and staff members before paying outsiders to deliver training and "professional development." I lost track of teacher hours wasted during my years in public education, hours during which my peers and I felt belittled or treated as if we knew nothing about the students in our care—by people who knew nothing about us nor about our students. We preach differentiation for students, so why not extend the concept to teacher training? More often than not we sat through information we already knew or could have presented ourselves, with no opportunity to "test out."

A potential stipend or continuing education credits for someone already employed in a school district would do much to improve morale and would cost significantly less than paying a program-pushing agency. If we truly want to develop as professional educators, we should explore every opportunity to develop from within.

School administrators who are ignorant of their internal assets will also undoubtedly struggle with organizational communication, increasing environmental toxicity and destroying morale.

For years I taught my students how to use figurative language elements to give readers a clear picture of what they are trying to express. "Unclear communication is like an outdated road map; it can leave you lost and confused," I'd say, and some of them even appreciated my simile. The ability to communicate effectively is critical for building effective relationships, and effective relationships inherently require trust between parties. Without an atmosphere of open and honest dialogue in an organization, it is nearly impossible to develop trust between members of that organization.

During my first back-to-school meeting with district staff and faculty in my new school, my boss, who knew about my West Point education and Army background, encouraged me to lead a group activity. That was the start of my involvement with the district instructional leadership team. For two and a half years in that school I collaborated with my peers and those above me on topics ranging from curriculum design to school spirit. I sent weekly emails to all staff members with topic recaps, suggestions and reminders. My peers knew they could share concerns and questions with me and I would represent them the best I could.

Turning around a corrosive atmosphere in which members believe information is being withheld can be as simple as sending out routine status updates, minimally once per week. To be truly effective as a leader, those you lead must believe you value them as individuals—a belief worth more than any price tag—and by keeping them "in the loop," you demonstrate that respect.

Sure, there will be times when closed-door sessions take place, but leaders must still find ways to share even the most difficult conversations in a way that keeps the best interests of the organization in mind. Secrets will always breed contempt and destroy trust among those who feel left out, and we all have witnessed or experienced the wildfire effects of rumors.

What kind of investment is necessary to improve communication within a school district? Time. Even 15 minutes each week dedicated to sending out an update and perhaps even highlighting a success, however small, could start transforming the morale in an organization where employees have felt in-the-dark for too long.

Shawn Achor, author of *The Happiness Advantage,* demonstrates several examples of organizational leaders who have deflated the mood of otherwise buoyant employees by communicating in a way that inadvertently failed to emphasize anything positive. He reminds us that "Just as important as *what* you say to employees is *how* you say it."[1] The premise of *The Happiness Advantage* is that success follows happiness, not the other way around; it is a book worthy of designing a professional development session around.

*Involve local communities to improve the environment in your school district!*

Those who are able to participate in community outreach programs should do so. Outreach is vital, especially in school districts with limited funds, and the most creative school leaders find ways to expose students to the world outside their classrooms before launching them into that world with a handshake and a piece of paper.

Local businesses and art galleries were delighted to open their doors to my students for field trips and writing opportunities, and the local newspaper welcomed articles and pictures of those free fieldtrips. Exploring opportunities for visits, internships and community service would cost only an investment of time—and the rewards would be invaluable.

Leaders and teachers owe it to their students to develop relationships with community members in an effort to realize a shared vision of growth and success for all members of their district. Ultimately, schools in which community involvement is valued will be more successful, and a school's success, in turn, will improve the whole community.

**Assess, yes, but in moderation.**

A school district that fails to assess its students is like a proctologist whose magic wand explores the wrong end; both will lack the vital information necessary to improve the lives of those in their care. Now more than ever our students must understand their public education is designed to prepare them for a workforce increasingly geared toward employing those with education beyond high school. Regardless of the type of further education—whether it be in a degree program or in technical training—assessments are an academic reality.

The challenge, then, is to ensure there is an acceptable balance between time spent assessing and time spent teaching and learning because our students—whether or not they are English Language Learners—will not perform well when assessed without sufficient time to learn and will rebel when they believe they are being used as guinea pigs.

Students and teacher alike know their schools will try anything to improve yearly performance on high-stakes testing, and "anything" generally results in a multitude of assessments throughout the year. These assessments often have no consequences for the student and reduce actual teaching opportunities for teachers.

What follows is an essay I wrote encouraging parents to rally together to opt out of the latest high stakes test designed with no other purpose than to keep a corporation's pockets full. It outlines my frustration with the current environment of over-testing in our public schools. Be forewarned. It is not politically correct.

### *Stop Outsourcing our Children!*

I'm not proud of what I'm about to share with you, but here goes. Many people in our little town know me as "Leadville Laurel," one of your local authors. I have taught English to many of your children in past years. So, when I started hearing about the new test—PARCC—which replaced the CSAP, I asked questions. My questions were answered with grumbles. "Take the 5$^{th}$ grade practice test," someone suggested, "and see for yourself."

Never one to walk away from a respectable challenge, and feeling quite confident I'm smarter than most 5$^{th}$ graders, I visited the web site and started the 5$^{th}$ grade English test. An hour later and with shaking hands (pretty sure my blood pressure was up several points), I got my score: 30/40, a solid 75%, perfectly "average" for a 5$^{th}$ grader. Granted, I didn't go back to check my answers, so I might have reconsidered some of my responses. And I suppose I might have earned an extra four points for two essays I wrote, one having to compile and compare information from three separate essays and one having to rewrite a narrative from a different character's point-of-view, but those portions would have to be evaluated by a faceless person and scored. When? Who knows!

Developed by (a huge corporation, you may discover the name yourself) the same company that earns its fortunes through the sale of textbooks to our schools, the test—in addition to being stressful—is vague, complicated, and confusing. So why am I sharing this with you? Why am I confessing that despite my MA in English, I didn't even score in the "Good" range on a 5$^{th}$ grade test? Because I'm asking you to do what I did. Pick one of the practice tests and see how you do. Then scream out loud. Then, if you have a grade 3-10 student, hug them. Then write a letter to their school saying, "I am opting my child out of taking the PARCC test (or whatever new acronym it will be called in the future) this year."

Schools across the country are already protesting the increasing insanity of the testing we've imposed on our children since the inception of NCLB. Proponents of these springtime tests (with results coming months later, never in time to alter instruction) say that testing is a part of life, and use the SAT college exam as a reason to pre-pre-pre-test. I say hogwash. If teachers were allowed to teach their students core material (teach, not test, because there is no instruction or learning happening during a test) like my teachers could back in the olden days, their students would do just fine on the SAT. Or not. Not everyone needs to attend a four-year college anymore.

Most parents won't take my suggestion. Most will continue to grumble, but will not want to "rock the boat." And without a dissenting majority, schools will continue to buy the latest "testing success" materials and children will learn less and less each year. And perhaps parents don't feel qualified to be vocal about what's happening in our classrooms, so here's my suggestion to those of you who don't like what's happening, but are unsure of what to suggest as an alternative to having your child sit through days of meaningless assessments.

For school districts implementing Expeditionary Learning, why not use testing week(s) to have students complete a project that is both meaningful and manageable to evaluate internally using the core standards at each grade level for English, math and science? At least have that as an "opt out option" rather than sending students wherever administrators decide to send those who are bold enough to "just say no" to the commercial tests.

Here's the thing: most teachers are "highly qualified" in their subject areas and in evaluation strategies. They know what their students should learn and where they are weak. They've endured countless hours of professional development on the same topics every year (from money-making companies who package old ideas with new names), and they've been forced to outsource the evaluation of their students to corporations that don't give two hoots about them or their classrooms. Why?

We can't afford to be complacent anymore. Whether we have children in the public school system or not, we pay for the schools in our district, and all of our graduates will impact the communities in which they live. We all should feel empowered to demand more: More learning, less testing. Opt out, and work with your elected officials and school board members to take back the education and evaluation of students from careless corporations.

~~~~~

Just as professional runners should not train at race-day pace every day for fear of injury or burnout, students should not be assessed so frequently that they experience burnout too. The student, like the runner, wants to perform well, but also knows that without the proper amount of time to absorb new learning, s/he will struggle. By evaluating and selecting the most efficient tools for assessing students and employing them judiciously, we can expect our students will do their best when asked.

Socrates is credited with saying the "unexamined life is not worth living." While perhaps an extreme viewpoint, it nevertheless is a strong suggestion that examination, assessment, thoughtful reflection on what works, what doesn't, and why, can bring about growth. School leaders and teachers, much like that proctologist I mentioned earlier, must use their examination tools wisely to benefit those they serve.

### The Ultimate Challenge: Discipline.

How do we solve the problem of discipline in our schools? We don't. Every year teachers will have to learn how best to handle new challenges brought to their classrooms with unruly and often emotionally disturbed students, but if teachers and school leaders present a united front, then not everyone has to become the victim when little Johnny and Janie act up.

While many in academia tout the advantages of using technology in classrooms to appeal to their students and keep them engaged, in a December 2014 article in *The Atlantic* by Alexandra Ossola, psychology professor Daniel Willingham mentions a study in which the majority of teachers surveyed believed technology posed a negative influence on their students. The professor's concern is that "kids can pay attention but they just don't want to. They have the expectation that everything should always be interesting."[2]

As an English teacher, I would suggest to the professor that the word "interesting" is as meaningless as the word "nice" when describing something, but I also know what he means. Students today do not tolerate boredom well, and why should they? We live in a world where the power to learn anything from soap-making to proctology rests in our pocket. Still, many a lesson has gone unlearned by students who have mastered the art of pocket-texting friends while pretending to listen to their teacher, and who believe their multi-tasking is not interfering with their learning. Studies have shown what we teachers already know: our students are wrong.

We've seen how kids of all ability levels turn into troublemakers when they are bored in classrooms. One suggestion, then, is to organize our classrooms in a way that helps teachers minimize the opportunity for boredom. Let's let students with similar academic abilities learn together. Let's finally answer the question of how teachers will differentiate for all levels of learning by differentiating our classrooms. This is not a politically correct solution, but haven't we all had enough of teaching to the average—or even lowest level learner in a classroom designed with only political correctness in mind?

Another suggestion is to stop the practice of advancing students who are not ready for the next level of education. Currently, community colleges are faced with enrolling students with high school diplomas who cannot test into the basic college classes. They offer remedial courses for no college credit, sometimes concurrently with first year classes, and the burden on unprepared students is tremendous. College professors are flummoxed by the lack of preparedness for higher-level learning.

Although we'd like to put the blame on the student for not being prepared, how can we if we've never expected them to demonstrate proficiency in their K-12 years? As a minimum, students advancing to high school should demonstrate they have mastered the fundamentals of reading, writing, and mathematics. Tenth grade English teachers should not have to teach the proper use of a period and high school principals should not find it necessary to give up their 28-minute lunch break to tutor students on multiplication tables.

Students who are passed along through the K-12 system should not show up to class each day knowing if they disrupt their peers or tell their teacher to piss off, or worse, they will be sent home for the day, a consequence students consider a bonus. Too many teachers' hands are tied by threats of lawsuits and by administrators who favor the notion of nurturing over discipline, as if the two were mutually exclusive. Discipline, something winning teams and organizations know is necessary for success, has somehow earned a bad rap in education circles and students know it.

So let's take back control of our school environments, my final suggestion. School leaders, do the right thing. Do the unpopular thing. Review your book of rules and student conduct, revise it if necessary, and then—most importantly—enforce the expectations you've established. If you don't do it, and do it consistently and across the board, then don't expect your students to comply. Expect them instead to decide which rules, if any, they'll follow, and then expect your staff and faculty to waste valuable time on disciplinary issues that rob them of their ability to teach effectively. Once you regain control, have the backbone necessary to hold students responsible for demonstrating their readiness at each level of education before advancing them to the next.

### *What more can school leaders and community members do to improve their schools?*

Whether your school district is small or large, affluent or struggling, it can always improve with increased effort and attention. I believe what works in a disadvantaged town also can help in areas more well-off. This is what I am asking you to do in your community whether you teach or have school-age children or not. Strong schools benefit the entire community, so share these suggestions with everyone you know:

- *Encourage community members to visit your schools.* Have them call ahead to find out about sign-in and security procedures. Let them visit classrooms, and if they have time and talents to offer—
- *Ask them to volunteer to help.* Could they tutor a subject? Make copies? Bring supplies to the art teacher? Listen to a child read? Work with math flashcards? Do a presentation on an area of expertise? Research ways to challenge advanced students? The possibilities in this area are limited only by what community members are willing to do. If you know someone who has their own business—
- *Find out how their local businesses can interact with your schools.* With limited funding, schools are often unable to provide field trips for students. Local business can provide a solution by opening their doors to student groups. Regardless of the subject matter, teachers

will find a way to tie in an academic standard, be it writing, research, calculation, art, history, and by exposing students to local businesses, their understanding of the practical applications of what they are learning in the classroom becomes more meaningful. With some planning, business owners will be able to answer the question, "But how will I use this in the future?" And if business owners are open to the idea—

- *Find out if there are opportunities for students to do internships.* Paid or not, internships provide students with goals beyond their K-12 education. Speaking of internships—

- *Consider and suggest ways students might intern within the school district.* Could the district's website be updated routinely? Might teachers need help researching future lessons? Are there custodial projects that could be completed with extra hands? Would the local news outlets like to receive routine articles highlighting school activities? There are many ways in which student involvement would enhance both their skills and their communities. If you can,—

- *Run for a school board position.* You do not need to be a parent of a school-age child, but you do need to care about the routine and future decisions of the school leadership. If you are not inclined to become a board member, you may still attend board meetings. Find out what decisions are being made about your schools and know the people who are making the decisions—they are elected to make smart ones. If you are not happy with the way things are handled in schools in your community—

- *Elect people who have the best interests of students in mind.* This goes not only for school board members but for other local officials as well. As a minimum—

- *Teachers, support your peers in whatever ways you can.* Let them know they are not alone and you understand their challenges. By becoming involved outside of your classroom, you can help to improve the environment in your schools. Good teachers work long hours for meager pay because they believe what they are doing will help their students, and ultimate the future of their communities.

Write a note. Make time to visit another classroom. Meet for coffee. Lend an ear.

On the last page of Achor's *The Happiness Advantage* we are reminded of the story of the hurricane attributed to a butterfly flapping its wings. "And each tiny move toward a more positive mindset can send ripples of positivity through our organizations, our families, and our communities. . . . the ripple effect is the perfect example of how there are no real discernible limits to our influence and our power (210)."[3] Recognizing I sound like Pollyanna, I still will ask each of you to believe you can bring about significant change by exercising your wings.

"Bernicia" ended up earning her diploma through a GED program after dropping out to raise the child she had as a young teen. She has a good job and a great relationship with the father of her child. She told me my belief in her and in her poetry inspired a belief in herself she never had before. Every teacher and every community member has the potential to change a child's world view.

Public schools will never be what they used to be when I was a kid, and in many ways that is a good thing, but schools should not feel like battlegrounds. There should be no "us against them" in places that prepare our students to become productive members of the communities in which they will live. We are all in this together. Educators are smart, tools are plentiful, and with the right team, any school system can improve. Together we must work toward improving the conditions of all who pass through and work in our academic establishments. Get involved and get your community involved. Offer what you can. Flap your wings. Do not leave the future to someone else.

[1] Achor, Shawn. *The Happiness Advantage.* New York: Crown Business. 2010. Page 59.

[2] Ossola, Alexandra. "Why Kids Won't Quit Technology." December 10 2014, 11:50 AM ET. http://www.theatlantic.com/education/archive/2014/12/why-kids-wont-quit-tech/383575/ Web. retrieved 01/02/15

[3] Achor, 210.

CPSIA information can be obtained
at www.ICGtesting.com
Printed in the USA
FSOW04n0256220916
25194FS